BIRTH OF THE TIPTONS

BIRTH OF THE TIPTONS

(Part One of The Tipton Saga)

PHILIP DAVIDSON

CONTENTS

INTRODUCTION

This is the first episode of the Tipton Saga and features the lives of the first generation of the Tipton family. Much of this comes, second-hand, from Frederick who told it to me, and I have to say he is a bit fruity. Much of it is my interpretation too. The original Tipton twins were born in England, in 1810. Of the second generation, one boy was born in England, and the other in the United States. All further generations were born in Pennsylvania, USA.

I have churned out three volumes of the Tipton Saga, as it is an extraordinary story. There will undoubtedly be two further books following the initial trilogy (five in total) due to some important information gleaned while in captivity. I should mention, this first volume was written entirely in captivity and if, at times, it seems a little strange, please give me some latitude because it was done in these highly unusual circumstances.

CHAPTER ONE

1 – Ten Minutes to Midnight . . .
(As told by Frederick)

Grunting, he stumbled down the cold stone steps of the ancient tower. Barefoot, breathless, overweight, and dressed only in a flimsy nightgown. The time was ten minutes to midnight on Sunday 31 December 1809, and the new decade was about to erupt. His feet shivered on the wintry steps, but down he went. His grunts ricocheted off the stone walls as he lurched from side to side, clutching at the masonry. The medication was driving him crazy, but he knew what he must do. Down and down, around and around. It was now or never. The meeting his great-great-grandfather had in the Bavarian Forest in 1685 confirmed it. Peace would only come to Earth after the two families united. He reached a half-landing. A further level down and she would be there, waiting.

2 – Kensington Gardens, 2019

On a sumptuous morning, in the early summer of 2019, I was strolling along the southern perimeter of Kensington Gardens on my way to a cryptocurrency conference at the Park Tower Hotel in Knightsbridge. The Park Tower is adjacent to Hyde

Park, and for those who are unfamiliar with Kensington Gardens, I would describe it as a particularly lovely London park with many graceful features. On the western edge, it has a small royal palace, and to its eastern boundaries, the gardens merge into Hyde Park. There is far more history here than most realise. I guess a bit of magic too, after all it was where Peter Pan hung out – the boy that never grew up – and there is a statue of him beside the park's gorgeous lake.

Because the day was so lovely and the temperature so perfect, I set out early, and alighted at the High Street Kensington Tube station, then walked the quarter of a mile into Kensington Gardens. It was the kind of day to spend as much time as possible in nature and off the traffic-choked streets. As soon as I entered the gardens, I felt at peace and glided across the gently undulating parkland into the rhododendron gardens. The air was sweet, the blossoms were out, butterflies were fluttering, bees were pollinating. It was like paradise in this traffic-choked city. I spent a few minutes soaking this in and restoring my equilibrium. Then moved off into the field that led to the Albert Memorial. Good heavens, that gold-encrusted monument sparkled dramatically in the morning sunlight. It surged a hundred and seventy-nine feet into the air like a nineteenth-century rocket preparing for launch.

Apart from being an ornately crafted monument, it summed up for me the nineteenth-century monarchy with clarity. The subject, Albert – Queen Victoria's husband – sat up high on a golden chair beneath a glorious canopy. Below him, the world went about its business in great harmony due, I suppose, to his great stewardship. Spanning out from the base were four great plinths, and on each plinth sat animals from the four corners of the Earth. To me, the implication was that Albert was not only responsible for all humans on Earth, but all animals too! Above the animals, were the humans in some kind of hierarchy, a great frieze of the greatest, and above the frieze, Albert sat underneath his spectacular canopy. Above this, no life at all, just an ornately decorated spire leading up to heaven. A direct connection with God. To me, the implication was that Albert had been chosen by God to rule his wife's realm with all its living creatures, and it seemed he was doing this task impeccably well. Either Victoria heavily idolised her husband, or really believed it.

I rested on the steps below the monument, taking in the sun, and deciding what to do next. I opted to head off to the Park Tower and take a coffee in one of their ritzy bars before the conference. I got up, saluted the crafters of this monument for giving me such a good insight into Victoria's vision of her husband and got on my way.

I made for the decorative Coalbrookdale Gates, and crossed the little road that separates Kensington Gardens from Hyde Park.

Once in Hyde Park, the elegant artistry of Kensington Gardens stopped, and the mundane features of twenty-first-century life took over. First, public tennis courts, then a huge grass field with no features at all. This stretched nearly a mile up to Park Lane. A curiously bleak field and almost totally deserted. Sometimes they hold concerts in this field, occasionally people play football, but usually it is deserted. I don't know why. Some way ahead, could be seen the rather ugly multi-storey Knightsbridge Barracks. I ploughed through this field towards my destination. About two hundred yards into the field, I tripped on something, and landed on the ground.

I came down with a great thump, and must have hit my head, because apart from having a sharp pain in my ankle, I had a pain in my temple too, as if someone had punched me. My head was spinning. I must have blacked out for a while because when I came to, the park seemed full of soldiers. Thousands of soldiers marching. Fortunately, this image faded quickly, and the field was as devoid of people as it had been when I took the tumble. This was a big disadvantage as nobody was around to help. My head cleared into a kind of headache, but my foot hurt badly. The pain seemed serious enough to warrant an ambulance. I eased the mobile phone out of my pocket and opened it. To my horror, the phone was dead. Nerves crept in as I realised the extent of my predicament. Needing medical attention and sprawled immobile in the middle of a massive field with nobody around. I yelled out, "Help!"

A few minutes later, a man appeared on the scene, and looked down. "Is something wrong?"

I looked up with relief. He was a strange sort of man dressed in a smart 1950's suit with trilby hat. He sported a bristly moustache.

"I have had an accident. Think I may have broken something."

"Dear me," he said. "I had better get you up. It is fortunate that I have medical knowledge. The thing to do is not to think of the pain."

"OK."

Under his arm, he carried a lightweight chair which he erected and got me into. Then I realised he did not have one chair, but two.

Surprised, I said, "You carry two chairs?"

"You never know when you may meet someone with whom you can have a good conversation. I am always prepared," he said.

He erected the second chair beside mine and sat himself in it. "That is better. Do you know where we are?"

"Hyde Park, I think. It is a little foggy as I may have concussion."

"Correct. Hyde Park, yes. A wonderful place. Sad to see it so deserted. Do you know what was once here?"

"Not really, no."

"Here, a fabulous glass palace once stood." He was indicating the large field we were in. "Inside this palace were thousands of astonishing inventions, and I will tell you a story of two orphaned boys. One had an invention, a fantastic new idea. His name was George Tipton . . ."

He launched into the story of George Tipton and his twin brother Charles Tipton. Oh boy, I thought, I have landed myself with a nutter. A lonely nutter who wants to tell me his stories. Once able, I edged in, "It sounds a wonderful story, but at this moment, I need to deal with my foot. That is my priority."

He looked upset. "I told you it is best not to think of the pain. My account of the Tipton twins is the perfect way to divert your mind from the pain."

"I need an ambulance."

"Have you summoned an ambulance?"

"No, the battery gave out on my phone. Can you call for an ambulance on your phone?"

He shook his head. "Alas, I do not have one of those devices. Never had the need. Let me have a look at your telephone. I may be able to get it going. I am rather special at a lot of things if you know what I mean."

A *special* type of nutcase I was thinking, but I gave him the phone, and he disappeared somewhere behind me, waving the phone around as he went. He returned a couple of minutes later looking very pleased with himself.

"I got your device functioning temporarily," he said.

I brightened. "Did you call for an ambulance?"

"Yes, I did."

"Did they say how long they would be?"

"Around twenty minutes I would imagine." He smiled. "Now your mind is at peace, let me continue with my story which will divert your body from the pain."

After a few minutes of relating his story, he stopped and peered at me as if he was inspecting me, assessing me.

"Things are beginning to happen," he said.

I asked nervously, "What things?"

"Things. Big things. Big important things. I need to get an opinion from someone on Earth."

"Someone on Earth?" I suddenly got a spooky idea he could be an alien. Maybe he was an alien. I confronted him. "Are you an alien?"

"No, you have the wrong idea. Naturally I am a Homo sapien, a product of the Earth, like you. I simply want to get an opinion."

"An opinion on what?"

8

"The rights of various individuals to rule the Earth. The legitimacy for them to do this. The legality of it if you like."

It seemed a peculiar thing to offer an opinion on.

He went on, "There is an urgency to this. It is starting to happen. There are two women in Brighton Heights. Descendants of the orphans I mentioned. The legend, the new world order, it is coming true. I need to discuss the legitimacy. These two women have received a trunk."

I was hoping the ambulance would arrive so I could get away from this lunatic.

He told me Brighton Heights was a suburb of Pittsburgh.

"Do you know anything about Pittsburgh?"

"No," I said.

"It is a steel city of the United States, in the state of Pennsylvania, and roughly three hundred and forty miles west of the Atlantic Ocean. Charlotte Tipton has a house there in Brighton Heights. I think we should call it Pennsylvania Heights so nobody can tell where we are talking about. Shall we call it Pennsylvania Heights?"

"If you want to," I said, trying to humour him.

"Good. As the name implies, Pennsylvania Heights is up high, high above the Ohio River. As suburbs go, it is a reasonably good one. As it was built in the early twentieth century, it is also a heritage one. Other than that, there is nothing particularly special about it. What I am telling you is that Charlotte and Georgina Tipton, direct descendants of the two orphans, are living ordinary lives, doing ordinary jobs, living in an ordinary suburb, and they simply do not know what is going to happen to them when they open the trunk."

"I suppose they would have no idea."

"The houses in Pennsylvania Heights are comfortable in a modest way. Detached dwellings standing in their own grounds with a lawned patch at the front and a

domestic garden at the back. The rear of Charlotte's garden backs onto the rear of the neighbouring garden, and Charlotte's house sits in the midst of a sea of similar sized houses and gardens. I mention this with regards to the security situation."

"Hmm, the security situation," I said.

"The security situation in relation to the trunk. This trunk was delivered an hour ago and left on the front porch of Charlotte Tipton's house. Do you know the type of wooden porches they have at the front of old American houses?"

"Yes," I said.

"A delivery company from Philadelphia placed the trunk on the porch and quickly left. I think they realised there was something strange about the trunk and didn't want to stay around."

"I suppose they wouldn't," I said, wishing the ambulance would hurry up, and longing to see those nice flashing blue lights, and maybe someone approaching across the field with an equally lovely stretcher for me. "How long do you think the ambulance will be?"

He shrugged. "Very hard to say. They could be caught up in traffic. Do you know how bad the traffic is in this town?"

"No," I said. "I mean yes."

"There you are. They are bogged down in traffic. There is nothing you can do but relax. Let me tell you about the trunk."

"Alright," I said reluctantly.

"The trunk is massive, like some great booty store of a pirate. The place where the chief of the pirates keeps his private hoard. Yes, where he keeps his personal stash in his great big trunk. That is what it is like. It has a huge rounded lid, studs and rivets everywhere, heavy leather straps, two discoloured brass handles at either end, it is just like a super pirate's trunk."

"Sounds quite a trunk."

"It is. Incredibly heavy too due to the contents inside. Maybe the delivery firm departed quickly because they thought the sheer weight of the trunk and its contents would break through the old wooden slats of the porch, and they would be forced to replace them."

"Yes maybe."

"Or maybe something else. Something inside the trunk. That is much more likely. The Tipton family have been in fear of what is inside that trunk for a hundred and sixty-nine years. Charlotte Tipton refuses to have it in the house because of what is inside."

"What is inside it?"

"Wouldn't you like to know," he sneered. "Excuse me, I need to check on something."

He wandered off somewhere behind me, and in my present situation, I found it hard to turn around.

3 – The Trunk Goes into the Cabin

There was a lot of heaving and huffing going on, more from Charlotte than Georgina. They had gotten the trunk down from their heritage porch in a number of manoeuvres trying to avoid damage to the woodwork, and down to the front lawn. Very exhausting for Charlotte. After a rest, they got going again and got the trunk around the side of the house. They put the trunk down again.

Charlotte wiped the sweat from her brow. "It is so heavy. What is in this thing?"

"We shall find out in a few minutes after we get it into the cabin."

After several more rest stops, they were outside the cabin. Charlotte had been trying to argue with Georgina to have the garbage men take away the trunk and have it burnt, but Georgina was saying, "Really, I don't mind the trunk being in my cabin. I consider it an honour. After a hundred and sixty-nine years, we finally get to find out what is inside."

"You should be careful. I think there is evil in that trunk."

"There is no evil. Just secret things that have gone wrong and ended in a bad place."

"It is alright for you. You live in the fantasy world of making films. I live in the real, harsh, everyday world, and have to take precautions."

"I am not frightened of the trunk. I embrace it."

The girls resumed hauling and got the monstrous trunk inside Georgina's garden cabin.

Charlotte, dripping wet, asked, "Where do you want it?"

Georgina surveyed her large oak cabin filled with film editing and special effects equipment. "Up against the far wall, away from the equipment. That'll be the best place for it."

With a few more heaves, the trunk was hauled up to the far wall. Charlotte collapsed into an armchair to recuperate. Georgina, on the other hand, stood gazing at the trunk in wonder. "We finally have it. After a hundred and sixty-nine years, it is in our possession. It is much bigger than I imagined. There is something magical about it."

"Spooky more like it."

A mist appeared to be rising over the trunk but was probably just condensation after sitting in a dank vault for all that time.

"I wonder if the cup of Heracles is in there?"

"What?"

"The cup of Heracles. It was given to Heracles by his father, Zeus. It's meant to have magical powers. It disappeared, and nobody knows where. It could be in here. You know how much I'd love to get my hands on a magical object. Something truly magical in my hands. Wouldn't that be great? I'd love it, really love it, yes that's what I'd really love."

Her hands were itching, and she cupped them around some imaginary object she could not quite picture, something luminous of red and yellow colours.

"You are weird."

"Do you think it's in there?"

"No," Charlotte said. "I do not think the cup of Heracles is in there. It is more likely to have classified government papers. Secrets about the British Empire that the British government didn't want to get out. Charles Tipton was a kind of revolutionary. He had done ten years in an English prison for sedition. He must have found something out. Maybe it's in there."

"Well let's get it open and see."

"No," Charlotte said.

"Why not?"

Charlotte, a bit rested now, got up and walked over to the trunk. She indicated the words etched into the lid. *NOT TO BE OPENED UNTIL EXPIRY.* Words that looked like they'd been hurriedly scratched on as if by a sharp knife.

"I think this means the expiry date of the trust."

Georgina nodded. "Yes, so?"

"So, I don't think we should open it."

Georgina groaned. "The trunk and the trust. Why has everybody been so scared of them. That's all I've heard all my life. Don't talk about *the Trunk or the Trust*. Pops shrivelled up like a baby and refused to talk about it. Generation after generation of the Tipton family have been terrified by *the Trunk and the Trust*. Nobody can explain why. Well, I am not scared. I want to know what's inside."

"Your ancestor, George Tipton the First, was assassinated because of something inside the trunk. That's why the first Charles Tipton had it locked up. He warned that if anybody opened the trunk before the expiry date of the trust, they could be assassinated too."

Georgina was exasperated. "The trust *has* expired. That's why they delivered it!"

"I think my ancestor, Charles Tipton the First, got the date wrong. He had just spent a harrowing journey escaping from England, lost his teeth and half his mind, and got the date wrong."

Georgina threw her arms in the air. "I don't believe this. Are we going to sit around like pumpkins for another hundred years on the strength of a rumour? This has gone on long enough. I want to know what is in that trunk, and I'm going to look inside, even if you don't." She advanced on the trunk, intent on opening it.

"Wait," Charlotte cautioned. "I'm having a security system installed. It will survey the house and well beyond the perimeter of the garden. There will be cameras placed around the garden and on the roof, and an alarm system connected to the Pittsburgh Bureau of Police Headquarters on Western Avenue. I have already negotiated with the police chief to treat any alarm with the highest priority."

"Why are you doing that?"

"We have to take precautions and take the threat seriously. I am a lawyer. I know what I am doing. We need timed photographic evidence if anyone tries to tamper with the trunk. I am asking you not to open the trunk until it is installed."

"When is it being installed?"

"Later this afternoon. I have rigged up a small CCTV camera trained on the cabin in case anyone appears before they arrive."

"You are taking this very seriously."

"After a hundred and sixty-nine years, we should. All I am asking is to wait until the security system is installed before opening the trunk."

Georgina shrugged. "What should I do until then?"

"Finish off the cinnamon cookie film. They are paying ten thousand dollars, and then you can get paid. I have to deal with an eviction. I will be back in two hours. Don't get assassinated."

Charlotte left, and Georgina gazed impatiently at the trunk, gunning to look inside.

The man in the 50's suit and hat reappeared. "They have got the trunk inside the cabin," he said.

"I understand."

"Charlotte Tipton is having a security system installed to thwart intruders."

I raised an eyebrow. "Is she?"

"I doubt it will thwart the intruders though, and now Georgina Tipton is anxious to see what is inside the trunk but has promised not to open it because of the security situation."

I shook my head, somehow getting sucked into this bizarre and silly situation, and stupidly asked, "What is inside the trunk?"

"Wouldn't you like to know?"

I didn't really want to know, but said, "Yes tell me what is inside."

"I cannot tell you, but it is not only about the trunk; that is just a small part. It is a much bigger story. It is huge. Do you want to know some more?"

"Alright," I said trying to keep my sanity.

He took off, walking around in circles, scratching his chin. "Will you keep it to yourself?"

"Yes, I will not tell anyone."

"Promise?"

"If you feel uncomfortable, I will definitely not be insulted if you decide not to tell me anything, not insulted in the least . . ." I was getting desperate, thinking why doesn't that bloody ambulance driver switch the bloody siren on. Put the bloody siren on, get through the traffic, and floor it!

"Very well then, I shall tell you," the man said, ignoring my hint. "I will start in the year eighteen ten. That is the best point to start. It is vitally important you keep this information to yourself. Now that I have let you into my secret, I shall tell you about the boss."

CHAPTER TWO

4 – *January 1810, England, The Boss*

The man in the 1950's suit stroked his chin and rattled his story out to me.

"The boss sat at his desk on a frosty morning in January 1810. To combat the winter outside, a handsome fire was roaring in a grate, which warmed the splendidly furnished room. The boss I refer to is, of course, His Royal Highness King George the Third, the third Hanoverian king of the new United Kingdom. Standing behind the king, were two courtiers who hovered patiently with state papers requiring a signature, but the king sat immobile, as if in a trance, because he had been informed a woman called Nefeli had conceived his child."

I sat like a lemon, listening, waiting for the ambulance.

"Now that I have let you into my little secret, we can be more informal and call the king by his personal name, George William."

"OK," I said.

"It is important to realise George William's state of mind regarding this woman, and other things going on at that time. Many things. The previous few months had been a mixture of triumphs and setbacks for His Majesty. The main triumph involved the Jubilee with him being the first British head of state to reach Golden Jubilee-hood. A milestone."

The man paused for a moment as though he was personally recalling the events.

"Yes, the celebrations had begun in India on his 'official' birthday of 04 June 1809. They spread to neighbouring countries of the Empire. Britain was a world power in those days, and George William was king to a large number of countries in the British Empire. Most of the Empire celebrated his 'official' birthday, although this was not his real birthday. George William instituted the 'official' one for the sole purpose of having a chance of decent weather in London so the public could witness an important parade. The Trooping the Colour parade. The ceremony where the Army publicly pledges allegiance to their king. It is important for the public to see this, and be familiar with where everyone stands, and bear witness to the Army being loyal to their king. In this way, the public can celebrate and relax with the wholesome feeling of peace and stability in the kingdom. The same procedure happened throughout the Empire. The British Army, along with millions of native fighters, pledged their allegiance to their king in England. I am thinking this could be the first building block of a divine order. A divine empire. Do you agree?"

"I don't know," I said nervously, wondering where this was going.

"The strange thing about the British system is that although armies pledge allegiance to the king, the king does not have the right to implement any major decisions. The government in London does this on his behalf. The king is obliged to agree with all decisions of the government even if he disagrees with them. Crazy, isn't it?"

"I suppose so, yes."

"This situation was reached after the English Civil War. For a short time, England lived without a monarch. Then the English wanted a king again, so a settlement was reached that the monarch would be the head of state, a figurehead with no real power. Crazy, eh? Do you think this should now be corrected? Do you think the monarch should be given the power to rule at will? It makes sense, does it not?"

"You seem to know quite a lot about the monarchy and English history."

"I do, yes."

"You appear to know a lot about King George the Third in particular."

"Well, I should."

"Why?"

"I am his father."

This was a shock that I had not expected. I was getting more and more confused.

He came closer, into very close contact, and whispered in my ear, "I am Frederick. Prince Frederick, the father of King George the Third."

I felt myself slipping into a parallel universe and didn't know what to think. Could this man in the 1950's suit really be who he said he was: Prince Frederick, the father of King George III? Had he somehow reincarnated on Earth? Was he paving the way for his son, the former king, to return to Earth, and in some kind of pre-planned coup, take over the world?

Frederick put his hand beneath my jaw and turned my head around, so his beady eyes were looking directly into mine. "Now that I have revealed this, I cannot let you go. A new world order is developing. It has been developing for some time, but now it is coming to a crucial stage. I have stupidly shot my mouth off and cannot let you go."

"That ambulance is not going to come. Is it?"

He shook his head regretfully. "No, it is not. I am sorry. I have let my mouth run away with me. I am very sorry for this."

Suddenly I became really scared. "What are you going to do?"

"I am not sure; I will have to think."

"What about my foot?"

Frederick turned surprisingly kindly. "Do not worry about that. I have medical knowledge. I told you. Superior knowledge, you will be healed quickly. That is one thing you need not worry about."

"What are you going to do with me?"

"Yes, what to do, what to do? This is a problem." Frederick stroked his chin in an agitated manner.

"You could simply let me go. I will not tell anyone."

"No, I could not do that."

"You can. You could get me to hospital. Even if I did tell anyone, which I would not, they would put it down to concussion."

Frederick considered this, concluding, "No, I cannot take that risk. Maybe you could join us?"

"Join you?"

"Maybe if I tell you about us. Me and George William, and the amazing Tiptons. Between us, we have the solutions the world needs. You will see what good ideas we have and join us. Join us in some trusted role that we can give you."

"Do I have a choice?"

"The way I see it, you can either join us and have a role, or I can lock you up until the new world order is complete."

"I see."

"Now I am thinking about this, it would be great to have a peasant like you in our ranks. Besides, it would give me someone from outside our circle to talk to!"

So that is how it began. I acquiesced. He had me listening to what a good bunch the Hanoverians were, and the surprising story of the Tiptons.

5 – Frederick Tells Me More About George William

Frederick said, "You must think we Hanoverians are obsessed with power and wish only to rule the Earth. Or maybe want to ride in a sea of privilege. It is true that most of us were carried away with entitlement, but it is not the case with my boy. Yes, my boy is a misunderstood man, and I will show you. Now, where was I? The king's state of mind, the Jubilee."

He walked around our seats in little circles stroking his chin, recollecting the Golden Jubilee in the latter part of 1809. (I found out later that Frederick had acquired an ability to hover through time and space, invisible and unseen, to acquire data for another role he had, a kind of spy.)

He stroked his chin and began his report.

"In the home counties of the United Kingdom, the Jubilee celebrations started on 25 October 1809 – this being the correct day to begin his fiftieth Ascension Year. George William flung himself into the Jubilee season with abandon. He pardoned crown debtors. He donated large sums of cash to charities who onwardly distributed them to the poor. He absolved army deserters and decreed prisoners of war be released. He gave funds for communities up and down the country to party, which they did. Nearly every town and village had bonfires. They had fireworks, and public banquets. Food for the rich to feast along with the poor. The whole country partied as one. It was a glorious time. A proud country at one with itself. Commemorative porcelain, coins and medals were struck. That was his biggest triumph for that time. There were setbacks too. His health. Yes, his health."

Frederick paused to recalibrate his thoughts.

"His health. By 1809 he was becoming an old man. Older than most in the land. Been on the throne for nearly fifty years! His health was not good. His illness can be put into two realms: physical health, and mental health. On the mental side, there were also two realms. A so-called normal realm, and a so-called madness realm. Madness! Who can say what is madness and what is genius? What is reality and what is delusion? I defy any man to truly state this. For George William, the two realms were distinct and incompatible, and this made it abundantly confusing. In the so-called madness realm, he connected with the legend of 1685; the only one in the family that could do this. The prophecy from a momentous night in the Bavarian Forest of 1685. The prophecy that forecast peace would only come to Earth after the two families united. A message from the divine? Is it not the true role of a monarch to be the conduit of the almighty? To be the servant and carry out the will of the divine? If peace on Earth is the will of the almighty, and you are placed in the position of conduit of the almighty, is it not your duty to carry out this role to the best of your ability? The Nefeli woman appeared at the castle. To him, all the signs pointed to Nefeli being the 'other' family, and what more perfect way for the two families to unite than to have a child? I shall now tell you how peace can come to Earth. Follow the train of events and you will see."

He paused again to gather his thoughts. "I shall return to that cold January morning in 1810."

6 – Birth of the Tiptons

In the stately office, with the fire burning in the grate, George William looked up at his courtiers.

"She is with child," he told them.

The courtiers looked at each other, shocked. Following an uncomfortable pause, one of them said, "It will be taken care of, Your Majesty."

Frederick commented, "George William knew what this meant. Children out of wedlock went to the orphanage. An orphanage no less! Not that he was a serial philanderer. Nefeli was the only one, and it was not for his personal enjoyment either. Simply duty. A duty visioned only when he was in the *madness* state. Nefeli, the legend, peace on Earth - all of these came into perfect clarity when he was in the *madness* state. Unfortunately, he was not currently in this state, and this made it confusing, so he cautiously went along with procedure, and plotted how to make the legend come true."

As 1810 progressed, it was, in many ways, a distressing year for George William. His health deteriorated. Along with bouts of profound *madness*, his physical health declined too, and there was the constant threat from Parliament of the Regency. The threat of him being replaced by his loathed firstborn son. There were problems with some of his other children too. In May 1810, one of his sons, Ernest, Duke of Cumberland, was attacked by one of his valets and left half-dead. At the same time, his youngest daughter, Amelia, his favourite and most loved, became seriously ill with tuberculosis and died. Distressing times. Along with all this, and with being head of state, he tracked the progress of the divine prophecy, and plotted for the birth of Nefeli's child. By September, came news of the imminent birth. Then it happened, the birth.

On September 20, George William was back in the office with his two courtiers, and he thumped on his desk, and roared at them.

"I want to see the child. This has been agreed, and I want to see him."

"It is two boys, Your Majesty. Twins."

"I know that, not demented yet. I shall see them both, but it is probably the elder I wish to inspect."

The twin babies were brought to him in a large, cushioned basket. The one nearest to him was the one that awakened his senses, which was indeed the elder, apparently by ten minutes. There was light about him, and in that moment, the king was ecstatic because he knew the prophecy was being fulfilled. He only got a few minutes with them before they were whisked off. Taken to an orphanage in the bleak north. An orphanage just outside the town of Tipton, in an area of England known as the Black Country. Colloquially termed the Black Country because of the heavy soot from smelting plants that worked night and day producing iron that powered the world's first industrial revolution. The choking, sweating heart that transformed the Earth into the machine-driven world we know today. The location of the orphanage was kept secret from George William as he knew it would be, and he brought the first stage of his plan into operation.

"I want a trust to be set up for the twin boys," George William said.

One courtier, James, asked, "A trust, Your Majesty? A trust?"

"Are your ears not operating correctly or are you simply looking for instant dismissal?"

"What kind of trust, Your Majesty?"

George William strode across the room. "I wish the twins to be fully educated. A superior education. In particular, I want special provisions for the boys to be introduced to the newest in the arts and sciences."

The first courtier, James, trying to be helpful, puzzled for a moment. "If we instituted a trust, it would have to be anonymous."

"Anonymous, why?"

"Because of the Prince of Wales, your firstborn son. This talk of the new and, err, illegitimate birth, this talk of him being your, err, *divine heir,* is making the Prince of Wales nervous and consequently, err, active."

"The baby in the basket *is* my divine heir. I am certain of it now."

"Yes, and I am not saying that he is not your divine heir, but this talk of *divine heir* is making the Prince of Wales extremely busy visiting Parliament, and he has gained the ear of the government who lawfully implement matters to do with the Regency."

"My firstborn is a useless overprivileged piece of vermin with no sense of duty whatsoever."

"That may be the case, Your Majesty, but the Prince of Wales has been very successful in pushing the case for a Regency. Him becoming the sole beneficiary of a Regency and inheriting the monarchy from you. It must be a discreet trust, otherwise content could leak out and give the Prince of Wales ammunition that could push the case for a Regency to a critical point."

"Very well. Make it an anonymous trust. Search for lawyers that do this kind of thing and report back to me."

Two days later, the courtiers reported back.

"We have identified a suitable framework for the trust. There are five of these trusts in existence. They are designed for would-be philanthropists to redeem themselves of ill-gotten gains by anonymously sponsoring an orphan. It is being sold on a 'personal salvation' theme. Not relevant in your case, Your Majesty, but on other counts would fit the predicament well. It is operated by an enterprising group of lawyers in Birmingham. They administer everything and ask no questions. One of their number is an expert on the secret Swiss banking system, and this is what makes them attractive to certain members of society."

The thought of opportunistic ragamuffin lawyers in Birmingham who sanitised their clients' wealth and made them look honourable by anonymously sponsoring orphans turned his stomach. "Can you not find anyone else?"

"They may be unsavoury, Your Majesty, but their discretion is impeccable. It is the best we can do."

George William grunted. "Fine, do it. Take funds from Brunswick-Lüneburg. The funds we hid from Napoleon. Use whatever funds are necessary. I want this trust operational for two hundred years."

"Two hundred years, Your Majesty?"

"Yes, two hundred years."

The courtiers looked at each other in puzzlement. Clearly the king was not right in the head. James said, "Why?"

"Science is advancing at a rapid rate. Given the right treatment, life expectancy could increase by up to two hundred years for those two boys. I am certain that, given the right science, life could be substantially extended."

Again, the courtiers looked at each other. "Two hundred years is most complicated for a trust, Your Majesty. We can specify an education yes, one to highlight arts and sciences. But two hundred years?"

George William went into a raging temper, thumping his fists repeatedly on the fine furniture. "Are you looking for severe and heinous punishments? Empty Brunswick-Lüneburg if you need to. Use the millions that are there. I want that trust up and operating and invested for two hundred years. If it is not implemented by the end of the week, there will be extremely serious consequences! Are you understanding me?"

"Yes, Your Majesty."

The king's will was enacted, and the trust activated within the week.

George William was not a well man. He was half-blind, half-deaf, and overweight. He was starting to have frequent fits and convulsions. This was not helped by the treatment he was receiving of the legendary Dr James's Powders, which contained arsenic, and was actually exacerbating the situation. Also, he feared he was about to be declared insane which would make life a lot more difficult. He frequently met with his physician.

"He is my divine and rightful heir," he told the physician.

"Yes, Your Majesty."

He preferred to meet the physician in the comfort of his curtained bed chamber, which is where he was. "Are you about to declare me insane?"

"I am not, Your Majesty."

"You say science is advancing rapidly, solving all manner of problems, and curing all kinds of diseases – why is it not making me any better?"

"I would recommend rest; a short rest away from the rigours of your duties would do a power of good." The physician began to administer the dreaded Dr James's Powders.

"This muck is not doing me any good," George William snarled. "It gives me convulsions. It is dangerous. I could have an accident. I need a restraining jacket."

"Yes, Your Majesty."

Monarchs must be careful of what they say. The next thing George William knew, he was in a straitjacket and locked into a small white room where his life changed dramatically. He screamed and kicked at the door with his only free limbs – his legs.

"Let me out, you conniving pieces of vermin. I am the king. I will have you hung. Let me out. I want to see my heir!"

A week later, he was declared insane.

The two courtiers continued with their duties meeting in his office. The second courtier, who had largely remained silent, became more vocal. His name was Kellewe, and he had a faint foreign accent. "Now the king has been incarcerated, we must add conditions to the trust," he said.

James was puzzled. "Conditions, why?"

"The talk of 'divine heir' is destabilising. You surely realise this. Has not the prime minister, Mr Spencer Perceval, approached you personally on this matter?"

James had to agree and nodded vaguely.

Courtier Kellewe went on: "We must make sure the twin boys never discover the identity of their father. Or their mother. We shall write this into a condition of the trust. There should be other conditions too, and the conditions must be enforced. I have identified the correct people to enforce the conditions of the trust."

"Have you? Who would they be?"

"An independent unit of the Prussian Army based in Königsberg. A superb unit."

"The Prussian Army? The Prussian Army!" James was astonished and looked at Kellewe with suspicion. "You are a Prussian. From Prussia, are you not?"

"In a sense, yes. That is how I know of this special unit. I guarantee they are the best available on this Earth to enforce the conditions of the trust."

"Your name is Kellewe. A strange name."

Kellewe smiled. "It means 'driver of the cart'. Now the king is incarcerated, we must push the cart."

7 – *Incarceration*

The legendary incarceration of the mad king had begun.

The room was white. George William pondered – was it meant to calm him? Well, it would not work, and he kicked the door with the only thing he could, his legs. He battered the door. His banging and kicking made no difference whatsoever, but he kept beating that door.

Time went by, and the king became dishevelled and unshaven. He was still the almighty king, but his requests and orders were totally ignored. He was not allowed to communicate and was alone for almost 100 percent of the day. Day and night became indistinguishable, and his eyesight was failing too. He was nearly blind. Such circumstances can cause a man to withdraw deep inside. His beard became long and white and reached his chest; his appearance began to look strange and mystical. No one expected the king to last for as long as he did. His incarceration went on and on. As the years went by, he surrendered to his fate and became strangely serene.

In his serenity, he discovered his mission. It was to assist, educate, and advise his divine heir in bringing peace to the Earth. In order to do this, he searched long and hard, and trawled through his knowledge of international affairs. As he had been king for over fifty years, his knowledge consisted mainly of the workings of the British Empire. In his higher state, he realised that one country dominating all others was not the answer. It was not the way the divine wished. Even so, he was amazed at how successful the British Empire had become, and how so many actually revered their British governors. He wondered how this was possible. Could it be the

Empire's love of the English game of cricket? Surely not. Could it have been the charisma of the British aristocrats? The British royal style is alluring, and may have contributed, but it cannot have been that alone. After sifting through a myriad of possibilities, he came upon something more substantial. The law.

Specifically, English common law. A law built on the customs and remedies of the people. A kind of folk law. In a sense, a peoples' law. The unique law of the English. A law built up over centuries of precedents. People appeared to recognise a degree of fairness about it. He became convinced this was the major factor contributing to the success of the empire. After all, people predominantly wanted to feel safe. Free from the threat of violence and intimidation. A law, with a suitable body to enforce it, could provide this safety. This could provide the building blocks of a perfect world for humans to live in. There were two obstacles to overcome. The first was the English common law itself. The problem with this was that it was an *English* common law. The second was, who would enforce the law, because he was convinced it should *not* be the British Army, or the army of any country for that matter. He could not immediately think of a solution to this second problem but got to work on the first. Devising a *common law* custom-designed for each culture. A truly *peoples' law* tailored to each country. This would be the gift to give his divine heir to put into his toolbox, and so help to bring about a glorious vision of eternal peace for the Earth.

His mission was starting to clarify. He saw this as the culmination of his years of ruling as a king and knowledge of the laws. He realised the purpose of his incarceration was to conceptualise on paper this world-wide system of law, the law of humans. With this realisation, he became energised, and transformed into good spirits. So good was his behaviour, that he was allowed to have a regular visitor – his former courtier James.

"It is good to see you once again, James, my man."

"It is good to see you again, Your Majesty." He gave a bow.

"Come, James, we do not need all this formal nonsense. I have been on my own for a long time, but now I am back. What year is it?"

"It is 1815, Your Majesty. Coming up for five years since you have been in here. We must get you groomed and washed."

George William clutched at his long beard. "I like my beard. It has been my friend all these years, but I would like a bath."

"If you pardon me for saying so, you do need one! I shall arrange for a team of washers to bathe you."

And so, he did. A team of young maidens. No impropriety you understand, simply maidens washing the body, but the king luxuriated in the hot water and soft hands that cleaned him, and requested the process be repeated each day.

"Now, down to work," he said to James. "I have discovered my true mission in life. It is to produce a universal law. A law that can be acceptable to all. Divine inspiration, that is what it is! I will need you to bring me books from the king's library, possibly obtain others from outside, and assist me in the reading as I am going blind."

For the next three years, James brought to the king various books on customs, traditions, and rites of Peoples from around the world. He studied ancient Indian law: The Arthashastra, The Manusmṛiti, and a myriad of other Indian laws and traditions. He studied ancient Chinese laws and traditions, ancient Hebrew laws, the laws, rites, and traditions from everywhere. It was an exhaustive task. By day, James read him the books, and by night, he contemplated and made notes. After three years, he had devised a basic framework, a common law for everyone. It had unique variations for every area, taking into account their own historical traditions. He still did not know what force would uphold the law, and this would eventually be a surprise to everyone.

As the great work was nearing completion, he said to James, "We have been working tirelessly for the last three years, now bring me my divine heir so that I may give him this body of work."

James lowered his head regretfully. "I am sorry, Your Majesty, that is not possible."

The king accepted this with resignation and dignity. "Would you be able to deliver this body of work to the boy when he reaches a suitable age?"

James nodded. "Yes, Your Majesty. That I will attempt to accomplish to the best of my ability."

The king was satisfied; his body of work was now complete with James promising to deliver it. He longed to speak with his son though, his divine heir. As it happened, his divine heir, George Tipton, longed to speak to his father too.

CHAPTER THREE

8 – Frederick Tries to Convince Me

Frederick looked at me proudly. "There! I told you he had a good plan. A common law for every country! What do you think about that?"

"Yes, I suppose it was quite a good idea."

"And that is only part of the plan. There is a lot more. Bags more. We are good people and want to rule for the betterment of the Earth."

"It might have been the most fantastic plan of all time, but it did not happen!"

"Ah yes," Frederick admitted. "It did not happen then, but it is about to happen now. All of it. A new improved version. Two hundred years in the making. It seemed a very good idea to me, and that is why I signed up for it. You could be part of it too if you behave yourself."

I started to doubt this man, again thinking of him as a fruitcake who went around telling fanciful stories. I said to him, "What if I don't sign up for your plan? Or behave myself? What are you going to do? Bump me off?"

"Please, nothing so crude. We Hanoverians are not normal people. We have a certain number of magical tricks to deal with issues like this."

"Like what?"

"Like dematerialisation. I have been shown these secrets. I could dematerialise you if I wanted, but I do not want to do this because I want to find out if you would make a good peasant to talk to. I am surrounded by my own people, some of them not very nice, and I long for an ordinary peasant to talk to."

"So, I am the peasant you would like to talk to?"

"Yes, that is right. More accurately you might be. I saw you studying Prince Albert's statue. You appeared to get an understanding of who we are. I witnessed you saluting him. Therefore, I followed you into this field."

"I was not saluting at Albert. It was the people who built the monument I was saluting to."

"Were you? Oh dear. I have misunderstood." He began urgently scratching his chin. "What to do, what to do?"

Suddenly, I got the weird feeling he really was who he said, and that he had caused the accident through some jiggery pokery. "You caused the accident, didn't you?"

"I am sorry, very sorry."

"You go around manipulating people and causing pain. You have caused pain to me. You pretend you are good people, doing good for the world, but you are not!"

He brightened enormously. "You are the peasant I have been looking for! This is exactly why I want a peasant to talk to. I need interactions, and grounding. Let me make it up to you." He vigorously rubbed his hands together and applied one hand to my foot. "I told you I have medical knowledge and I do. I shall three-quarters heal your foot as a sign of good faith. This will take away your pain. I will heal the other quarter after I have told you about the Tiptons."

I was amazed. The pain largely disappeared in an instant.

"I am the dumb one of the family," Frederick admitted. "But I do try. I keep trying. Because of this, I have been given a role, and to fulfil the role, I have been awarded two magical powers. Materialisation, and healing. I wish I had more, but I think this is my lot. We Hanoverians were given various bits of magic for our toolkit, but you have to be awarded them."

"Like what?"

"Like the stone."

"What does the stone do?"

Frederick puffed out, amazed. "What does the stone *not* do? The power of the universe is contained in the stone! The presence of the stone ensured our family rose to the top of the international power structure, but to use the stone personally, you must understand it. That in itself is a kind of award. Not many people ever understood the stone. I wish I understood it, but I have not been awarded the gift of understanding. George William understood it a little bit. George Tipton understood it more. I believe Georgina Tipton will understand it fully."

"What will happen if Georgina Tipton fully understands the stone?"

Frederick gasped, overcome with exhilaration at this thought. "The question is what will *not* happen if Georgina Tipton fully understands the stone! The possibilities are endless. I could guarantee we would see a transformation in Georgina Tipton the likes of which the world has never seen. I will give you a fifty-dollar bet she will turn into a superwoman extraordinaire."

"Sounds quite a stone."

"A fantastic stone! A bit unearthly too. Do you want to know where it comes from?"

"Alright."

"It was given to my great-grandfather by a Greek prince in the Bavarian Forest in the year of 1685."

"You mentioned the Bavarian Forest in 1685. Is that the same one?"

"Yes, it was the same night in the forest. Probably the most momentous night in the history of the world. The consequences of what happened that night in the forest are playing out now as we speak. The wheels have spun around and come into place. Everything has lined up. You will see. I had better tell you what my great-grandfather was doing that night in the forest."

"OK."

"My great-grandfather was a distinguished looking man who wore a gigantic bronzed wig. Very impressive. At the time, he was the duke of a duchy in what we now know as northern Germany. He was down south with a small army to help Leopold the First of Austria fight the Great Turkish War. Leopold was the Holy Roman Emperor of that time."

"Leopold the First? The Great Turkish War?"

"Leopold the First and The Great Turkish war, yes. It was a huge war and involved millions of souls. It began in 1683. Two massive armies fighting each other."

I had vaguely heard about this war, now Frederick explained more.

"On the one side was an alliance called The Holy League. 'The League' was made up of Lithuania, Poland, Russia, Hungary, Venice, and The Holy Roman Empire, which was not a Roman Empire at all, but a substantial German one in the middle of Europe. The opposing armies facing 'The League', were a number of countries mainly from the Ottoman Empire. Turkey, Syria, Egypt, Arabia. In fact, most of the Middle East and northern Africa. Tens of thousands of square miles in those territories, plus some countries in Europe which also belonged to the Ottoman Empire. Two huge armies facing each other.

My great-grandfather played his part in this war by leading his small army into battle on the side of The Holy League. In 1685 he was heading home to his Duchy of Brunswick-Lüneburg for a break. His name, incidentally, was Ernest Augustus.

My great-grandfather, Ernest Augustus, was weary after riding horseback from the front which was many miles away. His detachment camped in the Bavarian Forest for the night and pitched his personal tent which had three rooms. He was resting in his bed chamber, when a deposed prince from Greece whisked through the undergrowth, evaded security, and appeared under the flaps into his most personal room."

Ernest Augustus recoiled, and exclaimed in shock, "Who are you?"

The Greek prince moved swiftly to seal the lips of Ernest Augustus and whispered, "Do not raise the alarm, for I come in peace. I have information to impart of a most serious nature, which is extracted from the Secret Oracle of Olympus. It concerns the prophecy of the two families uniting."

The Greek prince went on to relate the prophecy, and the mission, and left by blessing Ernest Augustus and giving him a gift of a small rock. "Within this rock, contains a shining gemstone," the prince said. "The most precious gemstone in all the Earth. The true stone of the Earth, which contains all the wisdom of this planet, and the way humans should live on it. Those who truly understand the Earth stone are entitled to rule the Earth as they shall have the wisdom of the intended way to live in it. There is a sister stone to the Earth stone, the redemption stone, and this is held by the leader of the Aurora people. Treat this rock with supreme care and only employ the finest, most skilled craftsmen to release and polish the gemstone."

The Greek prince left as quickly as he had come and disappeared into the forest of the night. Other things happened that night too. Agents of Commander Zakamonsky visited, the absolute scourge of our family, but I will not go into that at this time and will complete the story of the stone.

In the morning, my great-grandfather left for his palace in the north and dismissed the story of the Greek prince as fanciful nonsense. As he retold the story, everyone treated the tale of the Greek prince as nonsense too. However, the promise of 'those who truly understand the stone are entitled to rule the Earth' intrigued several members of the family, and they all wanted a look at the stone to see if they could understand it. The stone was alluring and hypnotic with powerful red and yellow luminous colours radiating from within, yet nobody could truly say they understood it. Soon, the excitement died down, and the story was forgotten about. The stone was put amongst the many gemstones in one of our crowns. It was agreed the incident in the forest would only be told from father to firstborn son. The tradition went on until George William's son died in 1830. It stopped because his son, George the Fourth, never had a son of his own. Now, the only members of our family that are aware of this story are the Georgian kings and me. Our little group."

Frederick stroked his chin, thinking.

"While the story sounded fanciful at the time, there is no doubt that the stone contributed to the success of our family. Soon after receiving the stone, my great-grandfather became Elector of Hanover, and his son became the first Hanoverian king of the United Kingdom. We have remained on that throne ever since."

Frederick looked at me with a new seriousness. "I am telling you about our family and our secrets. This is a rare privilege that very few people will ever be privy to. I hope you will appreciate this."

I nodded vaguely.

"Concerning the stone; this is one of our biggest secrets. I count the people that know of this on one hand, but I cannot emphasise enough the importance of the stone. It is the reason I need to tell you the story of the Tiptons and was the reason George William was able to communicate with the young George Tipton."

9 – George William's First Communication

Even though James had promised to deliver the great document of law to George Tipton, George William longed to communicate with his divine heir personally, and a few nights later, he lay on his bed in his incarcerated chamber thinking of the great stone.

He had held the stone once, only once, and it had a warm magical effect on him. He was a young boy when this happened. His grandfather had let him hold it for an hour one afternoon before it had become coated. It was sumptuous yellow and red, and felt warm to touch. It sent him swimming warmly into a magnificent thermal cocoon. It was the reason he held onto the legend of the Greek prince: maybe the power of the stone had turned him mad too. Now an old and tired man, he lay on his bed thinking of the stone, and as he did, the image of the stone came to him. It bathed him in its warm red and yellow glow, like sunshine in the night. It calmed his aching body, and he relaxed into the shelter of its soothing rays. He luxuriated in this wonderful state for over an hour, thinking of his divine heir, then heard a voice.

"Dad?"

Astonished, George William yelped. "Is that you, George? Is that George Tipton?"

"Yes, this is George Tipton. Is that you, Dad?"

"This is incredible. This is your father speaking to you."

"I know."

George William knew it was his son. Certain of it. He could hear the young immature voice as clearly as if he was next to him. It was like telepathy, but more than that. The power of the stone, extraordinary! George Tipton, however, knew nothing of the stone at that time.

"It is strange, but this time of night I feel so alive," George Tipton said. "I just love the yellow and red flames from the furnaces."

Seven-year-old George Tipton was sitting bolt upright on his bed in the Black Country orphanage. Another eighteen orphans were asleep in their beds. Twin brother, Charles Tipton, was snoring in the bed beside him. The bright yellow-red light from the all-night furnaces blazed through the little window at one end of the dormitory. The light in that dormitory was bright and surreal.

George William smiled, overcome with joy. "George, finally I am able to communicate with you. I have plans for a Divine Empire."

"Have you?"

They communicated in this way for the next three nights.

CHAPTER FOUR

10 – *Black Country, September 1818*

"He spoke to me again," George Tipton said to twin brother, Charles.

"Do not tell anyone else about it or you will be taken to the nuthouse."

They were out in the street, sitting on a small pile of coal in the smoky, Black Country street. It was their favourite spot, and thick with smoke. Their legs were discoloured with the smoke due to their short trousers, and the black ever-present smoke made everyone look like coal miners.

"He told me about a divine empire."

"Yeah, well, do not tell anyone else about that."

"He said I should learn the history of Britain from 1702."

"That is something sensible."

"Can we look for them, our parents? Find out where they are living?"

Charles's mood changed sharply. "No, no, no! We have been warned. Our parents are dead. Just accept it - we are orphans."

"Why are we here?"

"That is a funny question."

George peered around the strange landscape; the flash of light from the foundries breaking through the thick black smog was weird.

"Why here?" George asked again. "This place is strange. It is very much smoky."

"It is smoky."

"I want to know why we are here."

"You ask too many questions."

"They hate us."

"Who hates us?"

It was an hour later, and George was sitting on Charles's bed, which was next to his in the dormitory.

"It is the other children. They hate us."

A line of orphans, about twenty feet away, were looking at them. Their contorted little faces were consumed with venom.

"Ignore them," Charles said.

"They hate us because of our privileges. I am sure of that."

"It is not the privileges. They hate us because we have each other. They do not have anyone."

"Do we have each other?"

"I am here. I sleep in the bed next to you."

George boldly stuck his tongue out at the orphans. Charles panicked, restraining him. "Do not do that," he said. "I am not a one-man army. You will get us both into trouble." He nodded to the orphans in an apologetic way, indicating George was a bit loopy. It seemed to work, and the orphans laughed and calmed down.

George asked anxiously, "Would you stand by me no matter what?"

"I do not know," Charles hissed irritably.

George dug a drawing out from under his bed. "I have done a drawing of you."

"Do I look like that?"

George lined the drawing up against Charles's head and looked at the drawing meticulously. It was an extremely good likeness. Almost exact. "It is quite good, but could be much better," he said, nodding to himself critically.

Charles nodded vacantly.

Then the matron came in and bellowed for everyone to get into bed.

Later, at 3 a.m., when all the orphans were asleep, as the roar of the furnaces shone their red-orange glows through the little window, George Tipton got in touch with his dad.

"Father, why do you not come and visit me?"

"I wish I could, but I cannot. I am locked up."

Although he did not question this further, George presumed his father was in prison.

11 – Beethoven's Fifth

The next morning, George and Charles attended their school. It was a class of just two: them. Their desks were all-in-one wooden contraptions with lids which opened into a compartment inside for books. Their teacher, another matronly woman, was up front near a blackboard.

"Today, we will have a mathematics lesson with Mr Wiggins," she said.

George groaned as he hated maths.

"Why do we have to come to school, miss?" George asked.

"Be grateful you do."

"Why do *we* come to school and the other children do not come? The other children hate us for coming to school."

The teacher's demeanour changed dramatically.

"I have told you before. You are not to question. That is a condition of the trust. Further questioning will result in you being taken to one orphanage and your brother taken to another orphanage. You will never see each other again. The men, the enforcers from Prussia, will take you. Other things may happen too. You will be very much on your own. Is that what you want?"

"No, miss, I do not want that."

"Another condition of the trust is that you do not ask about your parents. Maybe your parents were murderers or maybe something else that was bad. This condition is to protect you and give you a new life without the knowledge of the badness of your parents. All you need to know is that your parents are dead."

This troubled George.

"A further condition of the trust is that you do not embarrass the royal family." The teacher shook her head, puzzled. "That would seem obvious. We should all respect our monarch. We need to pray for our king that he may recover from his illness and rule us once again."

George and Charles nodded in a mechanical way.

"Be grateful you have a trust. A generous philanthropist has looked down and selected you from thousands of other orphans. Think of all the good things the trust provides. Tomorrow, I shall reveal your special birthday treats provided by the trust. You will love them."

That night, troubled by what the teacher had said, George got in touch with his father. It was 3 a.m.

"Father," George said. "Did you kill anyone?"

There was silence.

"Father?"

"I am thinking," George William said. "I have not killed anybody myself but given orders that may have resulted in some people being killed. I regret it, but sometimes it is necessary."

George was shocked. He did not want to hear more. The teacher was right; his father was a criminal. He must be the head of a big crime organisation. He vowed not to speak with his father for a whole week.

The next day, in the schoolroom, the teacher said, "I have arranged two treats for your birthdays. One in the arts and one in the sciences." She bellowed into the next room for Figgis. "Mr Figgis. Figgis? Figgis!"

Mr Horatio Figgis, a fragile little man despite his illustrious first name, entered the room, wheeling in a trolley that had a prized object on it, and addressed the boys.

"As you know, boys, I have been spending time in the village of Kew near London to help Mr Claude Niépce develop his motor engine. He lives close to where our king grew up in Kew Palace." He said this proudly for he was a fanatical royalist. "Mr Claude Niépce's engine is an internal combustion engine and will be fuelled by the chemical hydrogen. It is different from a steam engine which is an external combustion engine."

The teacher interrupted him. "Mr Figgis, please get on to the matter at hand. That thing on the trolley."

"Ah, yes," Figgis said. "The Niépces are a talented family because Claude's brother, Nicéphore, Nicéphore Niépce, invented this. It is a significant development from the camera obscura; in actual fact, something totally different. Mr Niépce simply calls it a camera. This is the only one in England."

He proudly spun the trolley around so the boys could see every angle of the instrument.

"Point the camera in any direction and pull this cord, and it should produce an exact image of what it is pointed at. A reproduction on a plate coated with chemicals."

George was mesmerised by the machine, and his eyes began popping. "Do you mean it can make an exact drawing of what it looks at?"

Figgis stuttered, "It is not perfected yet, but should do that in the end. I am working on it. The correct name of this will be – photograph."

The twins were being introduced to the latest in the arts and sciences, as per the king's wishes.

"Oh boy, oh boy, oh boy! This is what I have been looking for. Can we go out with it?"

"Go out? No, it is not ready yet. The plates need chemicals to make them permanent. That is what I have been working on. I worked all day yesterday and shall work all day today."

The teacher intervened. "Mr Figgis, you may go now. Take your device with you."

George had a glint in his eye, and Figgis had a worried look as he wheeled away the Niépce camera.

The teacher proudly introduced the next item.

"Your music teacher, Mr Brahms, will take you to Wollaton Hall to hear a musical concert. It is the very first performance in the north of England of the 'Fifth Symphony' by the famous composer Mr Ludwig van Beethoven. Prepare yourselves, boys. It will be a long day. You leave this afternoon!"

In the coach that afternoon, it was a treat indeed. The covered carriage had cushioned seats facing each other and was pulled by two horses. George and Charles sat on the back seat faced by Mr Brahms.

"I am so excited," Mr Brahms crooned. "I managed to secure the last three tickets from Mr Wollaton. It is so kind of him to host this concert in his music room. News from Vienna tells me this is Mr Beethoven's finest work. I am so eager to hear it!"

Mr Brahms was falling apart with excitement.

The boys were excited too. As the carriage passed out of the smoky Black Country into the pleasant rolling hills of Staffordshire, a new world opened up for them. George felt like he was in heaven. It got even better as they entered the grandeur of Wollaton Hall, built from Cager Wollaton's industrial wealth. The music room was lavish and bordering on the vulgar. It had the orchestra along one wall with a backdrop of gaudy drapes formed from expensive velvets. The audience, about fifty, were sat away from the orchestra on seats just a little too small. Hundreds of candles were placed in holders, waiting to be lit at the beginning of the fourth movement – all carefully timed as it got dark for a grand finale. The conductor indicated he was ready, and a hush fell on the room.

The hush went on and on for a full five minutes as the anticipation of the audience grew greater and more excited. Finally, the orchestra blasted into action.

Da da da darr! Da da da darr!

The dramatic opening notes of Beethoven's 'Fifth'. The audience gasped. The da da da darr's rang out like a call from God, or maybe some beast in the sky. Nobody gasped more than George.

Da da da darr! Da da da darr!

George imagined a series of pictures coordinated to those dramatic notes. Not just pictures, but photographs to be taken with the camera he had been introduced to earlier. Da da da darr! Da da da darr!

These notes kept ringing in his head throughout the concert. Naturally there was much more to the concert than those opening notes, but those were the ones he kept thinking about, and they were still ringing in his ears on the journey back to the orphanage.

In the carriage, George said, "That was great, Mr Brahms, thank you, it has given me some ideas that could change my life." Mr Brahms nodded as they sped back into the Black Country, and dozed off. Charles was tired and slept. However, George was wide awake with his new idea. Da da da darr! Da da da darr!

Some hours later, they arrived back at the orphanage.

In the morning, George was still full of inspiration. "Da da da darr!" He kept chanting this to himself.

He paid a visit to Figgis in the school lab to initiate the taking of the photographs. Not only would these photographs settle a serious issue in his life, but they would also be the world's first photographs. The boy was extremely excited.

He found Figgis hunched up against a bench heavily engaged in mixing chemicals. George crept up behind and shouted, "Da da da darr! Da da da darr! We shall take the world's first photograph and make history!"

Figgis recoiled in shock as if he had received a heart attack. His hands jerked up, and the test tube in which he was mixing chemicals flipped upside down, and the liquid started dribbling down the bench. His mouth dropped open in disbelief.

"Sorry, Mr Figgis, did not mean that to happen."

Figgis, staring at the disappearing liquid, gasped. "Thirty-two hours and seventeen minutes of work!"

"Sorry, Mr Figgis. What was in those test tubes?"

"The formula, Master George. The formula that would stabilise the plates and reveal the photograph. Without the formula there will be no photograph."

No photograph! The wind rapidly deflated from George Tipton's sails. All his enthusiasm stunted. It was worse for Figgis. Although a brilliant mind, he was a fragile little man, and he cupped his hands and buried his head, and began to sob. The strange thing was, he sobbed not for himself and all the wasted work, but for George.

It is hard to pinpoint what the strange relationship between George Tipton and Figgis actually was. Perhaps Figgis picked up on some primordial instinct of recognising George as a royal and felt the need to serve him. Even though George Tipton was pretty dumb, there was a sliver of magic about him that shone through, and Figgis reacted to that.

George said, "Is it not possible to make the formula again?"

Figgis raised his head and shook it. "There were so many steps, Master George. Thirty-two hours and seventeen minutes of steps. I would never remember them all. I am forgetting them already."

George scratched his head. "Do you remember the memory potion you showed me?"

Figgis looked at him, puzzled. "What memory potion?"

George shook his head. "I think we need to find that memory potion."

Together they went in search of the memory potion. At the far end of the lab was a storeroom, and this is where racks of Figgis's experiments were kept. Figgis selected a test tube from one of the racks.

"I think this is the one," Figgis said.

"Are you sure?"

"No."

"How will you know if it is the right one?"

"I will drink some."

George was nervous. "Be careful. Only drink a tiny little bit."

Figgis smiled. "Thank you, Master George," he said with reverence.

Figgis sipped a little and nodded. "This is the one."

"Sure?"

"Yes, I remember the taste. See, it is working already. I shall get to work and remember all the steps and recreate the formula as soon as I can."

"Wonderful, Mr Figgis. Together we shall take the world's first photograph."

Elated and back on track, George went in search of Charles.

12 – George, Charles, and Tom

George found Charles on the coal pile.

"I am going to put photographs to that music we heard last night. It will tell a story. Da da da darr! Da da da darr!"

"How are you going to do that?"

"With Figgis. He is mixing chemicals that will make the photographs come out. They will be the world's first photographs!"

Charles was impressed. "The world is changing fast. So many inventions."

"Yes, me and Figgis are going to make an invention that will change the world! I am going to look for places to take the photographs."

George went off in search of places to take the photographs. Meanwhile, Charles had interests of his own and visited Tom.

Tom was Charles's best friend and three years older than Charles, about eleven. He was a tall, gaunt lad and worked as a child labourer in a small metal casting plant. Charles ventured inside.

It was massively hot, and hugely noisy in there. Charles started sweating as soon as he entered. There was a roar of furnaces and flashes of blinding light. He found Tom drenched in hours of sweat. They were pleased to see each other.

Charles asked, "Can we go for a walk later? I like talking to you when we walk. It is too noisy in here." He had to shout above the roar of the furnaces. They both shouted.

"Charles Tipton, I cannot. Today I work until midnight. Too late to walk."

Charles was shocked. "That is bad. Very unfair."

"It is, I am only a child, but you could change that."

"I could?"

"With your schooling, you could be a lawyer. To defend and get laws changed. John Doherty is coming to town tomorrow eve. He will tell how we can get better conditions. He will show the way. It is secret, not legal. Come and listen."

John Doherty was a revolutionary Irishman who had come to Manchester two years previously and formed a secretive union of Manchester Spinners, which in effect was the very first trade union. John Doherty had managed to keep one step ahead of the authorities, for a union of workers was much illegal. John Doherty was due to hold a meeting in the Black Country the following night. It was a closely guarded secret.

"I will come," Charles agreed, intrigued.

"The world is changing, Mr Tipton. You want to be part of it. You want to be on the right side. You want to be a lawyer. Be part of the change."

Charles was inspired, which may not have been his best decision.

13 – *Careers Are Decided*

Two days later, at the school, their teacher asked for some decisions that would impact the rest of their lives.

"Today, I have been instructed by the trustees in Birmingham to decide careers for you. The more successful you become, the more money the trustees will make." She appeared to twinkle. "The more money they make, the more they give to me, so it is in my interest we make a success of this. It will be very much in your interest too." She said this last bit with a hint of menace.

The boys looked on in anticipation.

"Charles Tipton, have you thought about a career? A job to do for your future?"

Charles had. "I want to be a lawyer, miss. That is what I want to do for my future."

"That is good."

It was far better than expected, and she responded with enthusiasm. Charles did too. The previous night, he had gone with Tom to the meeting with John Doherty. It was tense and dark in the dingy little hall, and everyone was on edge. A lookout was on the door and a lookout inside the hall. The miners wondered why two boys were in there. Everyone was suspicious. Charles loved it. The fiery Irishman was brusque and unintelligible, but Charles caught there was a need for lawyers. Even at the age of eight, there was something in him to change the world.

The teacher was most pleased with Charles's choice. "I shall advise legal training for you. We can get started very soon."

The teacher turned to George.

"Master George, have you thought of a job?"

"Yes, miss. I want to do music-picture-stories."

The teacher's face dropped. "What are they?"

"They are stories in pictures with music."

"I shall put you down for training as a clerk."

"I do not want to be a clerk. I want to do music-picture-stories."

"We could get you into the East India Company. Think about your future."

"Music-picture-stories are the future, miss. I want to build picture-story-palaces. Soon there will be picture-story palaces everywhere."

"I see." The boy was clearly backward and an idiot. She dismissed the class and considered what to do about George.

George, undaunted, went to see Figgis.

He was careful to knock quietly on the lab door as he did not want Figgis to have convulsions and start all over again.

Figgis was in a cheerful mood, even though he looked a little demented. "I have redone much of the formula," he said. "I have used up a lot of the memory potion. I need to make more of it before I forget how to make it." He gave a little chuckle. "The formula for the plates should be ready soon."

George became jubilant. "When will it be ready?"

"It should be ready in approximately nine hours, four minutes, and thirty-two seconds."

"Can we go out with the camera tomorrow?"

Figgis said, "Yes."

George left exhilarated. He wanted to tell his dad, but he had vowed not to speak with him for a whole week which was not yet up.

14 – In the Incarceration Room

George William was in very low spirits. His son had disappeared. Each night he had begun a conversation and rambled on with his thoughts on ruling the Earth and the laws he had devised. Halfway through his monologue, he discovered he was talking to the walls. He tried repeatedly for the next three nights and realised his son had abandoned him, which sent him into a depression. He spoke with James about this, but James presumed the king was slipping into delusions. The bathing continued, but it did not prevent his steady decline.

As on many occasions, he tried to keep his spirits up by singing. He sang and danced his way around the room, kicking his legs up like a ballerina. He had been doing this for an hour or two. As he bounced his legs above his waist, he thought about the situation, and concluded he had come on too strong with George. Pressing him too hard with learning history. After all, the boy was only eight, and he must empathise with him. He thought back to when he was eight.

He remembered, at eight, being tutored along with his younger brother Edward at the family house in Leicester Square. So many subjects were being taught – chemistry, physics, astronomy, mathematics, French, Latin, history, music, geography, commerce, agriculture, constitutional law. Being the firstborn and first in line after his father, he knew some day he would be king, and he made an effort to study. In particular, he made big efforts to read, write, and talk in English, not German as was the custom of his family. He was determined to rule the four countries of the British Isles in English and rule by all the traditions of the English language. He would be English, not German. He remembered planning for these things when he was eight. That was in 1746. He remembered the awesome moment when he actually became king. Awesome as it was peculiar. It was early in the morning of 25 October 1760. His grandfather was on the toilet, and he fell off and was pronounced dead! From that moment he was king. He laughed recalling it, which raised his spirits a little, and he realised George was trying to contact him.

He quickly snapped out of his thoughts and got into communicating mode.

"George, wonderful of you to reach out to your old dad. Where have you been? Do not keep away from your old dad anymore."

George Tipton too was longing to reconnect. Although the week was not quite up, he could not keep his news from his dad. The yellow and red glow from the all-night furnaces flooded through the little window, and there was a warm feeling between father and son. It had only been a few days, but they were overcome with emotion.

"Father, I have made an invention."

"What is it?"

"Music-picture-stories."

"Tell me about them."

"There is a new instrument that can take an exact drawing of what you point it at. My science teacher has the only one of its kind in the country."

George William smiled, realising his wishes were being fulfilled. Science, he was convinced, was the way forward, and George was at the very forefront of it.

"It is better than a drawing because it is real. People will see it is real and not fake. Tomorrow I will be making my first music-picture-story."

"That is great news, son. What will be the topic of this music story?"

All of a sudden, George was not so keen to divulge the topic of his first music story. In his scrambled way, it was an attempt to answer a question that was vexing him, and he was strangely frightened to talk about it. In many ways George Tipton was an incredible idiot, and he went silent.

George William, in a desperate attempt to fill the silence, said, "Never mind, tell me when you are ready. I have thought of a game we could play. We can pretend we are in a position to rule the world. You can tell me your ideas on ruling the Earth, and I shall tell you mine. Does that sound like fun?"

Little George agreed it did sound like fun. The king related a few of his ideas, which George did not listen to, and he told him one of his own instead. "I am thinking about having music-picture-palaces where people can go to watch my music-picture-stories," he said. "I shall have them magnified and displayed on a big screen."

George William was swept away with pride. What a brilliant idea, he thought. Dazzle the population with the ways in which he would rule the Earth by displaying it on a big screen in an exciting picture palace! Brilliant, simply brilliant. "I am proud of you, son. You must sleep now so that your first photograph will be a success."

15 – The Day of the First Photograph

In the lab the next morning, George asked Figgis, "Is the formula ready?"

"I think so." Figgis clutched the test tube heroically. "It is a brilliant formula, a wonderful formula, the best formula in the world, and I did it all by myself. It was done by me alone, and me. Me." He waved the formula wildly like a madman.

George realised Figgis had gone nutty. "How much of the memory potion have you been drinking?"

"A lot. I have been drinking it all night."

"Where is the antidote?"

Figgis rapidly searched the test tube racks and pulled one out. "This is it," Figgis said. "I think this is the one."

"Drink some, Mr Figgis. Not too much, just enough to make you better. Get everything ready. I shall see you in one hour."

George left, worried about Figgis, and marched off to inspect the four spots he had chosen for the photographs. Each lurked spookily out of the Black Country smog. He satisfied himself they were all suitably odd and then doubled back to the first one where he had arranged to meet Charles.

Charles was standing in a doorway of a burnt-out foundry. "Here I am," Charles said. "Yes, good spot. Make a good photograph. Shows how dangerous these places are."

"I suppose it would," George muttered, although that was not his motive for choosing it.

Charles announced, "Historic day. Taking the world's first photograph. I'm glad you asked me to be with you."

"Yes, we should always do the important things together. Have you seen Figgis?"

Charles shook his head.

George was now really worried that Figgis had gone off his head, but his fears proved unfounded as, a few moments later, Figgis appeared through the smoke. He was carrying an object with three wooden sticks – a tripod – and was loaded up with various boxes.

"Good to see you, Mr Figgis. Are you better now?"

Figgis nodded.

"Can we get to work and take the photographs right away?"

Figgis agreed.

George demonstrated the setup for the first photograph and stood a few feet in front of the burnt-out building. He held a placard up against his chest. On it was written a single word – '*WHO*'.

"I want you to arrange your equipment," George said. "Arrange it so that it sees all of my head, my chest, and the notice, and the burnt-out building behind me. Can you do that?"

Figgis indicated he could, but cautioned the burnt-out building could look blurred. George said that was alright, and Figgis set about measuring the area of the photograph required and calculated the necessary distance between the camera and George. He erected the tripod, unpacked the camera, and set it on the tripod. "I am ready," Figgis said.

"This is a historic occasion. The world's first photograph," Charles announced. "I think we should have a ceremony. Shall we have a ceremony?"

"No," George said.

"Why not?"

"We need to take all eight photographs, two photographs at each spot, and then have a ceremony."

Charles shrugged. George got ready. Figgis was in place. "Are you ready, Mr Figgis?"

"I am ready," Figgis said. "Stand absolutely still until the photograph is done. Are you ready, Master George?"

George put on a peculiar expression of puzzlement and said, "Yes, go!"

George stood painstakingly still while Figgis engaged the camera and pulled a string. There was a flash and a small explosion and, many seconds later, the world's first photograph was completed.

Charles began clapping. "Hip hip. Hip hip hooray for George Tipton and Mr Figgis for taking the world's first photograph. Hip hip hooray for George Tipton and Mr Figgis for taking—"

George restrained him. "Save that until we have finished. We have to act fast otherwise the plates will go off. Mr Figgis, please load the second plate into the camera and take the second photograph."

Figgis wrapped the first plate in a black cloth and quickly loaded the second plate. The second photograph was similar to the first, except George's expression was now a scowl.

With the second photograph taken, George said, "Mr Figgis, we must move on to the second site and take the third and fourth photographs."

"Very well, Master George."

Figgis wrapped the second plate in a black cloth and packed up the equipment.

George marched off, followed by Charles and Figgis, who were struggling to keep up. George abruptly stopped. "It is here," he said.

Figgis re-erected the equipment at the second site, another damaged building, and George got into position placing another placard up against his chest. This placard read: '*IS*'.

The third and fourth photographs were taken, and George immediately got everyone to move off to the next site.

A little out of breath, Charles asked, "What is the rush?"

"We need to get this done quickly because the chemicals may go off."

They reached the third site. George raised the third placard against his chest. This one read '*MY*'.

The fifth and sixth photographs were taken. Charles was getting progressively puzzled. George raced off to the fourth and final site. Here, George raised his fourth placard and this one read: '*DAD?*'

WHO - IS - MY - DAD? This was George's vexing question.

He wanted to know if his father was the head of some vast criminal organisation that was going to take over the world. He felt if he asked this question he would, in some mystical way, get an answer.

"Hurry off to the labs, Mr Figgis, and process the plates before they go off."

Figgis packed up and marched off into the smoke. Charles was dumbstruck and shrieked, "Are you mad?"

"What do you mean? What about the ceremony?"

"You are asking: 'WHO - IS - MY - DAD?' "

"Yes. I want to know if our father is a criminal. I want to know why he is locked up."

"That is the exact question we must not ask. You will be taken to one orphanage, and I will be taken to another. Maybe something worse. Is that what you want?"

"No!"

"We have to get the plates back from Figgis and throw them in the canal."

George was devastated. "In the canal? They are the world's first photographs!"

"You can think up another music-picture-story but not that one. Prepare to advance on the labs. We must get the plates back."

Reluctantly, George had to agree, and like a couple of boy commandos, they stole back to the school and crept towards the lab. The lab had a glass window. They looked through it and saw Figgis nodding his head at the plates on a workbench. Charles was arched and ready to go like a viper. He whispered, "You keep him distracted while I grab the plates."

George whispered, "We have to be careful not to alarm Mr Figgis."

"Why is that?"

"He might have a fit and spill the rest of the formula and have to start all over again. Then he would drink too much memory potion and go bonkers."

"We will be careful not to alarm Mr Figgis." Charles carefully eased the door open, and they advanced a few feet.

"Be careful not to upset Figgis in any way."

"Why?"

"He is an emotional man. It could send him over the edge. Then he will be unable to help me with the music-picture-stories."

"We will be careful not to upset him."

They crept a few feet more. George started panicking. "Figgis does not like people creeping up on him."

"We will be as careful as we can be. What do you think will happen if we upset him?"

"He might start crying."

"Do not be ridiculous."

"What should we do if he starts crying?"

Charles snapped, "Do what we have to do and grab the plates."

They crept nearer to the bench where Figgis was working. The remainder of the formula was in a rack to one side, and Figgis was looking at it. At the other side were the plates. Charles saw the opportunity, and whispered, "I shall snatch the plates while you keep Figgis occupied."

Charles edged nearer to the plates and was about to grab them when Figgis turned sharply and looked at them. Charles froze.

"Boo hoo hoo."

Figgis started bawling out loud. Charles's mouth dropped open and he was unsure what to do. He went into suspended animation like a frozen Mona Lisa.

"Boo hoo hoo hoo hoo . . ."

Figgis blubbed away and gave out a series of moaning sounds. Then strange snorting sounds as he closed his mouth.

"Ahhh ahhh ahhh . . . Boo hoo hoo."

Charles thought Figgis was a pathetic blubber and decided he'd better grab the plates while he had the chance. As he was about to do this, Figgis buried his head in them and started bawling all over again, and the opportunity was gone.

"Boo hoo hoo."

George was puzzled. The test tube was intact with the formula still in it. Nothing had been spilled. He scratched his head and said, "What is the problem, Mr Figgis?"

"It is the formula. It did not work."

Charles unfroze, quickly seeing the implications of this. "Does that mean the photographs will not come out?"

Figgis nodded, sobbing. "It seems that way."

Charles, trying not to be cheerful, said, "That is a great shame. Must be very upsetting for you. Very sad. I can see that. Yes, very sad indeed. Never mind." He looked at the door and said to George, "I better get off now."

Charles happily skipped out of the door, and George was left with a blubbing Figgis.

"Alright, Mr Figgis, you can dry up now. We have work to do."

Figgis looked up at George like an anxious dog.

"Why did the formula not work?" George asked.

Figgis wiped his face. "There is a chemical missing. It needs an extra chemical to stabilise it."

"What is the missing chemical?"

"I do not know."

"Think about it, Mr Figgis. Think what that chemical could be. Think about it all the time until you solve it."

Figgis nodded.

"And hide the plates. The plates must not be found. Hide them well."

Figgis agreed to do this.

All in all, it had been quite an unsuccessful day for George. The music-picture-story had not been accomplished, and he had once again been frustrated from not finding out who his father was.

16 – George Gains Inspiration From His Father

Although the day had been a failure, he went ahead and connected with his father at 3 a.m. – the magical hour.

"I am sorry, Father. I have failed. The formula did not work. The image faded away."

George William was sympathetic. "It takes time."

"I have been pushing Mr Figgis to find the right chemical."

"That's my boy. Push him. Keep pushing. Always push them. Push them and push them hard. It is the only way to get things done. In my job you have to keep pushing and they seem to love it! So, keep pushing."

George loved it when his father spoke this way. It made him feel special. And powerful. Even so, he would love to know *what* job it was that his father actually did.

"Always take control of the situation. Take command. Assume authority. Be like a Hanoverian," his father said.

His father had told him about the Hanoverians. They were chosen by God and were a little bit superhuman. They had the magic touch and could assume command. It felt great to be like a Hanoverian.

"Just remember to do it with elegance and with grace. That is the trick. Elegance and grace."

"Yes, Father. I have been thinking of a way to make the pictures move."

"Tell me."

"I want to try it with Charles. Have him walking very slowly. Take lots and lots of photographs, one after another, and put them together so they move. He would have to walk very, very, very slowly because it takes about half a minute to take the photograph. He would have to walk so slow he would probably fall over. This is a big problem. Charles falling over."

George William thought about this, for it was a clever idea. Moving images, perhaps on a big screen. He considered the problem and came up with a solution.

"What we need is one hundred cameras all lined up and pointed at Charles as he walks. Then take a photograph from each camera every half-second, like a line of canons. It must be exact; precisely every half-second. Working down the line. By the time we reach camera number one again, fifty seconds would have elapsed, enough time to reload the plates and go back to the first camera and work down the line again. We would need a line of riflemen firing off shots every half-second to keep the time. This is what you will need: one hundred cameras and one hundred cameramen, one hundred rifleman and, let us say, ten thousand plates waiting to be loaded. Yes, ten thousand plates."

"That is fantastic. Thank you, Dad."

His father had such great ideas. He imagined things big. That is what he loved. One hundred cameras, one hundred cameramen, one hundred riflemen, ten thousand plates. Yes!

17 – Figgis Blows up a Chemical Works

"We need one hundred cameras," George said to Figgis.

"One hundred cameras? Why?"

George explained the moving picture concept.

Figgis gathered his hat and coat and a few other essentials. "I better get down to Kew and see Mr Claude Niépce right away."

George restrained him.

"Mr Figgis, no. First, we must perfect the formula. There is no point in having one hundred cameras if the formula does not work. Have you thought about the missing chemical?"

"Yes, I think I know what it is."

"Have you tried it?"

"No. The school does not have the chemical."

"Who has this chemical?"

"I think the Cradley Heath Chemical Works have it."

"Mr Figgis - go to the Cradley Heath Chemical Works and get that chemical."

That night, Figgis visited the Cradley Heath Chemical Works.

It was after dark, and Figgis hid in a bush beside the works and watched until he was convinced all the workers had left. Then he made his move and broke in. He found the main chemical store. There were thousands of chemicals, a hundred times bigger than the school store, but not one of the chemicals was the one he was looking for. He realised he would have to manufacture the chemical himself using a mixture of other chemicals. He grabbed several dozen chemicals and brought them upstairs to the testing lab. He worked like a maniac. After many hours, he got a mixture of a formula that worked. He added the mixture to the original formula and filled two vials. Then an accident happened.

Tubes of earlier experiments caught fire. Before he could do anything, they had ignited 200 experiments in other test tubes, experiments the chemical works were working on. Bangs and splutters and exploding test tubes were everywhere. One end of the testing lab caught fire. He stoppered up the vials of the successful formula and ran down the stairs and out of the building.

The first big explosion happened a couple of minutes later. Several others followed, and the building exploded into a fireball. He dashed into the dense smog and ran. The thick Black Country smoke obscured his escape. In the distance, he heard the bells of a fire wagon coming to the scene. He had been running for about eight minutes when he heard whistles too, the sounds of a hunting party. The party was coming closer, and he dived into a ditch. The hunting party went past. He took the vials out of his pocket and kissed them and looked out from the ditch in celebration. "I have done it! I have the right formula," he ranted. "A formula that works."

He knew now that he would have to go on the run.

In the morning, George visited the school lab. The lab was empty. He found Charles and said, "Figgis has gone missing."

Charles looked George in the eye. "The Cradley Heath Chemical Works burnt down last night."

"Do you think it was him?"

"Of course, it was him. Who else would it be? He has probably gone on the run."

"Where would he go?"

"I shall ask Tom. He has ears on the street."

A few days later, Tom reported back that Figgis was living in a fugitive colony near Liverpool.

In his nightly conversation, George told his father about Figgis and the chemical works, and a few days later he gave an update that Figgis had been spotted in a fugitive colony near Liverpool.

18 – George William Confides in James

In his nightly conversations with George, as well as the updates about Figgis, George William had been urging George to learn the history of the United Kingdom but wasn't getting very far with this. Moreover, George did not show any notion of how he would bring peace to the Earth. All he seemed interested in was music-picture-stories and the associated palaces they would be displayed in. Nothing else.

Then, the king was given a revelation from a celestial messenger that George was not the one; George was merely establishing the line for the one who would establish peace on Earth. It would be a descendant of George Tipton that would undertake this particular job, although there was no indication when this would be. This revelation caused George William to readjust his own role, and his legacy. He confided this revelation to James.

To James, he said, "None of us know the great beyond until we reach it. However, I have been reliably informed that kings do not simply expire. They are given time to explain their achievements on Earth so they can be listed in order of merit in the celestial memorial garden. I will do something different. Go one step further. I will list my achievements and give them observations of lessons learnt. With this, I will present my ideas on how human life should be organised.

While we are waiting for the one who will bring the heavenly age, I will request my return. In short, James, I have decided to ask for another go."

"Another go, Your Majesty?"

"I already have the document for universal law on Earth. I am ready to plan a step further. A vision of perfection on Earth. A perfect plan for the Earth. I want to present this as something I am uniquely placed to accomplish. I want another go."

"And I wish you success in that enterprise, Your Majesty."

"Thank you, James. We should not entirely cancel out George Tipton as it will be his descendants that are important. I want you to oversee that he does in fact have a descendant. We must not lose sight of the prophecy."

"No, Your Majesty."

"And I wish to give you a gift, James. A sanatorium."

"A sanatorium, Your Majesty?"

"The finest sanatorium in the country, and a most secure one. It is in the Ashdown Forest near the town of East Grinstead in the county of Sussex."

"Very kind of you, Your Majesty."

"It is not only a fine sanatorium but a very profitable one too. The odd raja has been locked up there for re-education. The potential in that sanatorium is great. I want you and your family to have a good income after I am gone."

James inclined his head in sorrow. "Gone, Your Majesty? No."

"Come, James, we must all leave our mortal bodies, it is inevitable. It will not be a goodbye, for I shall find a way of keeping in communication. You and your descendants will become part of my inner circle. There is also the question of Figgis."

"The scientist who blew up the Cradley Heath Chemical Works?"

"Yes, that one. He may be a blubbering idiot, but he has a fine brain, and he is at the very forefront of science. He who is ahead of science is ahead of everything. I want Figgis and his descendants to be part of my inner circle too. I want you to offer him assistance and make sure he does not fall into the hands of the authorities."

"I will do my best, Your Majesty. Now I have to inform you of something."

"What is that?"

"I am being reassigned to Kensington Palace. It is concerning your fourth son, Edward. His wife is having a baby. If it is a girl, it will be called Victoria. The nursery and everything for taking up residence is being prepared at this moment."

George William reminisced. "Kensington Palace, yes. I remember the place. Has pleasant gardens."

"Indeed, Your Majesty. The Kensington Gardens are amongst the finest landscaped gardens anywhere."

"I remember walking around them with my father. He had a particular fascination with them."

"Yes, Your Majesty."

"James, when will you be reassigned?"

"In approximately three months."

"In that case we must get busy."

For the next three months, the king and James worked on the perfect plan for the Earth. The king was in his legacy stage. Most people fashion their legacy so they will be remembered for the good works they did on Earth. For George William, it was all about getting back on Earth for a second go.

While he considered the plan would be perfect, there would always be exceptions: misbehavers that would not follow the conventions of good citizenship. For this, James's sanatorium near East Grinstead would be used to accommodate misbehavers. For the next few weeks, they had hours of fun planning the redesign of the sanatorium. In this period, they became something akin to best mates. The king never had so much fun in his life, and he discovered the delight of performing pranks.

"I have had a wonderful time, James."

"Me too, Your Majesty. I am sorry I have to leave tonight for Kensington Palace. I can no longer be by your side."

"That is something we can do nothing about, but we shall stay in contact."

"We will, Your Majesty."

Meanwhile, George Tipton, contrary to what his father thought, was studying history. He was making his teachers' lives a misery in the way he was cajoling them to do this. He would pull on their coattails like a rabid dog until they agreed. There were two motives for learning history. The first was to please his father. The second was his aim to make historical music-picture-stories. For some peculiar George-ism, history seemed to begin in Britain in 1702. He drew hundreds of pictures for these moving picture shows. A comprehensive history starting in Britain in 1702. For the music, he drew inspiration from visits to St Philip's Cathedral in Birmingham with Mr Brahms. He was particularly inspired by the music of Henry Purcell, George Frideric Handel, and Wolfgang Mozart. He was preparing all this material for when Mr Figgis returned.

During this time, the intensity of his conversations with his father waned, almost as if his father was no longer interested in him or his music-picture-stories. Then, at the time James transferred to Kensington Palace, the nightly conversations intensified once more. One night, at 3 a.m., George William announced to George Tipton, "Son, I am entering the next phase of my life."

19 – The Final Phase

"I am dying," his father said.

The king, his preparations for legacy done, was entering the next stage, the final stage on Earth, the dying phase.

"Do not say that, Dad, do not go."

"I have to, son, it is inevitable, there is no other way. It is the fate of all people. One day it will be your turn. Do you want an insight into dying? Do you wish to hear my experience of exiting from this Earth?"

George shuddered a bit and considered this morbid topic for a while. "How long will it take, the dying? How long?"

"I cannot say. Various diseases will consume my body, some known, some unknown. I estimate I will deteriorate terminally over the next month or two."

"Yes, Father, please share your experience of dying with me."

"Very well, you can be my dying consort."

"I will go on the journey with you, Father. I will stand by you and share in your pain. Share that with me. I will travel with you until you die. I can be your deathbed companion."

"My deathbed companion?"

The king was touched. Surprised and deeply moved. "It is kind of you, George, you are a sweet considerate boy and I do not deserve you. Thank you."

"You are my dad, what else could I do?"

"I know not what to say. I am feeling a love from you that I have not felt from anyone. It is wonderful, but enough for now. Illness is sapping my body of strength, and I am tired. Tired, so very tired. I must sleep, and so must you. I will speak with you tomorrow. Thank you, George."

In the orphanage dormitory, George could not sleep and spent all night thinking about his dying father.

In the morning, he spoke to Charles as they sat on the coal pile. "Our father is ill, very ill. He is dying."

"Our father is dead," Charles insisted.

"He is not dead, but he is dying."

Charles put his hands over his ears. "Do not talk to me about Father again. Stop. The trust says he is dead."

George realised Charles would not understand; the journey with his father would have to be a private affair with no one else in attendance.

"I am totally blind," his father told him the following night. "I cannot see a thing and I am almost totally deaf too. All my faculties are fading, and my enemies are probably having a field day."

"Who are your enemies, Father?"

"I do not want to go into my enemies at this moment, George. Too exhausting. Your support can keep me strong against any foul moves of my enemies. Enemies plotting against a blind and deaf man in his moments of weakness. My body is very weak."

Suddenly, George William began vomiting. Retching his guts out. For over five minutes, he vomited. "I am sorry, son, this is my condition at the moment." No sooner had he uttered this when the retching started all over again. After recovering from this bout, he said, "I have missed the bucket and been sick all over the floor. Nobody will clean it up until the morning."

"I am sorry about that, Dad."

Another bout of retching began, and his father moaned at the exhaustion of it all. This bout must have gone on for ten minutes, and at the end, his breathing was heavily laboured. He was wheezing as he took in air. Heaving for breath. "I am fading. Fading fast," he gasped.

"Are you dying now?"

He rallied, "Oh no, there is still a long way to go. This is what it is like. A long hard slog ahead of us. I am fading fast into the land of sleep. Very, very tired. Goodnight, son. I shall speak with you tomorrow."

The king's condition, by any measure, was quite horrendous. He had chest pains and abdominal pains. Blisters and boils multiplied over his body and itched enormously. His head ached, and he vomited most of the time.

"It is not the best situation," the king was fond of saying. "Rather unpleasant actually."

"You are coping well, Dad."

"It is because of you, George. You being at my side."

This situation went on for months, gradually getting worse and more painful. For most of the day, he lived a weird, haunted existence. Blind, deaf, and stumbling around his room relieved only by the warm familiar voice of George for an hour or so at night. Often, he descended into delirious fits. Epilepsy was one of his conditions. Frequently, he plummeted into hysterical ramblings and reminisced on the failings of his life. He was wailing in his sleep as he relived his greatest failure – the loss of America. His instructions for the colonists not to advance beyond the Mississippi River had been misunderstood. It was 1763. His intention was that a settlement be negotiated with the native population. An equitable settlement. He wished to be king to the native population as well as the colonists. He would be king to them all.

"I have failed and beg forgiveness," he wailed into the night. "Beg forgiveness for I have failed to communicate my plans correctly to the colonists. Please, Lord, put America right for me."

One night, he said to George, "I am being punished for my sins. This is why I am being tortured. It is punishment for my sins."

"What are your sins, Father? What have you done?"

"I have many sins, but mainly I have failed. Failed in my duties and failed you."

"How have you failed me, Dad?"

With the exhaustion of the communication, George William relapsed into unconsciousness and had once again failed, leaving his son mystified.

Sometimes, the king was lucid.

"Have you thought about children, George? Having an heir?"

"I am only nine, Dad."

"I know, yes. Children, keep it in mind, George. An heir, George, an heir."

"Yes, Father. I have composed a music-picture-story about 1702, like you wanted."

"That is good, very good. I would like to see that, George."

"You cannot see it because you are locked up, and I cannot make it because Mr Figgis has disappeared."

"Ah, Figgis, yes. That situation is under control."

"Is it?"

"Yes, the Figgis situation is being dealt with."

George was confused.

This batty situation continued for a while, and this was only when he was lucid. Mainly he was not. Most of the time, he was having frenzied fits and being ill. As his condition worsened and he lost the use of his limbs, he was transferred to his original luxurious bed chamber and attended by physicians. Other people were in attendance too, but since he was totally deaf and blind, he did not know who they were, and all he experienced was being poked and prodded which he accepted as he did not have any other options. The only real connection he had was with George Tipton in the middle of the night.

One night, towards the end of January, his father said to him, "I cannot hold out much longer, son. My life is going. I am fading."

George, sitting up on his orphanage bed, bowed to the inevitable and was, like George William, totally exhausted.

The red-yellow glow of the foundries flickered from outside. The strain of the 3 a.m. encounters was taking its toll, and the intensity was great.

"How long will it be, Father?"

"Maybe a day, maybe less."

"I have to go to school in the morning."

"You should sleep now. I will rest too. I shall be here when you return from school. I will hang on."

The significance of the coming event struck George.

"Do not go, Father. Stay."

"I have to go. It is the way of mortal life. All physical beings must someday die."

"What will I do? Please do not go."

George began crying.

In a rare moment of true and deep emotion, George William felt a huge wave of love for his son. A love he had never felt before. Poor innocent little George. A tear dripped from his eye. It turned into a flood.

"I must go, son. There is no other way. I will come back for you, George. I will come back and see your music-picture-story. I will find a way. I promise, promise to return."

"Will you, Father?"

"Yes. I promise. Now go to sleep and contact me again after you return from school."

Soon, George fell into a half-sleep.

20 – *Dying Day, 28 January 1820*

In the morning, George, half-rested, left with Charles to walk to school. It was a cold January day and just getting light in the smoky, Black Country street. Charles took two knitted waistcoats out of a bag. "Put these on," Charles said.

George put his waistcoat on. The clothing had been issued by the trust, and Charles had organised putting them on and off in the street so as not to cause more friction with the orphans. The orphans did not have such good clothes. There were ongoing problems and dangers with the other orphans. As they entered the school, the mood was solemn. The teacher announced lessons would be suspended for the next few days as news had reached the school of the king's imminent death.

"We must pray for the deliverance of His Majesty at this awful time," she said. "The school will be closed for the next two weeks. You must go home and pray."

She handed Charles two black armbands. "After he has ascended, we must wear black for several days of mourning. We will all wear black and pray as a sign of respect for his passing. The other orphans where you live may not have black clothes, and so it is acceptable to wear these. Everyone is being issued with them."

Charles thanked her for the understanding and took the armbands. He left with George. News had reached the orphanage, and all the orphans were praying. George and Charles tiptoed inside and maintained the silence. It was cold in the dormitory without their woollen waistcoats. Charles sat on his bed, not much into praying, but could not think what else to do. George sat on his bed trying to get in touch with his father. After a while he did.

"I am still here, son, but it will not be long." His father sounded very weak.

"Father, you never told me about Mother. Tell me now."

George William thought fondly about Nefeli. "She was a princess," he said. "A beautiful magical princess, Princess Nefeli."

George was a little puzzled.

George William became dreamy and hazy. "Maybe you could run a divine empire."

"Run a divine empire?"

"Have a think about divine empires. Have a good think . . . Ahhhchh!!" George William choked suddenly. "This is it. I am going, George. The moment has come." There was a pause for a few moments. Then a few grunts, and then, "Oh, it is really quite an unusual experience. Not bad. I am off, son, goodbye. Divine empires! See you in a while."

A few moments later, he was gone. George was stunned by the silence.

Gone. It had been very sudden.

He looked around the dormitory. It was silent. All the orphans were praying.

A few minutes later he stood up and walked out of the dormitory and entered the street. Teardrops formed. He dried his eyes and instinctively put the armband on. He headed for the coal pile and sat. A few minutes later, Charles appeared and sat beside him.

George was solemn. "Our father – he has gone. He is dead."

"You mean the king? Is the king dead?"

"No – our father. He has gone."

Charles looked away, but then said, "I think you are growing up."

"Our mother was a princess. A magical princess."

Charles looked away, realising George really did have a loose screw.

After he left his body, George William hovered above, saw the physician pronounce him dead and laughed at how solemn everyone looked. He saw his eldest son, in this instant becoming King George IV. He saw them making the preparations for his funeral. He soared above. He saw people praying for him. Ordinary people. He was humbled. Millions of people praying. He came upon the north and saw George and Charles sitting on the coal pile in the Black Country. What a smoky old place they had been put in. He saw that George Tipton was sad. He silently hovered over George and Charles, and listened in.

"I did not know much about him, not even his name," George was saying.

Charles empathised because, by now, everyone knew George was not quite the full shilling.

George went on, "Children should always know who their father is. I shall call my firstborn son George, so he will know who his father is."

Charles considered this because he thought it was a good idea. "Yes, that is sensible. You could call him George the Second."

"Yes, that is right. And he should call his firstborn son George too. He will become George the Third."

"What if the firstborn is a girl?"

George thought about this for a little while. "I would call her Georgina. Yes, Georgina."

Charles nodded. "I think I shall call my firstborn son Charles."

"He will be called Charles the Second, I suppose."

"That is right."

"But what would you call a firstborn girl?"

Charles thought about this. "I suppose I would call her Charlotte, yes, Charlotte," he said.

George William was pleased by what he saw. Satisfied, he soared above to begin his preparations. Freed from his crippled body, and the unbearable pain, he saw the divine order clearly now. Saw it laid out in front of him. He wondered who the divine ruler would be, which of George's children would be the one, and realised his next task was to prepare his pitch for his 'return'!

However, as in life, not all things go as planned. Especially in death.

CHAPTER FIVE

George Tipton's Pitch, 1850

21 – Frederick's Preamble

"As in life, in death nothing turns out exactly as you imagine," Frederick said. "George William could not return immediately. One may say he had given the boy false hopes. Nearly thirty years elapsed before the king had contact with the Earth again."

Frederick paused, shaking his head, and looked at me.

"As a result, life had not gone particularly well for George Tipton. He never gave up his obsession with moving pictures, but without his father, or Figgis, who had not yet returned either, he lacked the practical wherewithal to turn his work into public viewings. A galling experience for an important groundbreaking artist such as George. One should take a moment to feel the frustration of the artist denied the pleasure of anyone viewing their work. Nowadays, people love to revel in the agony of Dutchman Vincent van Gogh and pay millions to have a private experience of his torturous life as they wander through their personal galleries. George Tipton's genius lay not only in the moving picture sphere, but also in the way he combined music to his images. Brilliant. I am a man of music, so I have a particular empathy with this young man, not to mention him being a descendant of mine. All in all, I feel it incumbent of me to briefly recount something of his life and triumphs and to rescue them, if only for a few moments, from disappearing down the black hole of history.

"After finishing school in the Black Country, he was sent to the East India Company headquarters in London to work as a clerk, a job he disliked enormously. At night, he continued working on his moving pictures – or music-picture-stories as he called them – but got dismissed from the 'Honourable Company' (as it called itself) because he petitioned a wealthy tea merchant to invest in his moving pictures. I shall come to that incident later. In desperation, he begged the trustees for money and inadvertently betrayed his brother Charles, who received a long harsh prison sentence as a result. It was not George's fault as Charles supposed. You see, people were working behind the scenes, enemies of the king, the ones in Prussia. They had infiltrated the trust, and the trust had become a particularly dangerous organisation, something neither of the boys were aware of at the time. Obviously, after his brother was jailed, George became racked with guilt and hid away for many years. Living on a pittance in poor circumstances, he contracted typhoid. However, he fell in love with his nurse and had a child. Then his wife died when the child was two. I told you things did not go particularly well for George. He wondered how bad they could get.

"Obviously, he loved his son, but found it hard to look after him. His music-picture-stories became his anchor but made no money. His son, at the age of four, persuaded his father to give him a showing of the works. By this time,

George had built a number of projectors with magnifying lenses. The boy was bowled over by what he saw and became his number one supporter. Actually, his only supporter. In the interests of his father's mental health, and also for reasons of money, the boy, a very bright lad whom he called George the Second – funny that is also the title of my father – anyway, young George the Second pestered his father to go around the theatres and book some showings. Unfortunately, his father was not very good at selling himself. Always got sidetracked and constantly came home empty-handed. Finally, a few months later, young George the Second heard about the Great Exhibition, the greatest exhibition for inventions ever held. To be housed in a gigantic glass palace the following spring in 1851. Applications had just opened, and young George the Second insisted his father apply, which he did. His son impressed on him not to get sidetracked, which his father said he would try to remember.

"George Tipton, now forty years of age, was both excited and terrified by the prospect of auditioning for the exhibition. His great adventure was about to begin. Like a desperate gambler, he staked everything on this opportunity. He borrowed money to hire halls which were near to his old employment of the East India Company. He hired an orchestra and actors. Throwing the dice for one last go. Throwing dangerously for the jackpot. Rolling the dice for fame or destitution. One last go.

"So, my account of George Tipton continues in late November 1850 as he prepares to pitch to the Allocations Board of the Great Exhibition."

22 – *George Tipton Gives His Pitch*

At dawn, George took possession of the suite of halls and worked feverishly to get everything prepared for the arrival of the Allocations Board at 11 a.m. He began with the main hall, where a mixed media of his music-picture-stories would be presented. He wanted it dark and atmospheric, so when his show started, it would be exciting and mysterious. One strand of his show would include the royal succession of the United Kingdom, which was very odd, and more than a little spooky, as he was part of that family and did not even know it!

Once finished in the main hall, he turned his attentions to the reception area. There was a large ornate desk already there, and this gave the room some gravitas. Perhaps the gravitas was downgraded a little as George nailed a series of rails to the ceiling. These were fitted with runners and hooks, and he suspended dozens of his paintings on them, and they hung down from the ceiling like a wardrobe of pictures. He had a complex pulley system to lower each painting down with cords. Pleased with his system, he sat at the big desk, lit a cigar, and waited for the Board to arrive.

At precisely 11 a.m., the Allocations Board arrived. There were three of them: Gerald, Cedric, and Percy, each sedately dressed in black morning coats with tails. George showed them into the reception office and sat them on three seats in front of his big desk. Gerald, the head of the three-man team, stood up and explained how the audition would run.

"Mr Tipton, we give you one hour to present your invention. Explain it in as much detail as you need using diagrams and models and highlight its uses and benefits and anything else we need to know. We will assess its worthiness for the exhibition and present our findings to Prince Albert, who is the director of the exhibition. I should add that our recommendation will almost certainly mean it will be accepted."

"Yes, I know the rules," George said.

"Good, then proceed when you are ready."

"My invention will show how Great Britain led the world into the modern age!"

"Extraordinary," Gerald said, amazed. "I was not aware an invention could do that."

"Oh yes, mine can do that."

Gerald withdrew his pocket watch. "Right, let us begin. Your hour starts now."

"Here goes," George said nervously.

Rather absurdly, George Tipton had dressed himself as a British bulldog type of Englishman with a tight Union Jack waistcoat, tight trousers, top hat, and a cane. He braced himself and rose from his large ornate desk.

"England, England, England!" George proclaimed. "The country that propelled the world into the modern machine-driven age. What a fine country! I am going to tell you how all of this began. It began in 1702. Yes, 1702!"

The three members of the Allocations Board looked on, slightly perplexed.

George continued, "It is necessary to have a period of mourning for the passing of an age. A degree of respect for its dying way of life. The end of the medieval age, the start of a new age. The new age of the machine. What will it bring? What will be the outcome? I shall tell you."

Instead of telling them, he went absolutely silent. He closed his eyes and breathed in deeply. It was not a momentary thing but instead went on for about five minutes. If the Board had been perplexed, they were now full-throated baffled. George went through a series of pained contorted movements with the occasional groan. What was actually happening was, George was hearing the slow, sombre, and deeply mournful tones of 'Queen Mary's Death March' by Henry Purcell and imagining all the traditions of the medieval age coming to an end. While he was experiencing all this and imagining the music, nobody else was. Now, you can appreciate why George Tipton never progressed very far with convincing people of his music-picture-stories. Finally, after an appropriate period, George came out of his trance and asked the Board, "Are you familiar with 'Queen Mary's Death March'?"

Gerald, the head of the three-man Allocations Board, asked grimly, "Are you suggesting we are funeral directors?"

George shook his head vigorously. "I was not meaning that at all. I feel music deeply. Feel it as though I am composing it, and I intend to add the music of 'Queen Mary's Death March', so that it gives magnitude to the enormity of the change. Now, I will tell you how the change happened."

George turned his attention to his overhead pulley system and lowered two drawings. One of King William III, and the other a drawing of the original Bank of England building in the Walbrook enclave of the City of London. He got into his stride and slammed his cane into King William.

"Here is King William, William of Orange. The funeral music is very appropriate because William of the Orange died in 1702. Before he died, he started this."

Now, George slammed his cane into the Bank of England building, making it swing. "King William started the Bank of England, a financial system that would fuel the coming machine-driven revolution. Shares and credit – the oxygen of the coming age. A source of endless money that would realise a thousand inventions. I shall start with two inventions of 1702 that changed everything."

George sent the Bank of England and King William travelling off on a parallel rail and engaged another set of pulleys releasing another slew of pictures. With his confidence growing, he slammed his cane into the first picture, and then a second. "Here we have a chap called Jethro Tull who invented this: a seed-drilling machine. A machine that could accurately sow seeds in orderly rows, sow them faster, a machine that could increase food production many times over." He moved his cane to the machine in a field. "Here we have the machine in action in the fields of England, outside the village of Shalbourne in the county of Wiltshire. A seed-drilling machine, a momentous advance in farming. At the same time, several miles west, in the village of Saltford, another man – Mr Abraham Darby – was finishing off his new invention." George moved his cane to the Darby set of drawings. "He invented a new way of making iron. The material to make the machines of the new age. Now, England could feed the world with Mr Tull's seed-drilling machine, and all of humanity could be relieved of toil with the machines that were made of Mr Darby's iron. With mankind freed of toil and hunger, there could be a divine world. England could institute a divine operation on its empire, but did it? No. My father wanted me to run a divine empire, but how am I meant to run a divine empire? It would be nice to have a divine empire, but how am I meant to run it?"

George seemed to have gotten sidetracked and gone off on a tangent about divine empires. Ideas for divine empires, theories on divine empires, and the almost impossible task of getting into a situation of being empowered to run a divine empire.

Now, you can appreciate why George Tipton was not very good at presenting his moving picture ideas – he was always going off on tangents, and divine empires was usually one of them. He was jolted out of his rant by a series of loud raspberry sounds.

"Blooooph . . . Blooooph . . . Blooooph . . .!"

The raspberries were coming from the smallest member of the allocations trio, an impish little fellow called Percy. "Blooooph . . . Blooooph . . . Blooooph . . .!"

George Tipton's jaw dropped, alarmed. "Why is he doing that?"

Percy piped up, "Divine empires? The man is a lunatic. What have divine empires to do with us?"

Gerald, the senior member, stood up. "Yes, Mr Tipton, I agree. Divine empires are nothing to do with us. We have come to review your application for two stands in the Crystal Palace exhibition area. The exhibition is for inventions only and not for divine empires. Divine empires, or anything to do with divine empires, are not in our remit." Gerald flipped his eyes towards the door. "Come on, you lot," he said.

George panicked, realising his whole life was about to evaporate. "No, wait, sorry, I went off track," he said. "Please sit down. I promise not to talk about divine empires anymore.

No more divine empires. I will tell you about my application for two stands in the Crystal Palace. Please sit."

George quickly released more placards, ones of the Crystal Palace, and the Board reluctantly sat. The Crystal Palace was shown to be a huge, sparkling glass edifice with tiered layers like some vast transparent wedding cake. George pointed his cane at the first placard.

"I only want one stand inside the actual Crystal Palace, a ticket office to gain entry into my music-picture-theatre which will be on the grass area outside the Crystal Palace."

Now, George turned his attention to a series of dangling paintings of his music-picture-theatre. This was like a mini version of the tiered Crystal Palace. Apart from being about a tenth of the size, it had no windows and was made from shiny, white alabaster stone. The words 'music-picture-stories' were emblazoned in big bold letters along one side of the building, enticing people towards it.

"I want one stand inside the Crystal Palace that explains what is inside my music-picture-theatre, and someone to advise on showtimes and direct them to my music-picture-theatre outside. This man would also sell the tickets."

The three members of the Board looked at each other in incredulity.

Gerald said, "There is no theatre in the exhibition, and no plans for one either. It is not that type of exhibition."

"But there could be. I went to see a builder last Tuesday and showed him my drawings, and he said he could build one."

Gerald was a little overcome with this level of idiocy, and Percy began blowing raspberries again. "Bloooph, blooooph, blooooph!"

This time, George became aware of the stakes: his son, the money he owed. He simply could not be defeated. He remembered what his father had said to him so many years ago. "Be like a Hanoverian and take control of the situation. Take control. Simply do it with grace and you shall be fine." He felt a fire rising in him.

"I want that theatre, and I am going to get it. I know the rules – you have to listen to my application for one hour, and I demand that you stay and listen."

He began beating the drawing, making it swing, and roared, "I want this theatre! I need this theatre! I demand it!"

He hit the picture repeatedly. Hitting it so hard that it swung violently, knocking Percy and the chair onto the floor. Percy had the look of a surprised squirrel. The other two were taken aback with astonishment.

Cedric, the third member of the trio, looked at George in shock. "You have knocked Percy to the ground. Percy and the chair are on the floor!"

George roared at them. "I do not care. I want that theatre. I know the rules. You must listen to my presentation, and if you do not, I shall report you to Prince Albert. Report this to Prince Albert, do you understand? Follow me into the Hallowed Theatre of the Picture Story. Follow now!"

He said this with immense force, and the Board, bamboozled and a little confused, up righted Percy and followed him into the next hall.

George had certainly taken control of the situation but had forgotten about the 'do it with grace' bit.

23 – The Hallowed Theatre of the Picture Story

"Why did we not simply leave?" Cedric asked.

Miffed, Gerald replied, "He somehow took control of the situation. He threatened to report us to Prince Albert."

"We are allowed to leave if an applicant gets violent."

Percy whispered, "Tipton is mad, an unhinged maniac. We need to get out of here."

"Yes, well, we have missed that opportunity," Gerald said. "Next time he tries anything, we will certainly leave. If he starts throwing the furniture around or has some other fit of lunacy, we shall leave immediately, report him, and see that he is locked up."

"Agreed," Percy and Cedric said in unison.

George had led them into this large, darkened hall, and there were various things going on in a rather unsettling darkness. Percy whispered his concerns that it may be too dark to find their way out, and that Tipton was trying to disorientate them; Gerald, uneasy, acknowledged this may be the case. There was a ghostly hum about the place and the whine of an instrument tuning up. In the middle of the room, appeared to be two stumpy objects, and a few yards in front of them, some kind of stage with the faint silhouette of a woman seated.

Out of the darkness, George Tipton's voice came.

"To appreciate the glory of the United Kingdom, one must first be introduced to the majesty of the royal succession," he said.

At this stage, George Tipton had no intentions of doing dastardly acts on them; he simply wanted to get on with his show, which essentially was to portray the history of the United Kingdom in a way nobody had done before.

"I shall now add the depth of music to my show with the sounds of a full orchestra."

Very softly, the orchestra started up with the majestic music of Handel.

"I shall continue my show from the year of 1702, the year that King William of Orange died. Anne, from a family of the Stewards of Scotland, filled the empty throne. She became Queen of England. Her family had been the High Stewards of Scotland since the 1100s. Now, they entered the steward-ship of England too. As Queen Anne got settled onto her throne, the Court of Hanover sent over their court composer, a man we shall call George Frideric Handel, and I present to you an actor who plays George Frideric Handel!"

Now, a team of previously unseen lamp-holders illumi-nated the actor playing Handel, who bowed, and the sound of applause was heard. It was coming from an audience of fifteen men and women, actors, who became illuminated too. They were a select audience wearing exquisite garments from the height of 1700's fashion. As the genteel music got into full swing, the audience gently tapped in time with the genteelness.

"A genteelness descended upon London," George said. "No longer were these to be the bawdy lands of King Henry the Eighth but filled with the graces of Handel's genteel music. The airs and graces imported from the Court of Hanover. A miracle was achieved. England's genteelness. The secret magic of the British Empire. Britain ruled half the world with very little effort. Genteelness was to become the mark of Great Britain. The word of a Briton became his bond. He needed nothing else. Poise, grace, genteelness. It was a great talent perfected in Britain, but the Empire it ruled was not yet divine . . ."

He stopped urgently, aware of not mentioning divine empires. Instead, he coughed, moved on to divine queens, and shuffled the lamp-holders towards the stage which became illuminated, revealing Queen Anne sitting on a fine chair as a handmaiden delicately brushed her hair. The orchestra and a singer began performing Handel's 'Ode for the Birthday of Queen Anne – the Eternal Source of Light Divine', a cantata with deeply religious tones.

George continued, "Handel created the divine music for Queen Anne, giving her the divine image needed, all part of the magic of empire.

"The empire continued apace, because during her reign, England united with Scotland to form one United Kingdom. A powerful combination: a divine queen with Scottish fighters to conquer the world.

"During her reign, a law was passed that the monarch of the United Kingdom would never again be a Catholic. And George Frideric Handel's divine music carried on."

George paused for a while. Then his tone became sombre.

"Queen Anne ruled for fourteen years and then she was taken from this Earth. Seventeen times she incubated an heir. Seventeen babies, and not one of them made it to birth." He said this grimly with tragic emotion. "Seventeen babies, all dying. Hard for anyone to bear."

Handel's sombre death march began as the stage slowly darkened.

"Although there was no natural heir, there were over forty relatives, but they were all Catholic. The nearest Protestant relative was Georg Ludwig, the Elector of Hanover."

Very slowly, the stage re-illuminated, and sitting on the chair that Anne once occupied, sat King George I, dressed in fantastic robes and looking all pomp and splendid.

"The Hanoverian reign of the United Kingdom had begun. I have been told the Hanoverians are a little bit magical and will remain on the throne for as long as the United Kingdom exists. The Hanoverian rule did not start very well."

The orchestra started bashing pots and pans, the sound of civil unrest.

"The English did not like King George, and he did not like the English. Riots broke out in Bristol, Birmingham, and seventeen other cities."

Actor Handel entered the stage, sat at a piano behind King George I, and played his composition, 'Lotario'.

"Soon, the riots calmed, cajoled by the soothing majestic sounds of George Frideric Handel. What a joy it was for King George to have a fellow countryman in his court, speaking a familiar language, and playing the familiar music of back home. King George the First never liked England, never spoke English, and returned to his Duchy in Hanover every summer, year after year."

King George grumpily marched off the stage, and then returned. He did this repeatedly as Handel continued playing.

"King George did not like the English way of ruling either. Most of his commands had to be approved by Parliament, not like back home. Most of all, he was in constant arguments with his son. He thought his son was becoming too British, and not paying attention to the Duchy of Brunswick-Lüneburg back home. The rows became enormous. Sometimes, they did not speak for weeks. This is a common fault line of the Hanoverians: fathers and firstborn sons not getting along, hating each other."

The stage slowly darkened.

"The years passed, the king grew older and weaker, and bowed to the inevitable oncoming fate all men must face."

The stage re-illuminated. The king looked older. Handel, looking older too, was still at the piano.

"The king realised the throne must be secured with the Hanoverian bloodline on it. Despite all the arguments, his firstborn son must become the next king. He asked Handel to compose music for the coronation of his son. Something so strong and powerful that it would imbed the Hanoverian bloodline onto the throne of England forever."

Handel began writing feverishly. The orchestra struck up with the long opening preamble to the Coronation Anthem.

"Heirs and successions are very important to the Hanoverians," George said. "It is one of their major functions. My father told me to be like a Hanoverian and have an heir." George Tipton started reminiscing dreamily about his father and fell back into his major flaw. The flaw that had always dogged his presentations. Getting sidetracked and drifting off into tangents.

"My father was a prisoner," he went on. "He was locked up in prison and we never met. We discussed my music-picture-stories many times without ever meeting. He promised to come and see my music-picture-stories after he was dead. He died thirty years ago, but he never came. I am still hopeful."

The Board had been somewhat relaxed, but now that confidence fell apart.

Gerald whispered, "Tipton is a complete fruitcake. Once we get back to the palace, we shall find a suitable asylum that can look after him."

"Let us go now," Cedric said. "He does not have an invention. What he thinks is an invention is only a play. We are entitled to leave."

Gerald agreed. "You are right." He stood up. "Mr Tipton – although we believe your play is quite inventive, it is not an actual invention. It is actual inventions we are licensed to review, and your play is not one of them. Therefore, we must leave."

They all stood up.

George shook his head. "You cannot leave."

"Why is that?"

"I got a man to lock the door."

Gerald said uncertainly, "You did what?"

"Got a man to lock the door."

"Well, get him to unlock it!"

"That is not possible. I sent him off to lunch and told him not to come back for an hour, so you could watch my show. It cost me a lot of money, that lunch."

"This is a serious business, Tipton. Keeping servants of Prince Albert captive. Use the second key to unlock the door now!"

"He has both keys. You will have to stay until he gets back."

A panic began to descend on the Board.

"It was good that George Tipton had a backup plan," Frederick commented proudly. "Although he was thick as a stick and did not realise he was a Hanoverian, there is a certain magic to us Hanoverians, and we usually prevail. A little sprinkle of extraterrestrial power that usually cuts through."

George Tipton had a problem. Although he had managed to get the Board to stay in the room, they had lost interest in the show and were currently searching the hall for ways out to the street. He still needed them to recommend his invention to Prince Albert. In desperation, he called on his father to help. He remembered those nights in the dormitory as a child, the red and orange flickering shadows from the all-night furnaces, the pure conversations he had with his father. With all his will, he sunk into the simple, unadulterated red-yellow state, and with all his heart, called on his father with the simple plea, "HELP!"

Miracle of miracles.

"I am here, son."

The voice of his father was heard. It appeared to be coming from a tubular canister which mysteriously materialised at the side of the stage. It was about the size of a fire extinguisher and appeared in those magical red-yellow colours.

George was amazed. "Have you become a canister, Dad?"

"No, I have brought this canister as a gift. Although you cannot see me, I am carrying the canister. I have not yet found a way to get my body back to Earth."

"Where have you been? It has been thirty years."

"I have been busy, son. Busy up in heaven."

"Busy in heaven?"

"Yes, looking after business in heaven."

"You could have said hello sometimes."

"Very busy in heaven. I have been put in charge of a prison."

George was surprised. "Do they have prisons up in heaven?"

24 – George William Produces a Gas

"Oh yes, they have prisons up in heaven, except they call them rehabilitation centres. I am calling them re-education centres because, hahaha, I am re-educating the inmates to my way of thinking."

"I suppose you would know a lot about prisons, having been in one yourself."

"You are not wrong, son. Ten years in that blasted room, but it has prepared me for a role up in heaven – being the governor of a prison."

George was trying to get his head around the idea of prisons in heaven. "What kind of people go to prison in heaven?"

"All kinds, but the ones I am interested in are the scientists. They did experiments that went wrong. Not bad people, just unlucky. Now they have me to re-educate them, hahaha. I have them working on projects. This is one they did for me." He shook the canister. "Inside is a gas."

"What does the gas do?"

"It makes people feel good. If they feel good, they will like you and let you get on with what you have planned for them. Hahaha. One of my Hanoverian tricks."

"You and your Hanoverian tricks. You are so clever, Dad."

"I am sure you can do Hanoverian tricks too, George. Just be like a Hanoverian."

"Yes, I shall try to be like a Hanoverian."

George William moved the canister sideways so his son could view the lever and hose at the top, just like a fire extinguisher. "Depress this lever, and the gas will come out. Point the hose at the Board and spray them with the gas. Give them a good dose. After that, they should become intoxicated and approve your show. I would like to see how well this gas works in practice."

"Great, Dad. What a clever idea."

George William chuckled. "We cannot let the men in suits get in our way. Now get along and spray them good. Tell me, son - have you produced an heir?"

"Yes, Dad, I have a son. He is now five years old."

George William was gratified by this. And relieved. He gave George the canister. "Now go and spray them, son."

25 – *The Show Reaches a Huge New Level*

George, invigorated, sprang into action. He ordered the lampholders to illuminate the hall and saw the three members of the Board scurrying around the perimeter of the room, trying to find a way out. He swooped in on each of them, pointed the nozzle, and sprayed them, giving them a hefty dose. Within seconds, the gas pacified them, and they became like zombies.

"Come on, gentlemen," George said. "The show is about to recommence. Take your seats!"

The Board stumbled back to their seats, intoxicated, and George got the next stage of his show into action. He sped to the centre of the room and unveiled the two stumpy objects, which proved to be two big brassy projectors. They had big lenses on the front, and the brass was polished to a high shine.

The preamble to the Coronation Anthem was still playing, and George ordered the room back into darkness. The scene was being set.

Between the projectors lay a box. From it, he fished out two long strips of painstakingly drawn pictures on transparent paper that constituted the visuals for his shows. The *music-picture-stories*! He lit the gas-fired projectors, and instigated test images between the two projectors. Two vertical lines, one loaded into each projector. Accurate alignment was essential to produce the enchanting illusion of movement. When the two lines became one, they would be ready. On the big white screen at the other end of the hall, the two projected lines merged into one. He loaded the first set of strips into each of the projectors, taking great care the flame would not ignite them, and capped the projectors. The screen went black, and the room plunged again into total darkness. He clicked his fingers at the orchestra. They would continue the preamble for another thirty seconds. He counted down.

At ten seconds, he went into action by uncapping the projectors. The screen became a blaze of colour. The new King George II sat on a golden throne, about to be crowned. The coronation crown was a few inches above his head. George worked the film strips, causing the crown to slowly lower. The seconds ticked by as the crown lowered in extraordinary slow motion. The tantalising beat of the preamble lumbered on, but as the crown touched the head, the sensational roar of the chorale rang out with enormous drama. Perfect coordination. That was just the beginning. The blast of the chorales kept on and on, and so did the moving picture show. A rainbow of auras radiated out from the king's head, and his face fulminated in ecstasy as he realised he was the most powerful king in the world.

George Tipton noticed something else: in the middle of the crown, was a powerful red and yellow stone radiating luminosity. George went dizzy staring at the stone and realised some strange power was igniting inside him. Something he had experienced many times before, but never like this. He remembered having a similar experience when drawing that stone. It had taken 500 drawings to get the stone to radiate like it did. Now, in a hall with servants of Prince Albert, it took on a new and profound meaning. It was the coronation stone. Somehow, he connected with the magic of this stone. Maybe he was the only one in the world who could. All the other red-yellow light in the world was coming from this stone. In his simple little mind, he realised this. It was all contained in that stone. The experience of its rays made him feel warm and strong, wise and righteous. It was an intense experience which knocked him back for a few moments.

26 – George is Awarded a Theatre!

The crowning show ended with thunderous applause from the Board. Whether this was a result of the gas, or the sheer exhilaration of the visuals, or perhaps George Tipton himself, the outcome was: the Board loved it.

Percy said, "That was fantastic. I have never seen anything like it!"

Gerald nodded. "Well done, Mr Tipton, you have surprised us all. That is indeed an invention and permissible for the exhibition."

Cedric asked, "Do you have any more of these moving picture shows?"

"Oh yes, I have hundreds. I shall move on to the next one in this set and advance to my next composer. Two composers in fact. They wrote a song. In my next moving picture show, I will use this song to demonstrate how Britain gained an empire. First, I will set the scene."

The stage lit up and had been reconstructed into the music room of Cliveden House in Buckinghamshire. The music room of a fine stately home which was the home of Frederick, Prince of Wales, the son of King George II. The date was 1740.

Frederick sat in an ample chair while two men stood before him on a small, raised platform.

"Wer bist thou?" Frederick asked.

"We are Thomas Arne and James Thomson, Your Royal Highness, and we have a new song."

Frederick smiled. "Goot, very goot. What is der name of the song?"

" 'Rule Britannia', Your Roal Highness."

In Hyde Park, Frederick said a little sheepishly, "Me and that song. I was still a little bit German at that time. We all were. I was a little bit at war with my father too, something most regrettable. Reflecting on it now, I might try doing something about that soon, but right now, I need to put the record straight."

"Put the record straight?"

Sitting beside him, I was becoming somewhat hypnotised. I could do nothing else. I got the feeling this man was trying to justify himself. Why? It was rather odd.

"I am proud of that song," he said. "It was big and did huge things. I worked on it with them until it became perfect, so I have every right to use it as part of my curriculum vitae, so to speak. It reflected the spirit so wonderfully. England's time had come, and the spirit was there. The spirit was great and, it might surprise you to know, the spirit was freedom. It was simply a matter of becoming a Briton. If you became a Briton, you would be free. That was the promise. It inspired the British Army. Filled them with zest that their cause was true and would deliver freedom. That was the idea. For the cause of freedom. To an extent, it worked, but I will never do it that way again, for in the end, it failed. No, we shall not do it that way."

"We?"

"Yes, there are five of us."

"Five of you? Who?"

"Never mind about that."

In the hall, George Tipton was building himself up in order to present the 'Rule Britannia Moving Picture Story'. Still high as a kite from the heady experience of the coronation stone, he slumped down on the floor and did 100 press-ups.

Getting upright again, he chirped, "Ah, much better, all refreshed now!"

The Board looked on, dazzled by this almost superhuman character.

"My next music-picture-story shows how the British Empire was won in the name of freedom. This is also part of my history of the machine-driven world show starting in 1702."

George Tipton clicked his fingers and engaged the projectors. The song and the images roared into life. It was a big show involving more than 1,800 images.*

For the next five minutes, the song rang out with gusto going through all the verses, repeating two. The Board swayed along. People always swayed to that song. The Board joined in by singing along that *Britons never, never, never shall be slaves.*

After the show finished, The Board looked abundantly satisfied.

"We all enjoyed that," Gerald said.

Cedric and Percy nodded with cheesy smiles.

"We all like freedom."

"Yes, to be free and able to do what we want. We would like that."

"That is why we are helping Prince Albert get what he wants. We are guiding him into the direction of that song. The direction of freedom. The promise of the song."

"I would love to be free," Percy said.

---

* (Appendix 1: For the full show and how George Tipton coordinated the words of the song to 43 battles fought to gain the British Empire, go to Appendix 1.)

"Me as well," Cedric added.

Gerald asked, "Do you like the idea of freedom, Mr Tipton?"

George had to think about this. "I suppose I do, yes."

"Good. Then, we all like freedom and so we shall definitely recommend your invention to Prince Albert. We shall also recommend the building of your Picture Palace in the grounds beside the Crystal Palace."

"Really?"

George Tipton was surprised and swelled with elation. He had done it. The pinnacle of his career!

Gerald asked, "Can we see your next moving picture story?"

"Yes, you can! I shall prepare the next one in the set."

George sprang down to the floor to do another 100 press-ups. Going up and down on the floor, he introduced his next show.

"As you know, Prince Frederick died before his father, and so he did not become king. The next king was his son. So, my next music-picture-story is about King George the Third."

George William, still hovering in the hall, was not at all keen on this. He had no wish to be depicted in a show. In fact, he did not want any of the Hanoverian family depicted. He hovered over to the Board and got himself lined up with Gerald's ear. "Prince Albert will not take kindly to random depictions of the royal family," he whispered firmly down the earhole of Gerald. "Ask George Tipton if he has any other moving picture shows."

Gerald looked at Cedric. "Did you say something?"

Cedric said, "No."

"Something about Prince Albert not taking kindly to depictions of his family?"

Cedric whispered urgently, "We should think about that. Prince Albert would not like us offering depictions of his family."

Percy added, "Prince Albert would probably sack us for offering depictions of his family."

Gerald thought about this, stood up, and deliberated.

"Mr Tipton, we do like your music-picture-stories but feel depictions of the royal family would not meet with Prince Albert's approval. Do you have any music-picture-stories on other topics we could present to Prince Albert?"

George Tipton was a little confused. "Do you really think Prince Albert would disapprove?"

Gerald nodded grimly. "Probably. It is a very big risk."

Percy added, "He would probably sack us. He is a beast."

"Can you not give us something else? Something, anything?" Cedric asked.

George had a think. "Very well. I could do my evolving set. I have a set of evolving music-picture-stories."

Cedric was relieved. "Yes, Mr Tipton, that sounds suitable."

George William looked on cautiously.

George spent a few minutes fishing out his evolving set from his box.

In fact, his evolving set was like a day-by-day account of events that happened in the 1700s, both in the United Kingdom, and around the world. The difference was, it was like an accelerated flip chart, running very fast. It displayed inventions on the dates they happened, as well as novels and paintings as they were released. It flipped through changing fashions as they evolved - hence the evolving set. A momentous century evolving faster than any century before it. It dwelt on some events more than others, like the South Sea Bubble, a financial speculation of vast proportions that caused the greatest monetary loss in history, and the traumas that followed. It was a century of incredible inventions and fantastic fashions.

"For this music-picture-story, I shall use the first symphony of Wolfgang Mozart," George announced. "He composed it when he was eight. I was eight when I composed my first music-picture-story. Did you know he composed it here in London?"

"I did not know that," Gerald said.

George got the show in motion.

George William was relieved he had successfully changed the topic of the show. Pleased too, he had done something for George. Satisfied everything had worked out, he left the hall and travelled back to the prison in heaven to continue his work.

The evolution of the 1700s show swept over the Board like some exotic wave. Even at eight, Mozart composed a playful energetic piece that had all the grace of the 1700s. It suited the events and fashions of the show well. After it was over, Gerald said, gratified, "I believe that settles it. We shall recommend your invention to Prince Albert at the highest level. Congratulations!"

George's eyes popped out.

Cedric suggested, "Shall we award him the theatre in the Elephant too?"

Gerald agreed. "I think we should. Mr Tipton, there is a theatre we requisitioned in the Elephant Inn area of South London. You can use this theatre to practice your shows. Let us make your show at the Crystal Palace perfect."

George was overcome with excitement. In one hour, he had risen to dizzy heights *and* seen his father. He knew the theatre he was being awarded. It was a mile away from where he lived in Camberwell. He had failed an audition there months before. Now, it would all be his.

CHAPTER SIX

27 – George Visits the Crystal Palace

George Tipton started the weekend in an ecstatic cocoon. The day following his audition, he opened his newly acquired theatre with his five-year-old son, who was very proud. The day after that, he ventured over the river to view the big prize – The Crystal Palace – but went there alone.

He had chosen a Sunday to visit the glittering site in order that the construction workers, who were mainly Irish, would be in church, and the building would be empty. He wished to enter the building alone and savour the palace in all its glory; relish this palace of light in its crystal magnificence. The palace was being built on the southern edge of Hyde Park, but he did not approach it from the east, or the west, as it was a 'royal park', and he did not want to be arrested for trespassing. Instead, he chose to enter from the south, through the fields of the Gore Estate. Of course, he could be caught trespassing on the Gore Estate, but this was not as bad.

"Is this not amazing!" Frederick exclaimed in awe. "Here we sit in Hyde Park, on the very site of the Crystal Palace, and so few people are aware of this. Two hundred yards behind us, was situated the house and fields of the Gore family where

George Tipton got his first sight of the Crystal Palace. Yes, outside this royal estate were only fields. Fields as far as the eye could see. Only the small village of Kensington on the horizon. Now, it is the most expensive real estate in the world. Knightsbridge, Kensington, Chelsea. All of it built-up with the most exclusive shops and properties in the world. All because of the Great Exhibition of 1851. I tell you; we sit on hallowed ground!"

George Tipton was careful to stalk through the Gore Estate undetected. He made a detour to avoid Gore House and any of the outbuildings by creeping cautiously through the fields. On his right, about a quarter of a mile away, were the Gore Nurseries, and he was careful to avoid them too. Very soon, through the long grass, he witnessed the towering Crystal Palace appearing like some magical apparition. He shuddered at the awesome sight. The 'palace' was tiered like some giant wedding cake all made of glass. As he moved closer, he realised it was only half-built. More than half-built but nowhere near finished. He panicked as he knew it must be completed by January, barely a month away. He realised there was nothing he could do about this and simply had to have faith the builders would complete the job on time and his show could go ahead. He reached a bridle path, deserted as it was a Sunday, the bridle path which, many years later, was to become the major traffic-clogged artery of the A315, also known as Kensington Gore.

He crossed the bridle path and entered Hyde Park, and the giant Crystal Palace was before him. Much bigger and more complex than imagined. He felt tiny in front of it and became possessed with concern his little theatre would be lost as an off-site sideshow. The building had a central atrium and two giant wings to the left and right. He jogged along the right wing to the spot where his mini crystal palace would be constructed and had an idea. He would place brightly coloured stones leading from his ticket office in the main building all the way to his picture palace in the grounds. He would paint one set of stones with the words *'music-picture-stories'* and have alternate stones with the words *'this way'* and highlight them with a bold arrow. Satisfied, he walked back to the central building.

He found an opening where the glass had not yet been fitted and stepped inside. This central part was long, high, and proportionally narrow, a bit like the nave in Westminster Abbey. He gazed high above at the glass roof which was curved. It was sunny, and light flooded in from the roof and walls, everywhere, making little dancing patterns. He felt like he was in heaven. His show on the world stage. After thirty-two years of trying, it had finally happened. He felt a deep love for his son and gratitude for his persistence in getting him to follow the path of applying to the Great Exhibition. He had not brought him along because of the danger of getting arrested, but this had receded now he was inside the palace.

He paced around, luxuriating in this palace of light. He would have to badger the Board to get him stands very near the entrance. To make sure that everyone entering the building knew about his theatre, he would get a man to hand out bits of paper to everyone who entered. Satisfied with all this, he wandered further down the hall. The entrance and first part of the hall was nearly complete, but further down was still under construction, and a massive maze of wooden scaffolding was erected. Great interlocking blocks of scaffold with around thirty levels reached up to the roof. Fascinating. He gazed up at the outer structure, calculating what still needed to be done.

He suddenly became aware that he was not totally alone.

He thought this may be a security guard and ran into the maze of scaffolds, trying to lose him. The man followed. He saw some building materials, hid behind a sack, and used the cover to climb onto the scaffold. He levered himself up two levels and lowered himself flat onto a plank. On his stomach, he slid slowly along the plank, trying to locate the man. As he manoeuvred, the plank wobbled, and the immediate infrastructure creaked and teetered too. The man strolled towards the creaking sound and came to a standstill about eleven feet below him. George, facedown, went immobile, hoping the man would move on. The man did not move on. He shouted up.

"I thought I would find you here," the man bellowed.

With one eye, George peered down and nearly had a heart attack. It was Charles.

He had not seen Charles since the dreadful day in 1833 when Charles was sentenced to many years of hard labour in an extremely tough prison. He couldn't bear to think of it. For seventeen years, he was too traumatised to consider it. He'd hoped this day would never come, but always thought it might.

"So – here I am," Charles said calmly.

George was paralysed, unable to speak. Finally, he did. "I am sorry, but it was not my fault."

"Ah. So, tell me, who is responsible?"

"I do not know," George said, his teeth beginning to chatter. "I do not know how it happened."

Charles immediately became fantastically angry. "Tell me why you did it!" He rattled the scaffold, and George saw Charles's face had hardened. It had become like steel over the years and looked incredibly dangerous. George did not wait to answer; he shot up the scaffold, trying to escape. He bolted up three levels. Charles shook the scaffold again. "I am coming to get you!" he roared, and climbed after him.

George continued to put distance between him and Charles. The great tangle of scaffold stretched up to the roof, but also hundreds of feet sideways too. George climbed a few tiers sideways and a few levels higher. Charles climbed a few tiers sideways too, shook the very block George was climbing on and roared again. "Tell me why you did it!"

George was now five levels above Charles, and shouted down, "I will tell you if you calm down!"

"I am calm," Charles said, becoming almost motionless.

"Alright," George relented. "I got dismissed from the East India Company and went to Birmingham to ask the trustees for money."

"So?"

"They refused, saying you were more deserving than me."

"I was. Far more deserving. I had become a lawyer; you were just a clerk. Not a very good clerk. I had made something of my life."

An old rivalry ignited in George, and now he was angry, although it came out as a sulk. "You were always doing that. Always putting me down. Always taking over."

"I had to because you were an idiot. You have always been an idiot. You were an idiot then, you are an idiot now, and I want payback."

"What sort of payback?"

"Payback!" Charles growled, and he made a menacing leap to the next level of the scaffold. The calmness was over, and there was a fire raging in Charles. George shot up, climbing upwards as fast as possible. Charles climbed upwards too, but not as fast as George. George raced up. He was not sure what the plan was, but he kept going up. By the time George had reached the twenty-third level, Charles was about eight levels behind. In frustration, Charles stopped climbing, and instead, began shaking; shaking the stack so violently the whole block was in danger of collapsing and crashing down to the ground in a massive heap of poles and planks.

George yelled, "Stop it, you will get us both killed!"

"I do not care. My life is not worth living."

George realised Charles was serious and reckless, and raced sideways to the next block which was not shaking as much. He hatched out a plan to escape through a hole in the roof. He knew from the plans there would be an iron ladder built into the roof that would reach down to the ground. A horrendously long way down, and he hoped it would not be slippery; it was not much of a ladder, just bare rungs. Once on the ground he would rush to the farmhouse on the Gore Estate and try to raise assistance. That was the plan. The roof was about twenty-five feet above him, and he began climbing in earnest.

Charles began cackling, a weird bout of loud demonic cackling.

"You are yellow. Yellow, yellow, yellow," he cackled. "Come down and face me!" He wrenched at the structure once more for good measure.

"No," George yelled down. "You may want to die, but I do not."

"I do not want to die," Charles said. "I do not want you to die either. I want payback."

George paused in mid-climb. "What payback do you want?"

"Come down, and I shall tell you."

"No," George said.

"Then I am coming up."

George rapidly tried to think of the best thing to do. The big, curved roof was now only nineteen feet above him, and the open section off to one side. He wasn't clear what he would find when he got onto the roof. He would have to locate the ladder, which meant sliding down the curved part of the roof. It was a steep curve and probably slippery. He might end up sliding off the building and getting killed. Or he could be slaughtered by Charles. Difficult choice. The level he was on was just wooden poles, no planks, which made him feel vulnerable, so he climbed to the next level which did have planks. They were laid down. Here he felt slightly more secure, and he edged along to a crossbar which he clung to. In a great leap of faith, he announced, "Alright. Come up and tell me what you want."

Charles climbed up the poles, grunting like a gorilla. He climbed onto George's plank. George was shocked by how much Charles had weathered. His face was old and hard like wrought iron.

"Come towards me and fight," Charles said, standing a few feet away from George on the plank.

"No," George said.

"You do not get to choose." Charles cackled and began jumping up and down on the plank.

George covered his head in his hands. "Just tell me what you want for your payback," he said.

Charles came towards him. "I want the theatre."

"Why do you want that?"

"I want to show people my vision of the world at the Great Exhibition."

"It has taken over thirty years for me to get this. Finally, my music-picture-stories will be shown on the world stage."

"Now, it will be my show on the world stage!"

Charles grabbed him, pinning him tight against the crossbar. "I am taking over now. From now on, I shall be in charge."

Charles pressed George over the crossbar with such force that the pole was near breaking point. "I shall be in charge from now on. Is that clear?"

Charles bent his head backward, so George could see over a hundred feet downwards.

George was thoroughly depressed. He had been defeated by Charles again. At the point of his success, after thirty years of trying, Charles had taken it off him. It was supremely distressing.

He thought back to how this horrible mess with his brother had begun. Thought back to 1833, the year Charles had become jailed. It started the day Lord Bentinck visited the place of his work at East India House in Lombard Street.

CHAPTER SEVEN

1833

28 – Meeting with Lord Bentinck, 1833

The building of East India House was completed in 1729 and stood with various additions until it was finally demolished in 1861. The estate stretched from Leadenhall Street at the front, to Lime Street at the rear, which was a prime spot at the heart of the financial district of the City of London, a spot now occupied by the Lloyds of London insurance company. Although in a prime position, it was not huge considering the company ruled the whole of the Indian subcontinent, an area more than five times the size of the United Kingdom. It had a classical frontage, several offices, a courtyard, and two principal buildings: a Court Room, and a Trading Room. Both these 'Rooms' were large circular buildings with a big rotunda in the roof. The principal function of the Court Room was to be a space where directors of the 'Honourable Company' (as it called itself) could meet and discuss company business. However, the actual rough and tumble of governing the subcontinent of India was left to the governor. On this day, the governor of India, Lord Bentinck, was on a visit to London and addressing employees of the company's London office, including George Tipton. Lord Bentinck was doing this from a podium in the Court Room.

"It is wonderful to see the dedicated staff of our Company's London base at this pivotal time in our Company's history," Lord Bentinck said. "Many things are about to change in our India operations. Next month, I am to be invested as the first Governor General for the whole of India. All the separate states of India are about to become united into one governable whole."

The employees of the HQ all clapped at this statement. All except George Tipton who was busily drawing in a sketchpad. He was determined to keep a record of this important moment. He was twenty-two at the time and had been at the company six years. He never wanted to be a clerk. Charles and the teachers had relentlessly guided him into this position, and finally he was ground down, something he was resentful about, but he never abandoned his dream to make music-picture-stories.

Lord Bentinck continued, "Of course, it is unusual for a company to run a country, especially a country the size of India. Indeed, running a country like India, with its large and diverse population, is far more complex than running a normal business, but run it as a business we must, for we are a business with all the various rules and confines that successful businesses must adhere to. In my new role, I have come to realise that having companies running countries could be a splendid idea. For a country to live within the unemotional confines of company procedure would, I am sure, eliminate regional squabbles and enable a country to accumulate wealth and flourish. Once we master this in a profitable way, I believe that all countries in the Empire should be run in this way. Company Rule for Countries – I shall be suggesting this idea to the prime minister when I see him tomorrow."

George was intrigued with this idea and drew a map of the world and placed little markers suggesting *Company Rule?*

These markers or flags were placed over countries in Africa, countries in Asia, and one big one over Australia. *Company Rule* with a question mark over all countries Britain had control over. Was Company Rule a good idea for a world government? This was a question he wished to discuss with his father when he next showed up. He missed the philosophical discussions he had with his father on the topic of world governments, but he would keep a record of it for when he finally reappeared.

A Company Official noticed George sketching and alerted another Company Official.

Lord Bentinck continued, "Having companies administering the British system would be an attractive proposition, I am sure. Being from a military background, I am familiar with security. After securing a country, the first task of ruling is to keep it secure. Secure from invasion, religious squabbles, insurrections and so on, and as much as possible, thievery. India is plagued by 'Thuggee' gangs which I am determined to eliminate. In my new title of Governor General of India, my task will be to unite all the regions of India into one governable and profitable whole. Some troublemakers in this country are saying we are destroying the culture of India. Nonsense. I am a great admirer of Indian culture. I eat Indian food every evening and am very fond of it too. Apart from a few odious practices like burning women on their husbands' funeral pyres, I leave Indian culture to the Indians. India is free to practice their culture. In fact, my wife encourages natives to express themselves and holds monthly debates in the Governor's mansion. She once had the tenacity to put on a debate with the topic *Is Company Rule Right for India?*"

Bentinck went on to describe this debate in which the majority of his native Indian guests voted in favour, which further reinforced his idea of it being a good one.

George sketched a series of drawings of the reception room in which the debates were held. The Indian guests, about fifty, were seated on chairs and served tea in fine porcelain cups, while a turbaned servant kept the room cooled by waving a giant fan. He made a note on the final sketch where the vote took place. It said:

Did they really feel Company Rule was right, or were they being polite because they were the governor's guests? This would be another topic of conversation with his father when he finally turned up.

George was unaware of the two Company Officials now staring at him.

Lord Bentinck continued his speech:

"It may come as a shock for you to hear that the company is losing a great deal of money on its India Rule operation. This cannot continue. In the Bengal region, I managed to turn the company deficit into a profit, and I am now charged with doing the same for the whole of India. There are dilemmas in doing this. Our main expense is the Honourable Company's Army. To cut pay and personnel at this time would ferment discontent in the ranks and jeopardise security, which in turn, would cause the job of making a successful country very difficult. Tomorrow, I will ask the prime minister that the British government fill the financial gap as it should not be for the company to bear. India is a great asset to the British Empire and will eventually be profitable."

After Lord Bentinck finished, he left the room.

Immediately, the two Company Officials swooped down on George. Their attitude was hostile although George was unaware of this. The first official pointed at George's sketches.

"What are you doing?"

"I am making a record of Lord Bentinck's speech at this important moment in our company's history," George said.

"Who asked you to do this?"

"Nobody. I record things. Since I was eight, I have been making music-picture-stories. I have made hundreds of them. I am looking for money, so I can show them to the public. Would the company give me money to do this?"

"If Lord Bentinck wanted drawings of himself or illustrations concerning topics of his talk, he would have asked for them, and we would have provided one of the Company Artists to do it. Lord Bentinck has not asked for it."

"Oh well, I have them if he ever wants them. Would the company give me money to develop my music-picture-stories? This is what I want more than anything."

"Tipton - you don't seem to be getting the hang of what I am saying. You do not draw images of Lord Bentinck, or anyone else, unless we instruct you to do so, which is unlikely as we have Company Artists to do this. Your job at the company is confined to the auction room."

George nodded.

The other guard picked up George's drawing, the one with the note. "What is this? You are interpreting what Lord Bentinck's guests may or may not be thinking?"

"It is something I want to discuss with my father. It is a note to remind myself."

The guards looked at each other, concerned about the possible insurrectionary implications of this.

The guard asked in a severe tone, "Tipton – where is your father residing? We need to speak to him."

"He is dead. Me and my father liked to discuss divine empires. Would it not be fantastic to know what a divine empire would look like? Would you like to discuss divine empires with me?"

The guards looked at each other, relenting. "We realise you are a simple man, Tipton, and the company took you on in their generosity after your trustees paid them a substantial fee. However, you are in this company to do a job, and you must not stray away from that, otherwise you will get sacked."

"And we do not want to discuss divine empires with you either," the other guard added. "You have been boring us silly with your ideas on divine empires."

"Yes, sorry."

"I have to put you on official warning with this drawing episode. Only do the job that has been asked of you and do it now. Five thousand tons of tea have arrived at the company's warehouse in Shoreditch. There will be an auction of it tomorrow. Many important buyers will be attending. Go and prepare the Auction Room. Do your job properly or you will be dismissed."

George nodded obediently and left to prepare the room.

The Auction Room was almost identical to the Court Room with a similar rotunda in the ceiling and a series of inlaid statues set into the walls. There were tiered benches arranged in a semicircle around the room in which the buyers would be seated to issue their bids. George placed an auction catalogue on each of the seats and arranged his clerk's stand which was situated on the auction floor. He opened a clean page in the ledger and filled his inkwell.

The next day, the auction was about to begin. The tiered benches were filled with anxious buyers. The tea was being auctioned with two huge lots, and twenty smaller lots. The auctioneer described each lot in particularly fruity terms. George was seated on his clerk's stand and poised to record each bid in his ledger. The bidding started and was fast and furious. The atmosphere was tense as large sums were at stake. After the hammer came down, there was a clap for the winning bidder, then a pause while the next lot was prepared. The auction lasted around forty-five minutes. After it ended, George closed his ledger and got onto some other business.

He had been observing the bidders and sizing them up. Mentally making a note of how much each one of them bid, and what their limits were. He had an interest in a particular American bidder that had been outbid on three different lots. He commandeered him before he left.

"Commiserations, I am sorry you lost," George said.

"I cannot sell tea in the United States at that price. You think it was rigged because of what happened in Boston? That was over fifty years ago!"

"No, the price of tea has been rising – it has become very popular in the British Isles, but I have a proposition to make up for your loss."

"Oh."

"You Americans love new ideas in entertainment."

"Yes, we do."

"I have one. They are drawings and photographs set to music which tell a story. I call them music-picture-stories. They will be illuminated on a screen in a darkened room. The effect is magical."

"Images on a screen in a darkened room. Sounds interesting, I like it. How do I contact you?"

Just then, two Company Spies who had been embedded in the bidder benches, swooped down and grabbed George, frog-marching him out. A third one appeared out of nowhere and apologised to the American.

"I am sorry, sir, an errant employee," he said. "I will have a case of our finest wines sent to you as an apology."

On the way up to the executive offices, George passed the two security guards from yesterday who looked at George sheepishly. "Sorry," one said. "We did warn you."

George was unceremoniously sacked from the 'Honourable Company' and went into deep shock as the ramifications began to sink in. He was facing destitution. He sent a telegram to the trustees in Birmingham. Three days later he visited them.

29 – *George Faces the Trustees.*

There were three trustees, and they had a veneer of respectability. Their principal aim was to make as much money as possible from their trustee business, which at times was on the edge of legality. The first trustee, Frank Rudders, had a rudimentary knowledge of the law. The second trustee had expert knowledge of the Swiss banking system, and the third trustee was responsible for recruiting orphans and matching them with clients. 'Gain salvation through sponsoring an orphan' was their motto, which sounded quasi-religious, but the salvation bit was code for respectability and actually a cover for laundering a client's money, for, in addition to the orphan sponsorship, they offered banking services. It was not a huge business, and the majority of their clients took the salvation word literally and were genuinely charitable. That part of the business made money, but it was more work-intensive, for they offered a range of orphan management services for various fees. All clients would sponsor an orphan. Thirty-two clients were looking for salvation, and four to launder money. Another key part of the service was confidentiality and to ask no questions. They did not wish to know their clients' circumstances, as if they did not know anything, they could not be prosecuted. There were thirty-six accounts in these two categories, and then there was the Tipton account.

The Tipton was the most unusual and mysterious account. Even so, they adhered to their policy of asking no questions. Their banking arrangements were the opposite of the banking being offered to other clients. The Tipton account already had Swiss banking arrangements, and money for the different services was available to the trustees through various access codes. Requests by the trustees for money was done through correspondence to obscure addresses, was always accepted, and the money was always there. It was their most lucrative account by far. Besides, the quarterly fee would carry on for 200 years, which would come in very handy as a selling point when they wished to retire and sell the trust on. In view of all this, they responded to George Tipton's request for a meeting, and he was waiting outside.

The trustees sat on a long desk like judges at a tribunal as they waited to interrogate their orphan. They got into their severe 'guardians of orphans' mode. Rudders got the trust documents on the desk and spent a few moments studying them. He scratched his head.

"It seems as if we are acting for two clients in the same trust," Frank Rudders said. "One, calling himself James, who concerns himself with the welfare of the orphans. He specifies their education and requests guidance and support for their employment . . ."

"I met James back in 1810," the trustee in charge of clients said. "Seemed to be a decent man, which is unusual for us. He personally put all the funds into a Swiss bank account and gave us individual codes to access funds to carry out the different services requested. Never been any problems with money. That trust appears to have almost limitless funds. We get paid every quarter without fail. Our most reliable and lucrative account."

"The other calls himself Kellewe. He is an enigma."

"Kellewe - a strange name."

"I looked it up. A Prussian name meaning 'driver of the cart'."

The other two looked at him queerly. "What do you make of that man Kellewe - driver of the cart?"

"He states a list of restrictions for the orphan twins. Infringement of any restriction to be enforced by a special unit of the Prussian Army."

"The Prussian Army? Rather strange, is it not?"

"Very irregular, I would say!"

"Our policy is not to question. No-questions-asked."

"All infringements to be carried out by the Ettikeomisna Aiinibi on the strict orders of Mr Zakamonsky."

He had some trouble pronouncing Ettikeomisna Aiinibi.

"Ettikeomisna Aiinibi? What does that mean?"

One of the trustees looked it up in a Prussian dictionary. "It means the 'Redemption Unit'. I suppose it is the redemption unit of the Prussian Army."

"Oh God."

"It sounds like they have something to avenge. It does not sound pleasant."

"They want revenge for something."

"Eastern Europe. They have a lot of squabbles over there. Tribal blood disputes. We do not want to get involved."

"Who is this Mr Zakamonsky?"

"I suppose he is the commander of this horrible unit. Some kind of warlord, I imagine."

"Yes, it does mention Mr Zakamonsky is the Supreme Commander of the Ettikeomisna Aiinibi."

"I do not wish to know him."

"My wife has been reading to me about Vlad the Impaler. He does terrible things. A blood sucker and an impaler are some of them. Maybe this Zakamonsky is like him."

"I do not want to know about Vlad the Impaler. Not Vlad the Impaler nor Zakamonsky the warlord."

"Let us concentrate on the business at hand. George Tipton is outside. We need to find out what he wants. Send him in."

George Tipton came plodding in.

"You sent us an urgent telegram. What can we do for you, George?"

"I want some money."

"We would all like money." The trustees smiled at each other.

"I would like to buy a mansion in the country, and I would if I had the money."

"What do you want money for, George?"

"Music-picture-stories. That is what I want money for."

"What are music-picture-stories?"

George shuffled from one foot to the other, explaining.

After consideration, the trustee with the legal training said, "We cannot fund hobbies from the trust. It is not within the terms."

"It is not a hobby," George said indignantly. "It is the future of entertainment. I want to leave the East India Company and work on music-picture-stories full time."

This time, the trustees were indignant. "Leave the East India Company? We worked hard to get you in there."

They took a very patronising stance, looking George up and down.

"That is not something your brother would do."

"We are very proud of Charles. He has worked hard and got a senior position in an iron company. He is one of our most successful orphans."

George got in a sudden fit of jealousy. "You do not know anything about Charles. You have no idea what he is up to."

"Oh. What is he up to?"

"He is organising union meetings. He is persuading people to join a union."

"Is he?"

"Yes. Not only that. He is anti-monarchy. Not like me. I am very proud of our king. I think union people are anti-monarchy. They would do anything to embarrass the king."

The trustees looked at each other.

"George, could you leave us for a few minutes. There is a nice seat out in the corridor. Go and sit on it."

In the office, the trustees were thoughtful. "Is everyone thinking what I am thinking?"

"About the 'embarrassing the monarch' provision?"

"Yes. We collect one hundred and fifty pounds if we report either of the twins is embarrassing the monarch. We have not used any of the provisions of the trust. Christmas is coming. That would be fifty pounds each!"

"How would we prove that? He would deny it. Remember, he is now a lawyer. More qualified than any of us."

"We get witnesses. Find a few people on the street to say they overheard him plotting a protest. Something like him encouraging his union people to have a protest on the town square. They could have a banner saying *Down with the king*. Something like that."

"A banner saying *Down with the king*?"

"Yes, that kind of thing. It would go to a petty court. Tipton would get fined a few pounds – and then we would put in a claim and receive one hundred and fifty pounds from the trust funds."

"We are meant to hand over any infringements of the trust to this security firm in Prussia."

"We will not do that. We will not get involved with that Zakamonsky fella or his horrible Ettikeomisna Aiinibi operation. That is for sure. We shall do it ourselves. We can pick up four urchins off the street, tell them what to say, pay each of them ten shillings. Pay them an extra ten shillings after Charles Tipton gets fined. Is that a good plan?"

The three trustees mulled it over and gave it a tepid approval.

"We can give George Tipton a small monthly allowance. That is allowed in the terms of the trust. That should keep him happy. Is that agreed?"

It was agreed. George Tipton was recalled to the office. He walked in limply, a little embarrassed that he had betrayed Charles. However, he was grateful at being offered a small monthly allowance and relieved his destitution had been averted.

30 – *Charles Tipton's Situation in 1833*

While George's employment experience had involved enriching the imperial fortunes of the East India Company, Charles's employment was at the beating heart of early heavy industry. He was the chief legal advisor to a large iron-making company in the Black Country.

The ferocious pace of the Industrial Revolution had moved into a new sphere: the manic phase of railway construction. One production floor of the company was dedicated to pushing out cast iron rails for the last leg of the Leeds to Selby railway line. This floor was horrendously loud. Long, hot, and grimy. Charles's office was around fifty feet above this area, and slightly shielded from the row. There was an odd respectability about his office with a grandfather clock and quality desk, but it was tempered by a layer of grime that pervaded all of the Black Country.

The boss of the firm was a brusque entrepreneur with a wiry moustache, called Henry McIntyre. It was an age where ordinary untitled men were able to enter the business arena and make vast fortunes. Not without risk. Borrowing and share issues on the promise of future profits was the way to do it, along with a sweet tongue. McIntyre had sweet-tongued many, and over-extended himself enormously. He was in a state of constant sweat and fear, but secretly thrilled with the excitement of it all. He sweated now, worried about a man called Coker. Coker was the latest contractor for the final eighteen-mile stretch of the Selby to Leeds line. Like him, Coker was a sweet-talker who had also over-extended himself considerably. The whole industry was like a flimsy pack of cards.

Sweating nervously, McIntyre entered Charles's office and tensely strutted around.

"If Coker fails to pay up on time, the whole of my company goes into oblivion. He has a slippery reputation."

"Do not worry, Henry, we shall demand staged payments from Mr Coker. It will be written into the contract. I will try for a credit period of not more than two weeks."

"If he cannot pay, or fails to pay?"

"We will have the right to wind up his company. That will be written into the contract too."

McIntyre's eyes became glazed. "Wind up Coker's company, yes that sounds very good!" Then another thought. "If that happens, what do we do with the track we have already produced?"

"We sell it. It is a seller's market. Hundreds of miles of track are expanding everywhere."

"Expansion, yes! That is what we must do. We must have another floor producing rail track. Maybe another two floors. I will begin working on that. You are a smart man, Tipton. Would you join me in a partnership?"

"No, I am happy being independent."

"You could make a fortune, Charles. Join me. Become rich. I need smart men like you with me."

"No, Henry. I will just write contracts and try to keep you out of trouble. Now, if you will excuse me, I have an engagement to go to. My stagecoach leaves in fifteen minutes."

McIntyre licked his lips. "Is it a woman? Are you meeting a woman?"

"No, Henry, I am not meeting a woman."

Charles checked his pocket watch as the grandfather clock had stopped functioning a while back due to being clogged with soot. He rushed, collected his coat, and left.

If the truth be told, like George, Charles did not like his job either, but it gave him a certain status, and some ability to affect change. For a long time, he felt he had a duty to transform things on Earth.

He dashed out of the works and reached the coach stop just in time. His lanky boyhood friend Tom was there. They boarded the stagecoach for Bilston.

In the stagecoach, Charles asked, "How does it feel to be a foreman?"

"Not good. I do not like it. It feels like I am becoming one of them."

"What would you like? I could get you any job you want in the company. Nearly any job."

"I thought we were going to have a revolution."

"No need. We can do it through the law. It was you who persuaded me to become a lawyer. When we were children, the union was illegal. Now it is legal, and you are helping me to persuade more people to join. Because it is legal."

"I know it is legal, but it makes no difference. They look down at us. There is no respect."

"It takes time, but it will happen."

"Action, revolution. The working class needs to rise up and take over. We need a revolution. Make the bosses work in the factories, with us telling them what to do. Violent revolution, that is what we need. Give the upper class a taste of what we have been through. We need some revenge."

A sadness came over Charles because he could see they were drifting apart. In his bones, he knew his way was far different from his friend. He was not absolutely clear yet what his way was, but felt, however misguided, it would come through the law. Whatever way it was, it was not through violent class warfare. He knew it would be a battle to persuade Tom not to go down the road of class warfare, but he was not sure he could win him round. He was sad about this.

The coach arrived in Bilston. Tom helped at the meeting. A few people joined the union. The next day, Tom joined Charles on another recruitment drive in Wolverhampton. Here, there was a rumour going around that the king was coming to the Black Country – King William IV who had been king since June 1830 when King George IV had died – and there was some talk of organising a protest march during his visit with banners demanding better conditions for workers. Tom took note of this.

What happened next did not help.

31 – The Trustees' Plan Goes Wrong

The trustees had recruited four street urchins, given them ten shillings each, and sent them off to Wolverhampton. They were told to observe Charles recruiting members to the union, so the authenticity of their story could be proved, and they should make up the next bit. The bit about a demonstration in the town square with Charles holding a banner saying *Down with the king*. They were told to report this to the local court, and after Charles was charged with petty nuisance, they would each get the other ten shillings.

The urchins did attend the union recruitment meeting, but got there late, so didn't know who Charles Tipton was, and they stayed the night in Wolverhampton. In the morning, they went to the town square preparing to make up the story. One even made a banner saying *Down with the king*. They were surprised to find a real demonstration, not an imagined one. It was being led by Tom, who had recruited a few of the union men to his cause. Tom was holding up a real banner, not an imagined one. This one read *Shoot the king - free the people*. The urchins reported to the court that Charles Tipton was encouraging his supporters to kill the king.

In fact, Tom's meeting was quickly dispersed by the local guards, and everyone was given a warning. That was all that happened, and it would probably have been the end of the incident, except a reporter from the *Birmingham Journal* happened to be in the square and reported it to the Army. He wrote a piece for the next edition of the journal too. One of Tom's supporters got wind of this, and Tom disappeared into thin air.

After the incident was reported to the Army, a company of soldiers entered the ironworks and arrested Charles. Both Charles and McIntyre were horrified. Charles presumed there was some terrible misunderstanding and protested, but the soldiers took him away.

A week later, bruised and bloodied, Charles Tipton stood before a Birmingham court accused of seditious incitement. He was flanked by soldiers. The trustees were not present, and no mention of them was heard at the trial. George was present though, having heard of Charles's arrest from McIntyre.

In his trial, the testimony of the urchins was read out, and Charles's record of organising union meetings was catalogued too. Charles protested his innocence throughout, but his case was lost mainly because the article in the *Birmingham Journal* had been published the previous Saturday, and the court of public opinion was firmly against him.

"Charles Tipton," the judge pronounced, "you are found guilty of seditious incitement. I sentence you to ten years' imprisonment with hard labour."

Charles exploded in anger. "It is all lies. False witnesses! All made up!"

He pointed at his brother, George. "It was him. He has made this up! He is jealous because I have a career, and he has none!"

Their eyes locked. George went red with guilt, recalling his outburst with the trustees. Charles's eyes bored into him.

"You are despicable," Charles screamed at George as he was hauled down to the cells. "Despicable and treacherous. There will be payback for this. Payback, do you understand? Payback!"

The trustees were horrified at the way it had turned out. Their star orphan had been subjected to ten years' hard labour through their own mismanagement. They realised they were amateurs and playing a dangerous game in this dubious world of salvation. In the intervening years, they radically scaled down their operation and took no new clients. They honoured commitments made to existing clients and arranged for the small monthly allowance to be made to George Tipton.

For Charles Tipton, it was far worse. He was sent to a harsh secret prison in the far north, a prison for political convicts. By day, the inmates worked hard hacking rock in the quarries. The dust clogged their throats. The norms of conventional prisons were not observed there. The guards were many and thuggish. There were hardened murderers in there. To survive this place, one had to harden up too.

For George Tipton, it was not a good outcome either. He was racked with guilt and terrified of Charles. He had hidden away for many years on a small subsistence living. On the eve of his success in the moving picture business, Charles had finally turned up and taken it all away from him.

That was the situation George had got himself into on the scaffold at the Crystal Palace. Handing over the theatre he had just won. The theatre at the Elephant in Walworth.

CHAPTER EIGHT

1850

32 – The Walworth Theatre at the Elephant

The theatre had been something of an enigma. Constructed ten years previously by a benevolent benefactor, it was intended as a community cultural hub for the people of Walworth. The auditorium was relatively small for a theatre of the time, about a hundred and fifty seats which were covered with a red imitation-velvet material that looked plush when new, but had worn down in time and never been refurbished, so the place had a tired red look about it. It was not typical for a theatre of that era. Firstly, it was a single-storey building, and the main theatres of the time were big, elaborate multi-storeyed affairs with three, or even four, levels of balconies that were garishly decorated.

Secondly, it is fair to say, performances at a theatre in the late 1840s would fall into two basic groups. There were the dramas of Shakespeare and other notables that would form this group. High-brow opera could be included in this category too. The second group would be comic entertainment, either bawdy or, surprisingly, something resembling a circus. Freak shows and other entertainers doing daring exploits with animals, usually with lions. The Walworth Theatre at the Elephant was uncomfortable in both these categories. Audiences soon found Shakespeare a crashing bore, and numbers dwindled until it was not worth putting them on. The circus category fared much better; residents did like this. However, an incident where a lion escaped from its cage and chased the audience three times around the theatre had the place closed down for over a year.

Next, the location.

The Elephant, named after an old coaching inn, called the Elephant & Castle, lies on the northern tip of Walworth and is under a mile from the River Thames in south London. It lies on a main arterial and was the gateway to Kent and southeast England. A busy traffic-ridden junction. Adjoining The Elephant to the south, is the tightly populated working-class area of Walworth. Cramped accommodation with crowded street markets. Although poor, it has a cheerful population notwithstanding some dangerous elements. Later, in the twentieth century, Charlie Chaplin grew up in this neighbourhood, and for many years, the British Labour party had its headquarters there. That's the kind of area it is.

The Walworth Theatre of the mid 1800s was a failed project that spent most of its thirteen years of existence closed down. Its most notable and momentous time was the few weeks in which George and Charles Tipton inhabited the place. This time was as extraordinary as it was historic, although it is doubtful whether anyone recorded it.

It was boarded-up at the time the Exhibition had requisitioned it. It was boarded-up soon after George and Charles Tipton left it, and two years after that, the building was knocked down and replaced by a far grander theatre.

Despite its chequered history, George Tipton was thrilled to be awarded it. To him, it was confirmation of the escalating road to getting his music-picture-shows onto the world stage. Hours after obtaining the keys, he took his five-year-old son, George II, to see it.

Young George II was a very wise boy, and his father was very protective of him. The lad gave him all kinds of advice and was impressed with his father's achievement of getting the theatre. He shared in his father's triumph which pleased George no end. George II inspected the stage and advised where to put the screens for the music-picture-shows and where to put the projectors. All in all, George Tipton was in ecstasy with the situation.

Then, the incident with Charles at the Crystal Palace changed everything. Plummeting deflation. Charles had demanded the keys from his brother and had actually taken up residence in the theatre!

George spoke with his son about the grim situation. Young George wanted to come along to the theatre and resolve matters, but his father would not have it.

"It is far too dangerous," George kept telling him. "Uncle Charles is a wild man. Wild and dangerous. It is my problem. He is very strong and forceful. I cannot put you through that. I need to do it myself."

It was an intolerable situation with Charles, and it had escalated to boiling point.

33 – Charles Takes Charge

Charles had moved into the theatre and was throwing his weight around. His freshly washed underwear was hanging up all over the theatre. He would start every day by taking his shirt off and showing George his muscles. He pumped them up, displaying them in front of George's nose.

"See these muscles?" Charles would say. "They are big muscles, are they not?"

George had to admit they were.

"You do not have such big muscles, do you?"

George had to admit that he didn't.

"Better do as I say, or I will use these muscles on you."

In this way, Charles kept George in order and began treating him like a slave. First, he got George to teach him how to operate the projectors and then, perhaps in an attempt to humiliate him, he turned George's two-projector setup into a four-projector one. Then he taught four men to be projector operators and dressed them up in peaked hats and uniforms. Next, and most importantly, he got George to produce a long and complex show for him.

Presumably, Charles wanted to create some big splash in his life to make up for all the misery he had experienced in prison, and the unique opportunity to take over a theatre at the greatest international event of its time seemed to offer this possibility. It had the added bonus of humiliating George, which he prosecuted with relish.

For five consecutive days, he forced George to make his show, which involved several thousand drawings, and George worked like an overwhelmed donkey. By many accounts, the show was quite a revolutionary concept, proposing a revolutionary change in the world and, bearing in mind the exhibition was Prince Albert's brainchild to showcase Britain, the whole situation fermenting in that theatre was quite an explosive mix.

34 - Charles Starts His Show

By midnight on day five, George had finished the show in time for the first performance on day six - which was shown to some of Charles's mates whom he had met in prison. They were not all his mates, and not all of them had been in prison either, but each did belong to one of two groups. Two groups that did not necessarily like each other. Charles positioned them in the first three rows on either side of a central aisle. On the left side of the aisle were a group of communists, and on the right side a group of Quakers.

Charles built himself up to introduce the show and got up onto the stage. In a slightly deranged way, he was trying to fulfil a dual purpose. Fulfil the payback aspect and complete his humiliation of George, *and* introduce the show.

Charles cleared his throat.

"There is something deep in my genes that *compels* me to change the world into a far better place for me to live in," he said to his audience.

George flipped his eyes at the pomposity of this. He had been 'compelled' to sit on a little stool like a dumbo and was silently fuming.

Charles went on. "We are all regarded as outcasts here, so I have secured a place on the world stage where we can get our views across to the wider populations of the Earth. Comrade Marx," he said, casting his eyes on the bushy mop of hair in the midst of the communists. "Comrade Marx, would you consider unveiling your Communist Manifesto at *my* theatre at the Great Exhibition? It has been over a year since you finished it. People should be given the opportunity to discuss it. *My* theatre at this international exhibition would be the best place to launch it."

Karl Marx sat impassively, not responding.

"Maybe you will be persuaded when you see what comes next. *My* invention will be a feature of *my* theatre."

George was getting progressively irritated at Charles's use of the word *my*, when in fact it was *his* invention, and *his* theatre.

Charles rattled on. "I have a story which I will tell you in a moment. A story, an idea that would transport the world into a far better place than it is right now. We will have a discussion about it. We can have a discussion about your ideas, but we will discuss my one in particular. *My* theatre at the Great Exhibition will be a forum for all my best ideas. And yours too if you want to use it."

Charles clicked his fingers, and the four uniformed projector operators marched in with the four projectors.

"I am about to start my presentation," Charles said. "For the past hundred years, the British Isles have been at the centre of a transformation. A huge transformation unlike any other. The age of the machine. I am going to tell you a story that only a select number of people know. Very soon, many people will know it, and a superlative new age will descend on Earth as a result."

Charles clicked his fingers, and the show quickly powered into life.

The theatre darkened. The projectors lit, and two adjoining screens were lowered. An assimilated roar was heard from a concealed choir. The lens caps from the projectors were removed. There was a gasp of astonishment from the audience as the show blazed into life. What was seen could best be described as a fiery vision of hell.

"The Bedlam Furnaces of Coalbrookdale," Charles announced. "The birthplace of our industrial transformation."

A ferocious gust of fierce red and yellow flames soared into the night sky. The powerful, fluorescent animated glow flowed across the audience, bathing them in the light.

"I can see you are amazed, and the story I am about to tell you will amaze you even more. I have perfected a way to tell my story in motion. Now, I have secured a theatre for us in the Great Exhibition. I did all this for us. It has all been my work, and I urge you all to support me in this great enterprise."

The red and yellow glow galvanised George Tipton into action, and he sneaked out of the theatre to do something about the situation with Charles. He creeped out and ran back home, a mile away in Camberwell, to consult with his son.

35 – *Inspiration From George II and Nefeli*

George had a strange relationship with his five-year-old son. He was both a good father and a not-so-good one. On the one hand, he loved his son and did everything he could to keep young George II safe and healthy. He was in awe of his son and accepted him as his mentor and guiding light, an unusual arrangement for father and son. Because of this, the downside was, he rarely let his son out of the house. Perhaps he felt his son would catch something and die like his mother. Or maybe he was scared his son would be kidnapped by thieves and sold to a rich family. He was a beautiful boy and would be very much in demand.

George got home, seething with frustration and much in need of consulting with his son.

"Uncle Charles is unbelievable!" George raged to his son.

Little George asked, "Has he been showing you his muscles again?"

"No, not today. Yesterday he showed me his muscles, the day before that he showed me his muscles, but not today."

"What did he do today?"

"Today, instead of the muscles, it was something else. Today, Uncle Charles was claiming the theatre and music-picture-stories were all his. It is my theatre, not his."

His son said, "The problem is obvious and stems from Uncle Charles's muscles. I have been thinking about Uncle Charles's muscles, and I have the solution."

"Oh, what is it?"

"I have been looking through the newspapers you gave me."

With the help of his father, young George had learnt to read at the tender age of four. An exceptional child. Each week, George bought him a newspaper, and he devoured every word of it, even the obituaries; he simply wanted to know everything.

Young George soothed his father. "Once you stand up to Uncle Charles and his muscles, then it will be better."

"I know, but how can I? His muscles are huge, and he has learnt to fight in prison. Fight with the toughest people. I am no match for him. He has a hold over me."

"You must train. A month ago, Harry Wannop opened a gymnasium in Whitechapel."

"Harry Wannop, the prize-fighter?"

"Yes. I read this in the newspaper you gave me last month. I found the newspaper while you were at the theatre, look."

George II handed his father the newspaper, and he read the article, then gleefully punched his fists into the air. "Harry Wannop, yes! He was the top prize-fighter for over six years, and now he is teaching others. He could show me some moves. That would show Uncle Charles. You are an inspiration, George."

"You need to calm yourself, Dad. You are in no state to approach Harry Wannop. Do not stand up to Uncle Charles with the mind of a prize-fighter either. You should be calm on the inside. Approach Uncle Charles with the calm mind of a Ninjutsu fighter."

"Should I be seeing a Ninjutsu trainer instead?"

"I do not think there are any Ninjutsu trainers in London. Instead, you will need to train with a prize-fighter but have the calm mind of the Ninjutsu."

George thought about this. Once again, he looked at his son with an expression of wonder. It never ceased to amaze him how wise and beautiful he was. The lad had a shining glow, like a smiling Buddha.

"Thank you, George. I know not where you get this from but thank you."

Young George II smiled briefly and moved on. "Father, I think you should calm yourself completely before going to Whitechapel. Be alone in your room and be at peace with yourself inside. Calm yourself as if you were in a church."

George closed his eyes, briefly inclined his head towards his son in respect, and simply said, "Thank you."

George retired to his room and lay on his bed, attempting to calm himself from the traumas of the past few days concerning Charles. He breathed deeply and followed advice from his son on being calm. He spent several minutes doing this and gradually felt soothed. He spent some time in this state.

Slowly, he opened his eyes and saw a beautiful ghostly figure dressed all in white. Puzzled, and a little confused, he asked the figure, "Am I imagining things?"

"No, George, I am here."

"Are you God? Are you a ghost?"

"Hmm, interesting."

"Are you dead or alive?"

"Interesting but let us not dwell on this. I have important information to give you, and I cannot stay long."

"Who are you?"

"I am your mother."

George gasped. "My mother, Princess Nefeli?"

"If you like but let us not waste time on that. I need to impart important knowledge. First, you must realise you are the founder of a great line. A line that will eventually save the Earth. It is your duty to ensure no harm comes to your son, for he shall carry on the line. I have no information of how long it will take for the line to manifest this person and fulfil the mission."

George respectfully put his hands together as if in prayer. "I will do my best, Mother," he said.

"Now, for another important part of my visit."

With great effort, Nefeli pushed herself into full materialisation and presented George with a small white stone. The most beautiful, luminous white stone imaginable. It radiated its white magnificence, and George gasped at the beauty of it.

"Keep the stone safe and do not mention its existence to anyone."

"Does this stone have a purpose?"

"Yes – it is the antidote to the Earth stone. The red and yellow Earth stone."

George's jaw dropped in awe. "I have always felt a strange magic power coming from red and yellow light. Is it coming from the Earth stone?"

"I would think that is the case, but it is doubtful you will ever come into physical contact with the Earth stone."

"Where is the Earth stone?"

"It is set into the coronation crown of the United Kingdom. A well-guarded crown locked deep in the vaults of the Tower of London."

George was thoughtful.

"The Earth stone has immense powers that can only be fully discovered by the one chosen to save the Earth. It has a terrifying dark side too. That is the purpose of the white stone. To neutralise the dark side."

"Is it safe to think about the Earth stone without touching it?"

Nefeli considered this for a few moments. "I believe it would be safe, but if you encounter the dark side, the white stone is there to help you. Remember to keep young George safe. Remember to keep the white stone safe too. Do not tell anyone of its existence."

"I will do that, Mother."

"One last thing before I go . . ."

George was dismayed. "Do not go, Mother. I want to know you. I have questions."

"I cannot stay. I am starting to fade. That is the way it is. Let me tell you one last important thing. Beware of Zakamonsky."

"Zakamonsky?"

"Yes, and the Devils of Danzig."

"The Devils of Danzig?"

"Yes. Zakamonsky and the Devils of Danzig."

Nefeli began to go misty and ghostly.

"Will I see you again, Mother?"

"If I can come again, I will. I am nearly gone."

A few seconds later, Nefeli disappeared completely. George was stunned.

He lay for a few minutes, taking stock of what had just happened and contemplating what his mother had said. Then he got up and returned to his son in the other room.

"George, I am taking your advice and going to Whitechapel. We are going to deal with this situation concerning Uncle Charles."

Young George glowed with pride. "Thank you, Dad."

"Do not answer the door to anybody until I get back. Do you understand? You must stay safe."

"Yes, Dad."

36 – George Goes to Whitechapel

Harry Wannop was an unpleasant-looking man with a broken nose and cauliflower ears. His gymnasium was a foul-smelling place in the heart of Whitechapel, a tough area on the east side of London.

Wannop viewed George with suspicion.

"Entering the game, sonny? You ain't look the sort."

"I want to fight my brother," George said.

Wannop shook his head. "I only train ones I can put in fights. Make money in bets. Bets I know I can win because I train them." He laughed at this. "Train them to punch hard. I know the moves. Sorry, sonny, you come to the wrong place."

"I will pay you a guinea."

Wannop displayed his broken and dislocated knuckles. "I can sell you a duster and save your delicate knuckles. You can alter the look of his face with my knuckledusters."

Wannop fetched his collection of knuckledusters. They were lethal looking devices made of iron that, when attached to the fist, would substantially enhance a punch. Some had spikes that would tear the skin. George was horrified.

"No. I only want to learn some moves and I shall pay you a guinea if you teach me."

After consideration of the guinea, Wannop shrugged and taught George some moves. Techniques on how to land punches and how to anticipate others' moves and get out of the way.

"Now we shall try these for real." He laughed at this. "Take your shirt off, sonny, and we shall do it for real."

Wannop took his shirt off. It was not a pretty sight. Far worse than Charles's chest. George took off his shirt, as instructed.

"Stand straight and look him in the eye," Wannop said, and he levelled up. "What you want to do is take him by surprise. Weaken him right away with your best punch. Think about your brother and how much you hate him. Think of me as your brother and give me your best punch. Land me your very best. Then we move onto the next stage."

Wannop relaxed, awaiting George's punch.

George, instead of thinking about his brother, thought about his son and the advice given about Ninjutsu and being calm. He breathed in, becoming serene, and thought of his mother and the Earth stone. He felt the glorious yellow light, like sunshine, bathing over him, and with his other hand, felt the white stone in his pocket in case anything went wrong. The sunshine came surging up his arm, infusing energy, and like lightning, he dispatched his punch. Wannop went down, mouth gaping open like a surprised turkey.

George looked down at Wannop, motionless on the floor, scared he had killed him. A couple of minutes later, Wannop came to, shaking his head in shock.

"You pack a mighty punch," Wannop said. "Come into the game. We could make money. Big money."

George shook his head. "Thank you, but no. You have taught me what I need to know, and I am grateful."

George gave him a guinea, left, and ran back to the theatre, quietly confident he could challenge Charles. He bathed in the afterglow of the glorious yellow-red light, overjoyed he was discovering the power of the Earth stone.

In Pennsylvania Heights, Georgina Tipton had opened the trunk and was discovering the power of the Earth stone too. Although she did not know it yet, she was the *one* George Tipton's mother had been anticipating. The final link in the line that had the ability to transform the world.

CHAPTER NINE

2019 - Pennsylvania Heights

37 - The Trunk is Opened

Georgina could not resist the temptation. As it opened the huge lid creaked dramatically like some horror movie, but she did not care. For the first time in 169 years, the trunk was unsealed. Revealed inside, was a gigantic treasure trove of items, and she grabbed one - George Tipton's film strip from the crowning of King George II show. This excited her in many ways, and she immediately scanned all the images and turned it into a little film of her own.

She used George Tipton's original drawings, only modifying them slightly. As the crown touched King George II's head, she had the king open his mouth with words coming out in a childlike, chipmunk style. "I'm the king of the world . . . I'm the king of the world . . . I'm the king of the world." She jokingly had him saying this like some crazed megalomaniac, not realising he was one of her relatives.

She noticed something else. The stone at the centre of the crown. This sparked something awesome in her. The red-yellow luminosity of the stone was exactly as George Tipton had drawn it. It rapidly ignited her into a different stratosphere, a strange metamorphosis that transformed her for a few minutes into some superhuman, and she felt obligated to fish out the next item, Charles Tipton's moving picture show, the one he had coerced George Tipton to make for him. As she swept through the images, she began to visualise it, similar to the way it had been performed in that grungy theatre back in November 1850. Not an exact visualisation because the way you imagine an event that happened over a century ago will always come over slightly different. Even so, she felt she was developing a psychic connection to her ancestor George Tipton, and she felt compelled to transcribe the images into a film script. Soon after she finished, Charlotte returned.

Charlotte gazed at Georgina in shock.

"You have gone weird, sis. The trunk is open! I thought I told you not to open it."

"Calm down, sis. Nothing has happened. No little green men popped out. There are fantastic things in the trunk, and everything is just fine."

Although Charlotte was a pure and direct descendant of Charles Tipton – she was now the sixth generation of Charles Tipton's side of the family – and Georgina was a pure and direct descendant of George Tipton's side, technically they were cousins. However, they were like sisters and even called each other 'sis'.

"Everything is fine, sis," Georgina said reassuringly. "See outside, even the men are installing your security system without problems."

Indeed, they were. Georgina shuffled her outside to inspect. The men were busy at work on a system that involved a series of garden gnomes dotted around the garden. One eye of each gnome was shut, but the other open. The gnomes were programmed to recognise Georgina and Charlotte, but nobody else. If any other person trespassed into the garden, the gnomes would activate. The open eye was in fact a camera, and once an intruder was detected, they would begin taking pictures, two per second, and automatically send the pictures to the Police Headquarters on Western Avenue. There were dozens of these gnomes in the garden, all with one eye open that would start flashing and going clickety-clack once an intruder was spotted.

Georgina joked, "Creepy little things, aren't they?"

Charlotte led Georgina to the back of the garden which faced onto the rear of the adjacent garden in Cooper Street.

"Do you think we need to install an electrified iron wall coming up from the ground when someone is in a neighbouring garden?"

Georgina shrugged. "A little bit extreme."

"I am worried, sis. I have a feeling in my bones someone is coming for the trunk. We are in clear and present danger."

"Are we?"

"Yes. They are on their way. I know it."

"Who?"

"Strange people. Dangerous ones. Almost other-worldly."

"When they come, *if* they come, your gnomes will take pictures of them and send them to the police, and that will be that."

"It will not be enough. They are dangerous. They are on their way. I am sure of that. Perhaps they are the Devils of Danzig – the people our fathers warned of."

Georgina shrugged. "We shall deal with it – *I* shall deal with it. Leave it to me. I feel able to handle this. It does not scare me."

Charlotte was shaking. Georgina held onto her, soothing her. "Calm down, sis, and let me manage it. Come, I have something amazing to show you."

Georgina led her gently back to the cabin. Although Georgina was excited about her revelation with the coronation stone, this was not it. She knew that would probably weird Charlotte out and upset her even more. Once inside the cabin, Charlotte began shaking again. "Can we close the trunk, please?"

Georgina closed the giant lid, and it creaked. "Better?"

"A little, yes."

"Now let me show the surprise I have for you." She handed her the film script she had just transcribed. "Here are accomplishments from your side of the family, from your founder Charles Tipton the First. This will show you stuff you never knew!"

Charlotte started reading. After five minutes she looked up. "You are right. It does tell things I never knew."

Georgina raised her head proudly. "It is a proper historical document. How the machine world actually started, and how it went badly wrong, and how to put it right. This could alter the whole course of future history. An accomplishment by your ancestor Charles Tipton! You know you always wanted to make the world a better place to live in. This could be it."

With more enthusiasm, Charlotte continued reading, finishing twenty minutes later. "Yes, this is great, but where is Charles Tipton's solution?"

"Can you raise the money to make it? With $200,000 I could make a simple version. A few million, I could make something grander."

"It is a great story; one the world should know about. I think I have a client who could put up the money, but where is the solution to the problem?"

"The solution, yes. I have not found that yet. It is still inside the trunk."

They both looked at the closed-up trunk. The expression on Charlotte's face made it clear she was not keen to reopen it and was developing the jitters again.

There was a knock at the door which made Charlotte jump. It was the installers of the gnome system. "We're done," the boss said.

"When will it be online?"

"About two hours, maybe three."

"Can you make it quicker?" Charlotte was clearly shaking now.

"Why?"

This is what actually happened in the Walworth theatre . . .

CHAPTER TEN

1850

38 – George Tipton Gets the Upper Hand

The London fog had come down as George Tipton ran back to the theatre at the Elephant. He had become quietly confident he could stand up to Charles and claim his due credit concerning whose theatre it actually was. He ran across the River Thames at London Bridge. A cacophony of hooting was going on from vessels below as they came in to dock. On the other side, he ran through the crowded little streets of south London until he reached the Elephant and sneaked back into the theatre.

It was about three hours since he had left, and much had happened in the intervening time both for him and Charles. For Charles, a major part of the show had been performed, and everyone had been suitably impressed by Charles Tipton's technique of moving images, even though it was not his. The content of the show had impressed them too, but it was harrowing at times.

Essentially, the show demonstrated how the machine-driven world had come about, and how it promised a wonderful world without toil, and how it had been exploited by evil.

A long discussion followed on how to put this right and to ensure it never happened again. As George arrived back at the theatre, the discussion had ended, and the concluding scenes of the show had started.

In the darkened room, the audience was glued to the screens as George took a seat, merging unnoticed on the periphery of the Quakers' section. On the screens, the images chugged along at the endearing rate of five drawings per second (or five fps for the technically-minded), and George had to admit the projector operators were doing their job well. He was heartened to realise he had done his job well too. It was rare George ever got to view his own show as he was always operating projectors. Now he could. The changing expressions on the faces in the moving pictures moved convincingly, and they were suitably harrowing. The intense drawing of these images over the previous few days had resulted in a show he could be proud of.

(To explain the show: The start of the Industrial Revolution had started over forty years previously with the story of the revolutionary iron-maker Abraham Darby I. After he died, the bad deeds had infiltrated the company, and his son, Abraham Darby II, was living with these consequences. He believed he was being punished by God as a series of disasters befell him, including the death of his first child. A complete transcript of the whole show can be seen in Appendix 2.)

In the darkened room, on the panorama of screens, George gazed at his drawings of a children's bedroom.

Three child beds were in the bedroom. One bed was stripped of covers, and a small coffin rested on a table. Undertakers picked up the coffin and were followed solemnly out the room by grief-stricken Darby, his wife, and their two remaining children. His wife was sobbing. The screen went black and relit in the same bedroom. Now, two of the beds were stripped, and another small coffin lay on the table. The coffin of the second child. The coffin was lifted by undertakers, the screen went black, and relit. Now, all three beds were bare, and a third small coffin was on the table. Darby's wife wailed uncontrollably. The screens went black and lit again in the parents' bedroom. Now, a full-sized coffin, the coffin of Darby's wife Mary, sat on a table. Undertakers carried it out of the room with Darby following.

From behind a curtain, Charles Tipton narrated the ongoing story. He did it with dramatic zeal . . . "Abraham lost his family. Yes lost were his entire family. Every one of his family gone. None left. Is that not some form of retribution? Some message of 'what was done must be put right'? A message that it is incumbent on us to do it and put it right?"

A procession followed the coffin of Darby's wife along the banks of the River Severn. As the procession turned off towards the graveyard, Abraham Darby, alone, continued running along the banks of the River Severn, wailing uncontrollably. A small stone church came into view. The church came closer.

George nodded to himself at how well this moving scene of approaching the church worked on screen.

Darby entered the church and walked down the aisle. He approached a stained-glass window beyond the altar. Distraught, he addressed a stained-glass image of Jesus.

An actor voiced Darby's distressed prayer.

"Lord, I am overcome. Tell me what I should do. I have sinned, done wrong, sinned badly. I have participated in supplying arms for war which I know is wrong. Please forgive me. Please teach me in the ways of righteousness and put me on that path. I am broken, but ready to learn. Please give me the courage to learn."

A pastor saw Abraham and walked slowly up the aisle. He had a look of empathy and approached Abraham. They looked at each other.

The pastor said, "It is not the war you are being judged on, Abraham. It is your Quaker faith. Give it up. Give it up now. Come. Join us. Repent."

Abraham backed away, shocked, and ran out the church screaming.

The theatre was abruptly re-lit.

Rather an odd ending.

Both the Quaker group, and the Communist group, clapped as a bushy-haired figure rose.

"Comrade Tipton - it is obvious," Karl Marx shouted. "I have said it before, and I shall say it again. Religion, it is the opiate of the people."

Jonas for the Quakers sprang up and disagreed. A squabble broke out, and everyone started arguing with each other.

Charles raised his voice, appearing from the front.

"Please, everyone, sit down. We are meant to be cooperating on a solution to the machine-driven world. One day, it will become so bad that the one who controls the machine will control all of us. We need to devise a solution so we can have a world fit for me to live in."

"A world not just fit for you, but for everyone," Jonas said.

"Yes, that is what I meant, but first, I would like a round of opinions on how you find this new way of presenting things I have invented. I want your opinions of that first."

Perhaps Charles was split between the desire to get opinions on the content of his story on the one hand and extracting payback from George on the other hand. Whatever it was, George Tipton was sufficiently confident to put the record straight.

George rose from the shadows, making his presence known.

"I am sorry to tell you all, but my brother has been fooling you. It was me that invented these moving picture shows, and me that made this particular show. It was also me that was awarded this theatre," George said.

Both groups spun around to view George.

If George was expecting Charles to tell the truth, he was wrong. Instead, Charles exploded in anger. It was not verbal or even physical. Simply a huge welling up of emotion as Charles's face went a bright crimson. Rapidly, his body turned into wild-animal-in-attack mode, which was an unusual and terrifying sight.

A few moments of this, and Charles got his mouth working and told his guests, "You all need to leave, now! I need to see my brother in private!"

It was not a pretty sight, and the force Charles said it with got everyone onto their feet and heading towards the back door, fearing something ugly was about to happen.

As they shuffled out, George became nervous as to whether he could deal with this manic force that had overtaken Charles. He thought of the Earth stone, thought of his son and calmness, and the moves of Harry Wannop, and hoped he could contain this animal ferocity that had overcome Charles. Now was the time to put all these things to the test.

However, he could not put them to the test because something else took place. A trumpet sounded. It was coming from a lobby just outside the main area. A trumpet draped with a royal standard appeared. Blowing this trumpet, was a trumpeter, and he blew a royal fanfare.

"I come with a message for George Tipton Esquire," the trumpeter announced.

George looked around the theatre. It was now empty; even Charles had disappeared.

"It is I," George replied.

"His Royal Highness, Prince Albert, wishes to hear about your invention with a view to approving your application to the Great Exhibition of Works from All Nations, also known as the Crystal Palace Exhibition, which will be held in the spring of next year in Hyde Park. He requests the presence of your company at eleven o'clock tomorrow morning at Buckingham Palace. Will you attend?"

George glowed with pride. "Oh yes. Please tell Prince Albert I shall be there."

"That will be notified to His Royal Highness," the trumpeter said formally.

Slightly dazzled, George said, "I like the trumpet."

The trumpeter smiled. "Prince Albert wishes to make all applicants feel they are part of a royal show."

"He has done that. It feels great."

The royal trumpeter smiled, blew his trumpet, and withdrew.

George was thrilled with this news and hoped Charles had calmed down, but he was nowhere to be seen.

"Charles!" George shouted tentatively.

George was nervous, wondering whether Charles was hiding somewhere and was about to spring out and pounce on him in some wild animal frenzy. "Charles," he called out with a bit less confidence. "Charles?"

He tiptoed to the centre of the theatre, right in the middle of the rows, so he could have a clear view and as much advance notice as possible if Charles sprang out from wherever he was. "Charles!"

After George attempted shouting a few more times, Charles did appear. He had been hiding underneath the stage and had completely changed and did not look threatening at all. The opposite: he was shaking like a leaf.

George asked, "What are you doing under there?"

"Was he coming to kill me?"

"Kill you? Who?

"The royal trumpeter. Was he coming to kill me?"

"Kill you? No. He was bringing me a message. Why would he want to kill you?""

"I do not know. I think he wants to kill me. Ten years in prison has left me damaged. Damaged in my brain. I imagine things. I have delusions and flashbacks. You have no idea what it is like to be in prison charged with sedition. The guards beat you up all the time, and nobody cares. You should try it sometime."

"No, thank you."

Charles was shaking badly, and his jaw was chattering. George went to the kitchen and made him a cup of tea. Charles clasped the warm cup in his hands and stopped shaking so much.

Puzzled, George asked, "Who do you imagine wants to kill you?"

"The rulers. They want to kill me."

"What rulers?"

"Not sure. I feel it in my bones. Maybe I am imagining it. That is how bad it is."

Quite suddenly, George felt sorry for Charles and said, "Listen. I am going to Buckingham Palace tomorrow to meet Prince Albert. Come with me. You will see it is all in your imagination."

"I could not do that. They will want to kill me."

"No, they will not."

"I already have a record of wanting to kill the monarch. Prince Albert will want to kill me before I kill him."

George began to see the contorted logic of this. "I know what we can do. We can swap places. You can pretend to be me."

"Me pretend to be you?" Charles thought about this. "Does he want to kill you too?"

"No, he does not want to kill me. If you pretend to be me, you will feel safe and see it is all in your imagination."

Charles thought about this and said, "I will give it a try."

Almost immediately, George felt queasy about this and regretted it.

After settling Charles in for the night, George ran back to consult with his son and found him studying a newspaper. He told his son what had happened.

"Swapping places? I am not sure that was a good thing to do, Dad."

"I know, but it is done now. He is expecting to come to Buckingham Palace."

"I had better come with you, Dad. Make sure it is not a disaster."

"Children are not allowed. Besides, it is only meant to be me. Not me and Charles. It is already turning into a disaster."

"We need to write down what Uncle Charles should say to Prince Albert. He should say only what we write and nothing else."

George agreed and was abundantly pleased at what a sensible intelligent boy he had produced. They spent almost three hours writing a succinct account of what music-picture-stories were, and what would be shown in the picture palace, and exactly what Charles should say to Prince Albert.

Early in the morning, George ran to the theatre and let himself in. He found Charles snoring under the stage and woke him up. For three hours, they practiced what had been written the night before.

"Are you sure you can remember to say that to Prince Albert?"

Charles said, "Yes."

At ten o'clock, a cabriolet, as a taxicab was known at the time, arrived to take them to see Prince Albert. The little horse-drawn carriage trotted along the south side of the Thames towards Buckingham Palace.

CHAPTER ELEVEN

39 – George and Charles Meet Prince Albert

By ten thirty, the little open carriage was whisked through the gates of Buckingham Palace. George and Charles were given the royal treatment and seated in a lavish holding room. At the appropriate time, they were escorted to the presentation room to meet Prince Albert.

It was more of a long corridor than a room and there were about three hundred people all lined up waiting to be presented. Prince Albert was working his way down the line. He was about ten applicants away from George and Charles. George stood a little behind Charles and whispered, "Are you going to be alright with this and remember what to say?"

Charles nodded.

"Do you want me to take over?"

"No," Charles said.

Next to George was an Italian. "I am Felix Abote from Napoli," he said to George. "I have a burnishing machine. Very good machine. Polish metal like new." He smacked his lips, indicating how good the machine was. He went on about it. George wished he would shut up so he could concentrate on Charles, but Abote did not.

The prince, accompanied by a courtier, reached Felix Abote, who now extolled the virtues of his burnishing machine to the prince. The prince nodded politely and began to move away, but Abote continued to list the features of his machine. The courtier said, "Thank you, Mr Abote. That will be enough. I believe the prince has understood the essence of your application."

The prince approached Charles, and the courtier read from a list.

"A Mr George Tipton, Your Royal Highness. Mr George Tipton's application is for a theatre to be built next to the Crystal Palace. We have an artist's impression of the building," he said, and handed George's impression of the picture palace to Prince Albert.

The prince laughed. "A mini-Crystal Palace. I like it. Is this your drawing, Mr Tipton?"

"Err, yes," Charles said. "My drawing."

"And what will be inside the building?"

Charles hesitated for a bit, then said, "It will be a workers' theatre."

The prince checked. "A workers' theatre?"

"Yes."

George's face dropped. The idiot had gone off-script. Had he flipped?

"What a great idea," the prince said, turning to the courtier. "Is that not a great idea?"

The courtier nodded respectfully. "A great idea. One of the best."

The prince chuckled. "A little palace for the workers. It shows the world how much we respect our workers."

"It does indeed, Your Royal Highness," the courtier said.

"Well done, Mr Tipton." The prince prepared to move on.

"I shall be organising union meetings for the workers," Charles said.

"Jolly good."

"I will encourage the workers to organise. Organise strongly and effectively."

"Very good. That is what we need. Well organised work patterns to increase production. I look forward to seeing your workers' theatre at the exhibition. Keep up the fine work."

As the prince moved on, the courtier whispered to Charles, "His Royal Highness loves your idea. Prepare the theatre well. He is bound to visit."

George and Charles left Buckingham Palace and made their way back to the Elephant. Both silent.

Finally, George said, "Why did you tell the prince it was a workers' theatre?"

Charles did not say anything.

"Did you flip? Forget what to say? Have one of your memory problems?"

Charles nodded.

"It is a fine mess," George said. "I suppose it suits you though. That is what you wanted. A workers' theatre. You and the workers."

Charles shook his head.

As they re-entered the Walworth Theatre, and the implications sunk in, Charles became increasingly jumpy.

"Do you think it's a trick?"

"It was no trick. We have to get material for a workers' theatre. Prince Albert is coming to watch. What a mess."

Charles started shaking. Trembling, and his teeth chattering.

George thought he must be having another flashback and was unsure what to do but fetched him a cup of tea. Charles managed to control his mouth.

"I have something to tell you," Charles said. "I wanted you to go to jail. I told Prince Albert the things I had been doing that got me jailed. I thought he would send you to jail like I had been sent."

"You did what?"

"I wanted you to go to jail, like me, so we could be equals."

George gaped in silence, shocked at what he was hearing. It took a while to sink in, and when it did, it was like a slow-motion explosion. George's fist came at Charles's jaw like a sledgehammer. Charles was flung into the air, and there was a look of surprise on his face as he landed with a thud and saw his teeth splatter across the floor.

"Do not ever do that to me again!" George roared. "You may think I am an idiot, but I'm maybe not as much of an idiot as you think."

Charles became aware of his jaw. Putting his hand against it and feeling something was very wrong. Like it was broken. He looked up at George like a sorry puppy. "Please, could you get me a doctor?" It came out garbled as he could not open his mouth properly.

George agreed and left in search of a doctor. After making this appointment he ran home to update his son.

40 – George II Finally Meets Charles

Young George II shook his head. "I knew it was a bad idea, Dad, swapping places. If you had taken me along to see Uncle Charles like I said, it would not have happened."

His father had to agree.

Young George II carried on. "You should take me to see Uncle Charles before you get in any more trouble."

George thought about this and realised he could protect his son now. "Yes, I shall bring you to see Uncle Charles. We shall leave now."

Young George's face lit up. It was the first time he had been out of the lodgings all week.

Charles was still splayed out on the ground as they entered the theatre.

"Hello, Uncle Charles. I heard you spent a long time in prison."

Charles tried to answer, but another tooth spewed out as he tried to speak.

"Think it best not to speak until the doctor has seen you."

The doctor arrived a little while later and patched Charles up. He administered a comfrey pack which was held on by a large bandage tied around his head and chin, and made Charles look like one of those soldiers walking back from war minus the crutches.

The doctor left, promising to check on Charles in two days.

"Right," young George II said. "We need to decide how to move this situation forward."

"Well," George Senior said. "I promised the Allocations Board I would show my year-by-year history of the world, but now Charles has said it is a workers' theatre."

Charles mumbled something. With no teeth and a broken jaw, he was having difficulty getting anything out. After several attempts of garbled words, young George was able to decipher it.

Young George II translated this to his father. "Uncle Charles is saying that Prince Albert is expecting to see a moving picture show about *workers.*"

"Yes, that is the problem. I have not got any music-picture-stories about workers."

"I have an idea, Dad. You showed me some drawings you made of workers in Tipton. You could make them into a music-picture-story."

It was a lightbulb moment.

"You are right, George. I could, and I know the exact music I should use. A song. A beautiful song about the love the people have for their grimy old Black Country."

George paced around the theatre in a flurry of creativity thinking about this new show. When he rejoined them, young George had a further idea.

"Dad, I have an idea. We have use of this theatre for the next few months. We should use it to show your music-picture-stories to the public. We could show your music-picture-stories to other theatres too."

Strangely, Charles saw the potential for this. Over the next few days, after a rocky start, the family began to come together and embark on creating a family business involving entertaining the public with George's moving picture stories. It had several prongs. The first prong was to give a performance to the local population, and the next day they got to work in earnest.

Young George saw a problem. "Nobody wants to come to this theatre. It has a bad reputation, and they do not know what music-picture-stories are either. How are we going to get people to come and see it?"

"No problem," Charles claimed, and although his words were stunted, he had made a steady recovery due to being overjoyed at being part of a family. "I know people who could help with getting people into the theatre. After I was released from prison, my licence to practice law was revoked and I became destitute, until I offered legal business advice to anyone who needed it on a donation basis. That is what I do now. That is how I survive. Many get advice and walk off without giving a donation. Some do not, and they get good advice whenever they want it at very little cost. I have some clients who are promoters of big theatres. I can offer them a percentage of the first year's takings if they make a success of our business. What we need is the help of a professional theatre promoter. I know some. Do you want me to arrange that?"

George and his son agreed it would be a good idea. An hour later, Charles stumbled off to Drury Lane in search of his theatre promoter clients. He returned later that afternoon with the news that two big promoters would be arriving to see the moving picture shows the following day. George flew into a panic wondering what he could show them and worried that there was no music. George II had found an old piano in a dressing room, and they wheeled it in. George left to track down one of his musicians to play it and spent the rest of the day rehearsing one of his music-picture-shows. It was not ideal, and needed the full orchestra, but it would have to do.

The next day, George and the pianist performed the show to the two promoters who agreed it was a thrilling concept, but they could not see an entertainment market for it in the local working-class audience of Walworth. Charles quickly intercepted, explaining about George's *Black Country* production, and handed them George's 'in-progress' pictures for the show.

One of the promoters agreed to give it a try. Thursday 12 December was chosen as the date for a trial performance. The promoter agreed to prepare publicity for this.

Things were moving fast. They were already in December. After the promoters left, George went into a frenzy to get his first public performance ready for a week on Thursday. He thought about two other music-picture-stories to be shown alongside the Tipton show but concentrated on the Tipton one. He dug in deep and obsessed that he should take actual photographs to mix with the drawings in order to go in and out of a heightened reality. He insisted he needed to go to Tipton to take these photographs. Both George II, and Charles, thought there was not enough time for this and agreed there should be a second show just before Christmas, featuring an enhanced Tipton show with the additional photographs. It was agreed that George should take the overnight train to Tipton after the show on 12 December, take the photographs on Friday 13 December, and return on Saturday 14th. A date of 21th was tentatively set for the second show. During the week, Charles jogged down to the railway station in Vauxhall and bought the train ticket for George.

The theatre became a hive of industry.

George arranged three trestle tables in the theatre to work on his music-picture shows and began drawing with a feverish intensity. Young George II helped him.

Charles was busy too, coming up with new business ideas. He wrote letters to theatre owners, letting them know about this 'amazing' new entertainment form and inviting them to come for a showing in the new year. He came up with a money-making idea for the exhibition too. This was an offer to make picture shows of inventions at the exhibition. To show how they worked, and their benefits. Animated advertising if you like.

Meanwhile, at Buckingham Palace, things were developing too.

CHAPTER TWELVE

41 – Trouble at the Palace

It was two days after Prince Albert had met the latest round of applicants, the round in which he had seen George and Charles Tipton. The prince was reviewing this batch with Gerald, the head of the Allocations Board. Files had been arranged in the order the prince had seen the applicants. Gerald opened the file on Abote.

"A Mr Felix Abote from Naples, Your Royal Highness. Do we reject him?"

"Tiresome little man," the prince said.

"Yes," Gerald agreed. "Does that mean a rejection, Your Royal Highness?"

"Have we an application for a British burnishing machine?"

"Yes, Your Royal Highness, we do have one."

"Is it a better burnishing machine than his?"

"I am not an expert on burnishing machines, but I am informed it is better."

"Let Abote have his machine, but make sure his stand looks dull, and our one attractive," the prince chuckled.

"Very good, Your Royal Highness. We now come on to Mr George Tipton. I can highly recommend this one."

The prince stretched back, recalling. "Yes. I liked that one. The little palace for the workers."

"Not specifically for workers, Your Royal Highness."

"Oh yes, for workers, that is the purpose of it."

"I think you are mistaken. Mr Tipton's application is for his new invention. Music-picture-stories. They are glorious. Pictures put to music that tell a story. They wash over you in an amazing way. He displayed a glide through the 1700s. It was most uplifting."

"He never mentioned music-picture-stories."

"That is odd, Your Royal Highness."

"Yes, odd." Prince Albert rose and walked around the room. "If that was his invention, and it is as good as you say, why would he not mention it?"

Gerald was mystified. "I cannot say."

"Is he trying to fool me and *embarrass* me in some way?"

"I do not know. It is most strange."

"There can be no embarrassments."

"No, Your Royal Highness."

"Set this application aside and investigate. I wish to know why Tipton did not mention his invention." The prince walked thoughtfully around the room and then returned. "Do not let Tipton know we are investigating. It should be done without him knowing. There can be no embarrassments."

Gerald initiated an investigation and discovered from the list at the door that George Tipton was accompanied by a Charles Tipton. He related this finding to the prince.

Prince Albert stomped around the room, thinking. "Yes, I remember there were two of them. One stood behind the other. Possibly, for some reason currently unknown, they swapped places. Investigate Charles Tipton."

Gerald initiated this and was presented with an alarming police report that Charles Tipton had been arrested for sedition and served ten years in prison.

Gerald delivered his findings delicately so as not to alarm the prince too much. "It appears Charles Tipton is anti-monarchist," he said.

"Is he?"

"Yes. He has a record of protesting against the monarchy."

"Does he?"

Gerald stopped short of telling the prince that Charles had done ten years in jail for sedition. Instead, he said, "I discovered Charles Tipton has trustees in Birmingham. I understand trustees have ways of disciplining their charges."

"They do," the prince agreed. "Are you suggesting we lean on these trustees and see how they discipline Charles Tipton?"

"It would be interesting to see, Your Royal Highness."

The prince wandered off to think about this. "Charles Tipton is obviously trying to disrupt the exhibition and embarrass me in some way. There can be no embarrassments. The exhibition must progress without flaws. As a first step, send a stern letter to these trustees, signed by me, and insist they discipline Charles Tipton thoroughly. Make it clear that Charles Tipton must not be allowed to embarrass me."

"Yes, Your Royal Highness."

Gerald prepared a letter to the trustees. After three drafts, Prince Albert approved it, signed it, and had a royal messenger dispatch it in person to the head trustee. It arrived in Birmingham the following morning. In panic, Frank Rudders quickly convened a meeting with the other two trustees.

42 – The Trustees Convene

The three trustees were now entering advanced years and spending their later life in semi-retirement. Rudders and the two other trustees arrived at the office. The other two trustees were anxious to find out why an urgent meeting had been convened.

"I have received an alarming letter," Frank Rudders announced.

The Swiss banking expert cowered nervously. "Is one of our clients accusing us of embezzlement?"

"Worse. It is a disturbing letter from Buckingham Palace."

"Buckingham Palace?"

"What does Buckingham Palace want with us?"

"It concerns Charles Tipton."

A groan came from the other two trustees. The Charles Tipton affair was one big sorry incident they hoped had been left long behind.

"Charles Tipton has been causing problems for Prince Albert."

"Does he want to kill him?"

"Charles Tipton did not want to kill anyone. We never said he wanted to kill the king. Simply that he held up a banner saying *Down with the King*. We made that up."

"Now he actually does want to kill. Oh Lord!"

"Maybe he always did, and we did not know it."

Rudders clarified the matter. "It does not say he wants to kill Prince Albert. It says he wants to embarrass him. It keeps mentioning there can be no embarrassments."

"Embarrassments? That is the exact words in the trust. Strange."

The Swiss banking expert cheered up, seeing an opportunity. "Eh, we can make a Christmas bonus from this. It is clear-cut. The trust actually lists 'embarrassing the monarch' and is eligible for a bonus. Here we have it on Buckingham Palace headed paper!"

Rudders shook his head. "We are getting out of our depth here. We should do as it says in the trust. Hand it over to that special unit of the Prussian army. We should have done that in the first place."

"Put him in the hands of this Zakamonsky character? Zakamonsky the blood sucker?"

"Is he a blood sucker?"

"Yes, he is a follower of Vlad the Impaler. Dracula the blood sucker. All the warlords out there do it now."

"Whatever they get up to in their spare time is their own business. Just as long as it does not involve us. I vote we forgo our bonus and let them get on with it."

"Leave Charles Tipton in the hands of Zakamonsky the blood sucker?"

"It is his own fault. He should not go around embarrassing Prince Albert. He ought to have learnt his lesson by now."

"I vote we detach from this business altogether. Whether Mr Zakamonsky does his blood sucking at night, eats testicles for his breakfast, and devours virgins for dinner, I do not want to get involved in any of it. We had an offer to buy the trust from his field commander, a man called Albrecht. I vote we accept the offer and disappear."

The other two thought this was a very good idea and planned disappearing into the Highlands of Scotland.

"Right," Rudders said. "We shall get the sale into motion immediately."

"What about Prince Albert? He wants us to discipline Charles Tipton."

Rudders said, "I shall write a letter to Charles Tipton that will put the fear of God into him."

"Good. Agreed."

43 – Walworth Theatre 8 – 12 December 1850

The furtherance of the family business was going ahead in complete ignorance of what was happening at Buckingham Palace. Or, more sinisterly, with Mr Zakamonsky's secret redemption outfit in eastern Europe.

Charles had set up home in the theatre and slept underneath the stage. His office, two trestle tables, were at the back of the theatre. Here, he wrote letters to theatres, not just in London, but all over the country, each letter becoming progressively more persuasive. He tentatively planned 'the firm' should take a tour of the whole country in the new year and demonstrate the moving picture shows to all the regions. He had also managed to obtain a list of exhibitors at the Crystal Palace for the promoting of inventions idea. He had ideas on licensing the moving picture concept on an international basis but had not formulated his thoughts on that yet. He was planning for the business to expand exponentially.

Meanwhile, at the front of the theatre, George had set up his music-picture-story production office, which consisted of three trestle tables, and his son was by his side, helping.

"Dad, it will look fantastic. Your first public show!"

"Let us hope the public will think that too."

"They will, do not worry."

In so many ways, the boy was such an inspiration, and George felt an enormous love for the lad. "I am sorry I did not bring you along sooner."

"I am here now. That is all that matters. Now, we have to make sure everything is finished on time. We have only four days until the show."

There were huge piles of drawings on each of the tables, and George II was mounting the transparent drawings onto the French invention of cardboard. It was a very long strip of cardboard with exact cut-out squares that would hold the pictures. The completed strips would be fed through the projectors and display the animated show on the screens. George Senior was arranging the sequence of drawings while George-the-son was doing the mounting. A true George & Son operation. They were working at pace because a singer, Sherry Long-Barrow, was coming that afternoon for a trial run of the show.

While the mounting operation was going on, Charles's promoter, Montague Winkel, showed up with a poster and laid it out on Charles's table.

Charles called out to George, "The poster has arrived. Come and look."

George Senior and young George II made their way up to the back.

It was a large poster with a variety of bold, flowery Victorian fonts and decorative curls.

SEEING IS BELIEVING

NEVER BEFORE SEEN

THE TIPTON SHOW

Thursday 12 December, Walworth Theatre, Elephant

Special introductory offer 6d

(Money back if not totally satisfied)

EXTRAORDINARY NEW SHOW

George was thrilled at seeing his show promoted on a professional poster, and Winkel asked, "Everyone happy?"

Everyone agreed, and Winkel departed.

Montague Winkel got 100 posters reproduced that afternoon. He was anxious to gauge whether this moving picture idea would have legs or not. He sent three lads to place posters over a wide area, not just Walworth. This included Camberwell in the south, and Bermondsey a mile to the east.

In the afternoon, the singer arrived.

Sherry Long-Barrow was from the Black Country. She had worked in a factory during the week and sung in taverns of the Black Country on Saturday nights. She had a sweet, yet earthy voice that sent your heart soaring. She had been talent-spotted three years previously and enticed to London. Now, she only sang in the taverns of London. George had first encountered her the previous year and made a mental note. In fact, one of her songs, 'The Black Country Song', was what his Tipton Show was based upon.

He was rather nervous after she arrived.

"I have based my Tipton Show on your Black Country song. I hope you will approve."

Sherry was noncommittal. "Let me see how it looks," she said.

Charles's projector operators arrived and got the projectors fired up. They pushed the strips through the projectors at the appropriate rate. Like everyone, Sherry was enchanted by the moving picture technique, but it was the actual images that touched her the most.

"I love it," she said. "It would fit my song well."

"Can we try it with you singing?" George asked.

Sherry unpacked her guitar from its case. "Let us try."

She sat on a stool, and the projector operator reloaded the projectors.

Charles moved down the theatre to watch.

The images started flowing, and Sherry started her song. Her beauty and simplicity were as pure as her voice. Her Black Country song sent Charles into a world of nostalgia, a world of his childhood. The honest toil of the workers – it was there in the song, and the weathered faces George had drawn. In that moment, Charles gained a respect for George he never had before. A tear dropped from his eye. He kept watching the show.

The workers – there was pride in their ways, in their eyes. Despite the heat and the smoke, there was a love for their town, and they worked on despite their oppressors. It was the reason he became a lawyer – to better their conditions – but he realised they would carry on despite him. They were the Black Country. Like rivers and rocks, they were part of the land. Fathers and grandfathers, they had been there for ever, and would remain till the end of time. When everything was gone, they would still be there. They were the workers of the Black Country. Everything was there in the song and the images of George Tipton.

It was an emotional experience for Charles, and he looked at George in a new and almost reverential way. It was an emotional experience for everyone, even the projector operators. As the song ended, there was silence.

After a while, George said to Sherry, "After the first performance on Thursday, I shall go to the Black Country to take some photographs. I want to add a sequence with real photographs to give a heightened sense of reality."

Sherry nodded in an understanding way. "I will do an instrumental piece between the verses for that sequence. Just photographs and music."

George was amazed. "That is exactly what I would like."

"We should practice the song and the pictures until we get them perfect."

Again, George was amazed. "That is exactly what I would like," he repeated.

"We are both artists, and I know what works," she said. "We must work until it is perfect, and then it will be a success."

Over the next few days, they practiced and practiced and began getting closer. George's son, George II, began to think Sherry would become his step-mum, and he liked the idea.

Charles looked at George and Sherry like a lovesick puppy and vowed to look for a woman of his own once his jaw had healed. He added a new strand to the family business:

working-class motion picture music shows with 'George and Sherry'. Sherry had many songs that could lend themselves to George's pictures. He rattled off another slew of letters to theatres up and down the country with this idea. Also, Charles became in charge of selling tickets for the 12 December show.

The day after Montague Winkel's boys had put up the posters, a trickle of enquiries came into the theatre. Charles had put a notice on the entrance which read *Tickets and Enquiries This Way* with an arrow pointing inside. Charles was very persuasive at selling the tickets, and whether it was due to his sales techniques or the fact he still had a bandage wrapped around his head and looked intimidating, it was hard to tell. When someone would ask about the refund offer as stated on the poster, he would answer, "You must keep the ticket. If you want a refund, you must show me your ticket. No ticket, no refund." He was very insistent about this.

After Sherry Long-Barrow joined the show, word got around, and the trickle turned into a flood. Usually, people came for tickets in the afternoon, after work, so after doing his morning work with the letters, he would take a nap under the stage. Occasionally, people would come to buy a ticket when he was still napping, and George would have to venture under the stage to wake him. Charles would reappear, half-dazed, from under the stage in his underpants, which people found odd.

This anomaly did not adversely affect anything, and Charles settled into a routine. In the morning he would do his letters. Then receive his newspaper and read it, then receive the postman and read his letters, then retire under the stage until the afternoon. One of his letters was to Figgis. Being a fellow outcast, he had kept in touch with Figgis and told him about the show on 12 December. He invited Figgis to come. It was to be a surprise for George. All in all, Charles was relaxing into family life and developing the family business.

It was while reading his newspaper on the morning of 11 December that Charles came upon a disturbing item. He walked down the theatre to tell George about it.

He said, "George, there has been a crash on the Great Northern line."

"Is that the line I am travelling on tomorrow?"

"Yes."

George was anxious. "Would that affect my journey tomorrow? Is the line still running?"

"I am not sure."

"Please go to the station and find out."

Charles ran to Vauxhall Station and asked about the crash. He returned an hour later.

"They are not sure whether trains will run or not. They are still clearing the line."

"When will they find out?"

"I do not know. They did mention there is an overnight stagecoach to Birmingham if it is an urgent journey."

"It is an urgent journey," George insisted. "I have to get those photographs and get back in time to prepare for the second show on 21 December."

Charles informed him, "It is a complicated journey. A two-hour wait in Birmingham for a connection to Tipton. You will become very tired. You do realise you will be travelling overnight and into Friday 13th!"

"I do not care if it's Friday 13th. I have to get to Tipton and get the photographs. Please get me booked on that stagecoach."

With some reservation, Charles ran off to the station, got a refund on the train ticket, and on to the stagecoach terminus where the man in the ticket office smirked. "You realise you will be travelling on Friday 13th?"

"I know. It is not for me, but for my brother. He was very insistent about going."

The man in the ticket office shrugged and issued the ticket.

The next day, Thursday 12 December, was the day of the show, and it would prove to be a momentous day.

44 – The Day of the Show

Obviously, all focus was on the show, and Charles abandoned further letter-writing in favour of getting the theatre cleaned up. He started by sweeping the aisles, then let a cleaner in and supervised her in dusting all the seats. His newspaper arrived, but he did not read it. An hour later, the postman arrived. There were twelve letters, but he did not read them either and instead, carried on with the cleaning. He became a little concerned about the letters, wondering if there were any last-minute items that could affect the performance that night. He had invited a reviewer from an entertainment magazine, and of course, there was Figgis. He thought he had better have a read. He put his broom down, sat at his desk at the back of the theatre, and briefly thumbed through them. They were from around the country, all the regions, presumably from the theatres. It was the fifth letter in the pile that caused him concern. The markings indicated it was from Birmingham. Although he had written to theatres in Birmingham, he knew it was not from a theatre.

In the back of his mind, he knew the incident with Prince Albert would catch up with him. The last few days had been so pleasant and normal that he thought he had dodged that particular bullet. Now he knew he had not. He instinctively knew it was from the trustees, and he had flashbacks of prison and the quarries and the beatings. This time, he knew it would be worse. He began shaking. This time around, it would be fatal. Every fibre in his body told him this would be the end. He was absolutely mystified as to why they wanted him dead, but he knew it was true.

He could not stand opening the letter in the theatre. He controlled his shakes and called out to George, "I am going out for some air."

CHAPTER THIRTEEN

Thursday 12 December 1850

45 – Life Changes Dramatically

Clutching the dreaded letter, Charles sneaked into the Walworth Road and did not stop walking until he reached a steamed-up café where he ordered a cup of tea. A few seats down, an unkempt man with a straggly beard slurped a bowl of soup. The café was full of workers taking a break, and also a few other slurpers.

Charles was not fully aware of the other occupants. He clasped his hands around his cup, staring into space. The letter lay unopened in front of him. He was as white as a ghost. Finally, he braced himself and opened it. His fears were more than realised. The trustee confirmed his punishment would be worse than the first time, and in a strangely apologetic tone, Frank Rudders asked why he had embarrassed Prince Albert as it was a specific condition of the trust that he did not do that. The letter ended with a demand that he should answer why he had embarrassed Prince Albert, so that Prince Albert could dispense the punishment. Charles supressed a scream and bolted out of the café.

He ran aimlessly, imagining what the punishment would be. Floggings, protracted beatings? Whatever it would be, he knew it would end in his death; he felt this in the depth of his bones. Before long, nearly out of breath, he found himself near the River Thames.

He reached the river about a hundred yards east of Waterloo Bridge at Iron Dock. The main docks were further up past London Bridge where there were not any height restrictions. Iron Dock had burnt down in 1845 and was currently being rebuilt. It was still in use, and a few independent lines still used it as it was much cheaper. As he reached the quayside, a 200-foot vessel with low sports funnels methodically steamed into the dock. The mast and sails were down to get past London Bridge, and it flew an American flag. In a flash, he knew what he must do. Escape. Get out of Great Britain as fast as possible. Hitch up with old prison buddy, Jeremiah, who was now living in Quakertown Pennsylvania. He thought about it – The Commonwealth of Pennsylvania. Freedom.

He watched as it edged its way into a mooring. Two men were standing on deck as it pulled in. One had a peaked hat worn at a jaunty angle, probably the skipper; the other had a thick polo-neck sweater that was probably once white but was now thick with soot and salt.

"Ahoy there," Charles called out. "Welcome to England."

"Thanks," the one with the jaunty hat said. "What do you want?"

"Where you sailing to?"

"Back to New York tonight. Why?"

"Need a crew member?"

The jaunty hat looked him up and down. "You on the run? What you done?"

"Nothing," Charles said, but he had to raise his voice over a hooter that was sounding. "Not exactly nothing. I have embarrassed Prince Albert."

The jaunty-hatted sailor looked at the polo-necked one, and both chuckled. "You have embarrassed Prince Albert? Is that Queen Victoria's husband?"

"Yes."

"Get away."

"I really have." Charles ran up the gangplank and passed them the trustees' letter. "I think he wants to kill me."

The one with the polo-neck read the letter. "He really has. He has embarrassed Prince Albert. He's done it before too."

"Is that a habit of yours? Going around embarrassing monarchs?"

"I did not mean to."

Both men burst out laughing. "He did not mean to. Goes around embarrassing monarchs not meaning to. I like it, mister. Can you shovel coal?"

"Clean engines?"

"I could do those things."

"We have five loads to take onboard, and coal. We shall leave by 9 p.m. If you get here before then, and you can work, you can come."

Charles felt a huge weight lifting.

"Can I bring my brother along?"

"What has he done? Embarrassed Prince Albert too?"

"No. He is just a penniless artist."

"Can he shovel coal?"

"He could if he agrees to come. Trouble is, he has set his heart set on taking photographs in Tipton tomorrow."

"Where is that?"

"Up north."

"We have our sister ship arriving in Liverpool on Monday 16th. That is up north. He could get on that. Means he would spend Christmas in the Atlantic though."

"Gee, thanks." Charles found himself talking like an American. "One other thing. Could he bring his girlfriend and five-year-old son?"

"Blimey, old chap," the skipper said, imitating a cockney. "You want to bring all your family and their dogs."

"No dogs, just them."

"We have work to do. We leave at 9 p.m. tonight. If any of you are here by 8.30, you can come."

"Thank you."

Charles punched the air and ran off thinking of all the things he must do between now and 8.30. The first was to buy a trunk big enough to hold all their precious items. The place to buy leather and travel goods was on the other side of the river on a thoroughfare called the Strand.

46 – The Situation Becomes Unexpectedly Bizarre

Charles jogged along the river to the next bridge, Waterloo Bridge, which he joined. He jogged over the river. Midway across, he caught sight of Somerset House on the other side. A grand building which was once a royal palace. It had now morphed into government offices. One of these offices was dedicated to records of births, deaths, and marriages which, in his early professional life, he had cause to visit. He had a sudden overpowering urge to discover who his father and mother were. He was aware this was another forbidden condition of the trust, but as he was about to leave the jurisdiction of the United Kingdom, he felt this was the appropriate time to do this. Probably the only time. The Somerset House complex was entered through a trio of stone arches on the front side of the building, which was on the Strand, about a hundred yards inland from the river. He came off the bridge, reached the Strand, turned right, and ran through the arches.

The arches opened into a large classical courtyard. The buildings were built around this. The records office was the first building on the left. He was overcome with a sudden sharp twinge of fear – the breaking of another condition of the trust. The doors of the record office were about fifteen feet ahead of him. He braced himself and marched towards them. At a distance of six feet, he was unable to move, blocked by some weird invisible force. He shrieked with dread at disobeying a condition of the trust, convinced they were employing some supernatural force against him. A few moments later, a figure began to emerge. An elderly apparition with a long white beard and a cloak; a servant of the trustees, no doubt.

Charles shrieked in terror. "I am sorry. I will do anything you ask."

"Calm down," the figure urged. "I have important information to impart. I am not here to harm you."

Charles was trembling. "Are you a ghost?"

"Not exactly," George William said. "I am your father and have a lot to get through in a short period of time."

"My father?"

"Yes, Charles. This is what you came here to find out, and now I am here. I have managed to break through the material barrier, but I am only allowed a short time. We need to get out of here. There is a church over the road, and there we shall talk."

Charles was utterly confused and unable to resist being pushed back through the arches and over the busy thoroughfare of the Strand. He was pushed onto a little island in the middle of the road where a beautiful little church stood. St Mary's le Strand. He was pushed through a small graveyard, and into the church, and firmly settled down onto a pew.

"Ah, much better," George William uttered. "Beautiful." He beamed up at the magnificent curved roof that had exquisite Italianate inlaid panels. "Before my time, I hasten to add."

"Before your time? What do you mean?"

"It was finished in 1724, the first church to be built under a plan to build fifty new churches. It is beautiful, but I would have done it differently."

"How could you do that?"

"I was head of the Church of England. Head of many things. Hold onto your seat, Charles, and listen. I was the third Hanoverian King of the United Kingdom. I was King George the Third."

Charles gaped in shock, and things moved on fast. He remembered that day at the end of January 1820 when King George the Third died. Being on the coal pile in Tipton. George, wearing the black armband, had said their father had died. He had not taken any of that seriously.

"Yes, Charles, you are of royal stock. Far more than you can possibly realise."

Charles was about to receive a number of serious revelations and simply said, "What do you mean?"

George William stroked his long beard and considered how best to frame this.

47 – Serious Revelations

In the small, exquisitely designed sixteenth-century church of St Mary le Strand, George William stroked his long beard and considered his words carefully.

"Thirty thousand years ago, there were two branches of the humanoid model. The regular Homo sapiens branch, and the Aurora. For thousands of years, the Aurora branch was living on the island of Ocea-ana and were sometimes called the Ocea-ana People."

"The Ocea-ana People?"

"That is where they lived. On the island of Ocea-ana, but their race was Aurora. A light and advanced people. In many ways superior to us simpletons. More intelligence, better looking, more instincts, and they lived for one thousand years compared to Homo sapiens of around seventy. It was set up that way. The big celestial plan was the Aurora would instruct the Homo sapiens to be like them. Homo sapiens would aspire to become Aurora, and the Aurora would teach them. Through diligence, appreciation, and a sense of awe inspired wonderment, they would attain Aurora-hood. The world of the Aurora was like paradise. Ocea-ana was the epitome of heaven on earth. Their beaches and abundant vegetation were like something you could only dream of nowadays. Life was virtually stress-free. Nobody had nasty jobs because living was taken care of through advanced technology. People were free to enjoy themselves, and they did – endlessly. There were crystal towns and floating transport. They were not dependent on food either."

Charles looked at George William, dumbstruck. "You mean there was a civilisation on Earth before our own civilisation?"

"That is exactly what I am saying. The Aurora was the pinnacle of living beings, the crown of all creation, the way mankind was meant to be, the species all creations would aspire to. A civilisation on an island where the luxury of human form could be experienced without limits. People were not even bound by the need to eat, with no hunting or growing of crops necessary. Fruits and plants were available only for experiencing the luxury of taste. It was the ultimate state of the material and the infinite at the same time, and the greatest privilege imaginable to be bestowed with a thousand years of Aurora-hood. Where we use peat and coal to heat our homes, the Aurora had unimaginable forms of energy. They had superior awareness. Homo sapiens would come to the island to be taught the knowledge of the Aurora and seek to attain Aurora-hood."

Charles was agog. "What happened?"

"Ah, downfall. Yes."

"The paradise came to an end?"

"Yes. The Homo sapiens did come to this island, and many achieved Aurora-hood. This happy situation went on for many generations until a handsome warlord from Balta arrived on the island and established himself as Emperor of the Homo sapiens."

Charles shuddered, almost as if he knew what was going to happen.

"In time, this individual ingratiated himself to the Empress of Ocea-ana and they became lovers."

"And they fell out?"

"It has not been revealed to me yet what happened, but basically yes. They had a disagreement."

"Did war break out?"

"Apparently, there were skirmishes, and all of these were contained by the Aurora. All may have been resolved in time if it had not been for one incident."

George William paused, visibly shocked.

"What was the incident?"

"Special fighters from the Homo sapiens in the north – the Homo sapiens lived in the north; it was a large island, a small continent – special forces from the Homo sapiens in the north stole material from Aurora laboratories in the south. A new energy material the Aurora were developing. They took this material and developed it into something it was not intended for. A weapon. The Homo sapiens did not know what they were dealing with. Once they detonated it – the whole island blew up! An explosion so big and power-ful it was almost beyond imagination. The island of Ocea-ana, and eight hundred miles of sea surrounding the island, was quickly vapourised. Sucked up into a great vortex of vapour. Land and sea became vapour. The island of Ocea-ana, and nearly a thousand square miles of sea, all turned to vapour. Nothing left, just vapour. The explosion caused a huge crater, and to fill the void, an enormous amount of sea flooded in. The vapourised sea turned to mighty storms in other parts of the world. The giant hole in the sea caused ferocious tidal waves. Tidal waves that went on for months. Once it settled, the earth was a wreck. Two thirds of all living creatures perished. All knowledge Homo sapiens had acquired vanished. The few remaining elements of the Homo sapien population were savages who returned to their caves. The cycle of humanoid existence began again on a battered and not fully functioning Earth. Ocea-ana was the epicentre of the blast, and all trace of it disappeared – vapourised."

Charles said, "I suppose the Aurora People became extinct."

"Not exactly, no. That is the surprising thing. Generally, souls remain in some way or another. With the Aurora, a ghost imprint of their previous humanoid form survived and began the incredibly slow evolutionary process of reforming. Their form was covered with a thick coating of sludge. This was the effect of the blast and their last moments on Earth. They have to work their way through this sludge as part of the evolutionary process."

"So, they are still on Earth?"

"Not exactly, no. They are in a special zone. A recovery area. A redemption realm."

"A redemption realm? Where is this redemption realm?"

"It is here. Where we are."

"What do you mean?" Charles asked nervously.

"It occupies the same space as Earth, but in a different dimension. It is everywhere the Earth is, even in the church."

Charles recoiled, a little twitchy. "You mean they are in here? In this church? On the altar and in the aisles? Can they see us? Are they looking at us?"

"Sometimes they see us, but it is very blurred. If they see us, it is with a longing. And sometimes they are calling 'help me, help me get back on Earth.' They say this with pleading and look at us with longing. Longing to get back to Earth. Not many people ever hear this. It is a futile cry."

"If they long to get back, why do they not do it?"

"They cannot. They need to be led back by an appointed leader, a saviour."

"An appointed leader?"

"Yes."

"When will this leader be appointed?"

"He already has. His name is Zakamonsky."

"Why does he not bring them back?"

"Good question. He has gone totally psychotic."

"When? How?"

George William stroked his beard, thinking how best to explain what he had heard.

"The wise men of the redemption realm appointed Zakamonsky and secretly anointed him to be the emperor. They ordained him to redeem the Aurora People and bring them back to Earth. He was only eight years of age, and it was done in secret. In time, his father found out and was furious, incandescent with rage. His father always presumed he was next in line. Next in line to be emperor of the Aurora People. Zakamonsky's childhood was horrendous. His father tried to kill him on over one hundred and fifty occasions. This turned Zakamonsky psychotic."

"His father sounds like a monster. I thought the Aurora People were advanced, enlightened."

"Potentially they are, but war brutalises people."

"Why did his father want to kill him?"

"Buck up, Charles, it is obvious. He wanted to be emperor himself. Power struggles. I have seen plenty of them. His father wanted the top job for himself, get his hands on the rudder."

"It sounds ghastly. Zakamonsky is not yet on Earth?"

"No, he is still in the redemption realm. Towards the end of his childhood, after one hundred and fifty attempts on his life, he finally managed to get his father locked up, but had already become psychotic. He has never recovered. It is a sad situation. The Aurora People live a half-existence in the redemption realm. Sad for the Aurora People, and very sad for the Earth. The whole course of life on Earth could have been very different if Zakamonsky had not gone psychotic. All because his father wanted to be emperor. Tragic for Zakamonsky on a personal level too. He was anointed to carry out the mission of rehabilitating the Aurora People and delivering them back to Earth. He is failing miserably due to his psychosis. It is an incredibly sad situation. The misery for the Aurora People goes on and on."

"How long has Zakamonsky been emperor?"

"Zakamonsky has been emperor for over five hundred years. He is halfway through his life and nowhere near accomplishing his mission. One thousand years may seem a long time, but it is surprising how quickly it vanishes. The more time goes by, the more frustrated and reckless he becomes. All because of his psychosis. His first attempt at fulfilling his mission was in 1604, when he managed to get a taskforce of two hundred men back on Earth. It was something of an unusual scheme. Sending an expeditionary force to Earth to form a bridgehead for the return. People do strange things when they are psychotic. It had taken a huge amount of scientific effort to get them through the barrier, and a little bit more effort to have them disguised as Homo sapiens. They look just like me and you."

"So, there are Aurora already here on Earth?"

"Yes, there are two hundred of them, and you cannot tell them apart from normal Homo sapiens. One of these blighters infiltrated my office and made it to become one of my courtiers. Kellewe was his name."

Charles shuddered a little as he pieced together the mysteries of his childhood. He asked, "Was he a Prussian?"

"He came to Prussia, but he was Aurora. He was one of them. Zakamonsky's taskforce landed on the Baltic Coast in East Prussia, and initially, they joined the Teutonic Knights."

"I thought you said the Aurora People were advanced and enlightened."

"Yes, potentially they are, but Zakamonsky had failed to rehabilitate them. They still have the memory of the Homo sapiens starting the war that got them sent to the redemption realm. Without someone rehabilitating them, they retain hatred in their hearts for Homo sapiens. It is a desperately tragic situation."

"So, if they found their way back to Earth, they would want to kill all the Homo sapiens?"

"That is not the way it is meant to be, but with Zakamonsky running the show – who knows? Let me continue with the two hundred men of the Earth expeditionary force. They joined the Teutonic Knights and became corrupted in the ways of Homo sapiens. Of course, they take their orders from Zakamonsky, whom they obey implicitly. As time went on, they began leaving the Knights and formed into two groups. One group fanned out and performed some covert operations. One of which was to get Kellewe into my office as a courtier. Others formed a secret brigade of the Prussian army. This brigade made an agreement with my great-grandfather, but I shall not talk about that now."

"Was this brigade called Ettikeomisna Aiinibi?"

"Yes, how did you know that?"

"The teacher at the school you sent me to, was fond of reminding me of them often. Was she part of the taskforce too?"

"No, the taskforce are all men. The leader of the taskforce is a man that goes by the name of Albrecht. He is their Field Commander, but he gets his orders from Zakamonsky."

"The psychotic Zakamonsky?"

"Yes."

"Will Zakamonsky order to kill me as part of my punishment?"

"No, why?"

"Because the Ettikeomisna Aiinibi are charged with enforcing punishments for the trust. I feel in my bones someone is out to kill me. I guess it must be Mr Zakamonsky, not Prince Albert."

"Ah, I see what you are getting at. You are speaking of the current time and your present predicament, yes? The restrictions on the trust and the enforcers."

"Those are my urgent concerns at the present time."

"The restrictions on the trust were mainly instituted by Kellewe after I was locked away. You are in luck, Charles. Maybe it is providence because currently, Zakamonsky is experiencing an extremely serious bout of psychosis. He is in no state to give orders about anything. It normally takes Zakamonsky six to eight weeks to recover from this state."

"Are you sure about that? Maybe he could get in an uncontrollable rage?"

"Yes, I am sure about it. Zakamonsky is totally incapacitated right now, so you are safe for a few weeks. Now is absolutely the right time to escape, but eventually, he will want to kill you."

Charles breathed a sigh of relief. "That is good to know, but why does he want to kill me? Why me?"

"Hold onto your socks, Charles. Here is the next and most important part of the revelation. Your mother was part of the royal family of Ocea-ana. It was only last week I found this out."

Charles gasped. "Was she the empress of that ancient place? The empress of Ocea-ana?"

"No, I do not think so. Just part of the original Ocea-ana royal family, and of High Aurora stock. An elite part of the High Aurora who are able to materialise in various guises. She travels through the ages. When I knew her, she was a scullery maid in our castle at Windsor. She managed to get a message to me that previously she had been Princess Nefeli of ancient Greece. Well, that was the code I was looking for, and it fulfilled the prophecy. Naturally, I had to do my duty. You are the result. She never told me anything about Aurora or Ocea-ana.

Charles, you are part of the Hanoverian royal family and part of the High Aurora royal family too. It is the reason Zakamonsky will eventually seek you out for elimination."

"Why?"

"Buck up, Charles. It is obvious. It is the same reason Zakamonsky's father wanted to kill him. You and George are the only ones on Earth with the unique genes. The genes of the Aurora, and the genes of the sapien. Genes of each branch of the human race. You are the family that will bring peace to Earth. You are the bridge that can make that happen. You are the final attempt to return the Earth to the way it was meant to be. The Tiptons will become the Divine Rulers of Earth."

Charles Tipton always felt there was something strange and unusual about his life, and he felt something shift and open inside him. Something awesome.

"That is a surprise. Something I was not expecting. Wewph!"

"Glad to reveal this. I am proud of you, son."

"Wewph. Divine Ruler of Earth, wewph! I am not sure I am fit to be Divine Ruler of Earth."

"Do not worry because it will not be you. This will be George's side of the family. Your side will be the spare, the back-up, the helper."

He was somewhat mystified. "I see. It will be George. Thing is, George does not appear to be fit for this great role either."

"It will not be George. You two are simply establishing the Tipton line for the one who will bring peace to Earth. The one that returns the Earth to the way it was intended to be. This could be the last chance. It could be George's son, or it could be someone beyond him. A sign will come when the time is right. I want you to protect George's side of the family from all the dangers posed by Zakamonsky."

Charles was suddenly a little deflated. "So, I am exposed to all the dangers of being the ruler without ever being the ruler. Stuck with being the spare! My side always being the spare!"

"It can either be your great privilege or your great horror. It is up to you to decide. That is the situation circumstances have placed you in. I would recommend it to be your great privilege. I am revealing this to you, not George. You are the sensible one, the rational side of the family. The anchor. The one that will guide and protect George's side for the momentous change that could save the Earth. Right now, I wish to give you this great responsibility. The fate of the Earth depends on it."

Many momentous things had happened to Charles on this poignant day. A truly topsy-turvy few hours, but this was probably the biggest of them all. Slowly, he began to see it for the enormous privilege that it was. The one who would enable the Earth to transform into the paradise it was meant to be.

George William carried on with more instructions and revelations. "In order to carry out this great responsibility, I request you do it with one supremely important condition. That you keep what I have revealed to you an absolute secret. That you do not tell this to George or his son. That you do not let them know your heritage. In short, you do not reveal I am your father, and that Nefeli is your mother. You must not reveal who your parents are."

"Strange, that was a major condition of the trust. That we never look for our parents. Never ask about our parents."

"Yes. It was a condition that Kellewe added to the trust on the orders of Zakamonsky. It was a strangely benevolent act by Zakamonsky when he was in one of his better states."

"How?"

"You must understand, if you did not know your heritage, you would not be a threat to him, and he would not need to liquidate you. He does not want to liquidate you if he does not have to."

"And now I *do* know."

"That is exactly why you must keep it a secret. It is why I am telling you, and not George. I believe you could keep this secret where George may be unable to do so. You need to keep this secret for your sake, and for George's sake. And particularly for the sake of George's son. It must be kept a secret until the sign comes."

Charles took a deep breath. "I suppose I have no choice, but maybe Zakamonsky will want to dispose of me anyway."

"Maybe he will, but right now you have the opportunity to escape and disappear. I have told you that Zakamonsky is too psychotic to do anything at the moment, so you are safe for a few weeks. It is excellent you are going to America tonight. Change your name and lie low until the word comes. Take the family to America and do not reveal anything."

Charles was struggling to assimilate all this. "Thank you for revealing everything. It is a great relief to know I am not about to get killed."

"You are not out of the woods yet, Charles. There is the small matter of embarrassing Prince Albert."

"At least he is not the one that wants to kill me."

"Do not be too sure about that. You embarrassed him, did you not?"

"Yes."

"Why did you go and embarrass Prince Albert? Nobody likes to be embarrassed. That is why I put that as a condition in the trust."

"It was you that gave that condition?"

"Yes, that was my condition. The only condition I made. I thought it would have been obvious not to embarrass the royal family, but in case it was not, I put it in. I know those Saxe-Coburg-Gotha, and they are very touchy about being embarrassed. You could not have embarrassed worse people than them."

"Will he want to have me executed?"

"I do not think he will go that far, but you never know. I think it will take a few days before he orders your arrest. You are leaving tonight, so you should be alright."

"Thank you, Dad."

"I am starting to fade. I have told you everything you need to know. Take the family to America and lay low. Do not reveal anything to the family until the sign comes."

Before Charles's eyes, George William began to evaporate, and Charles was left alone in the church.

He spent a few minutes silently on the pew thinking through what had just happened. He had entered an unexpected new world. The keeper of the secret. The knowledge of the enlightened Ocea-ana People and the early Homo sapiens. A forgotten Golden Age of Light. The devastating war that ended it. Him being the product of two royal families and having to keep all of this secret.

After a few minutes, he got up from the pew to begin his new life of awesome responsibility.

48 – Charles Buys a Trunk

Outside the church, an endless stream of little horse-drawn carriages swarmed up and down the Strand. A different world. The world of London of the 1850s. Further down, past the street's elegant shops, Charles came to a row of three leatherware shops and marched through the door of the middle one.

"I need a trunk," Charles said. "One large enough to accommodate all of our most precious items."

The well-dressed shopkeeper looked at Charles and his bandage suspiciously, one may say sneeringly, but showed him the range of trunks. Charles chose the largest and ordered the man to summon a horse and cart to transport the trunk back to the theatre. It took two complaining men to manoeuvre the trunk onto the cart.

As the cart clip-clopped back to the theatre, Charles racked his brains as to how to persuade George to come with him to America.

Charles directed the cart down an alley at the back of the theatre, ordered them to wait, and entered through the stage door.

The theatre was a hive of activity. Sherry was practising her repertoire. The projector operators were firming up on the synchronisation for the umpteenth time. A small orchestra was practising a Rossini piece, and George Senior was engrossed in directing everything. There were to be three music-picture-stories followed by forty minutes of Sherry

Long-Barrow singing her songs to round off. Young George II was on a front row seat watching the activities. Charles approached him.

"George, we are going to America," he whispered in a sharp hiss.

"What?"

Charles got the boy out of his seat and to the back of the theatre where he gave him a cock-and-bull story that he had met an American that was going to pour money into the moving picture idea and have it performed at a major theatre in New York. Young George was intelligent enough to realise this was not true, but also sufficiently aware to know there was some important reason why this had to be done.

"Uncle Charles – what is the real reason we have to go to America?"

Charles panicked at how perceptive the lad was and was also conscious of the solemn vow he had made to keep the boy safe and not to reveal the unique family heritage until it was safe to do so. He began to realise what an awesome responsibility he had been charged with, and the desolate task of keeping the overwhelming family heritage a secret until it was safe to reveal it. This staggering responsibility descended upon his shoulders. He needed to give the lad a serious and convincing reason for the need to go to America. Trembling slightly, he handed the boy the letter from the trustees.

"I have embarrassed Prince Albert. As this is my second offence, he will probably have me killed."

Young George read the letter, looked up, and said, "You have made this mess by embarrassing Prince Albert. You go to America and leave us alone."

Charles said, "It will not stop there. Your father is complicit in this too. He will be punished as well. Maybe not as harshly as me, but he will go to prison and leave you as an orphan."

Young George looked daggers at Charles.

"I am sorry," Charles said. "Very sorry for what I have done. I promise to make it up to you in America. You must come, and you must convince your father to come to America too. His girlfriend as well if she wants to come."

Staring awkwardly at Charles, the boy saw the logic in this.

They took the horse and cart to George's lodgings in Camberwell, and for the next hour and a half, packed his most precious belongings into the trunk, including all of his music-picture-stories. They returned to the theatre.

A few early birds were beginning to arrive for the show. Young George went off to talk with his father.

"Dad, we are going to America."

"Are we? Why?"

"Uncle Charles has embarrassed Prince Albert. He has to escape to America, leaving tonight."

"Tonight! What about the show?"

"After the show. He is booked on a boat leaving from the Iron Dock."

"But I am going to Tipton tonight. I have to take the extra photographs."

"You are booked on a boat leaving from Liverpool in three days. I am coming with you."

George was confused and disorientated. "Let us discuss this after the show."

"Yes, we shall do that. First, you have to pack everything that you want into a trunk on top of the horse and cart which is waiting outside the back door."

Perplexed, George instinctively did what his son asked and gathered his few possessions from a dressing room. He climbed on top of the cart to do this. Finally, he packed the precious white stone which was in a velvet bag. He placed this deep in the trunk.

Meanwhile, Charles continued preparing the theatre and sold the few remaining tickets.

"You must keep the ticket if you want a refund," he told each purchaser. "No ticket, no refund." He made sure everyone was aware of this.

In between ticket-selling, he caught sight of two suspicious people with their faces against the wall. One adult, one child. Charles approached them.

"What is your game?" Charles challenged.

The adult turned around. He had a long black beard that came to a point at one end.

"It is me!" Figgis said, lifting up the beard which was attached by a bit of string. "See – it is really me! You told me to come in disguise, and I have."

"Oh yes, Mr Figgis. I forgot about you, and who would this be?"

The child turned around. He too had a long black beard held on with a bit of string. "This is my five-year-old son. I have brought him along in disguise too."

Charles felt a bit overcome with the silliness of Figgis.

Figgis touched his nose and said, "I am working for your father now."

"What do you mean?"

"Me and your father are working together. That is what I mean."

It was now sounding ominous, and Charles was getting jittery. "My father is dead," he said.

"I know," Figgis said merrily. "That is what makes it so exciting."

Charles was now nervous and confused. "Are you aware of who my father is?"

Figgis nodded with his eyes popping out like a sparrow. "Yes, a king! We are doing scientific experiments together now. Does George know who his father is?"

"No," Charles said sharply. "And you are not to tell him either."

Figgis touched his nose. "Confidential, yes. Mum's the word. I have a surprise for George."

"Have you?"

Charles's nerves were seriously jangling as Figgis went off to find George.

George was overjoyed to see Figgis. They spoke for a few minutes, and George was even more excited with the surprise Figgis had brought.

Charles watched them and his heart started pumping and he wished the show would start so it could end, and he could get on the boat and out of the country.

A few minutes later the show did start.

CHAPTER FOURTEEN

49 –The Show Begins

The theatre was full to overflowing, and there was much noise and chattering.

One of the projector operators got up on the stage with a stick and stamped it down.

"Ladies and gents, pray silence for Mr George Tipton so he can announce his show. Here he comes now."

George nervously got up on the stage and announced, "My name is George Tipton, and I am an orphan, so please do not be too hard on me."

Figgis and his son, both with beards still attached, sat with Charles and young George II on the front row, watching as George stumbled from foot to foot on the stage doing his announcement.

George stumbled on. "This is my first show to the general public. I have three music-picture-stories to show you. I hope you enjoy my invention. If you do not, you can get your money back as long as you show my brother your ticket. Please keep your ticket safe because he cannot give you your money back without the ticket. I assure you this is a risk-free show with a guarantee of your money back as long as you keep your ticket. I suggest you keep the ticket tightly in your hands in case . . ."

Jittery, Charles hissed to George II, "Why does he not just get on with it? He should talk up the show and not go on about getting the money back!"

"It was you that kept telling him there was a money-back guarantee if they kept their tickets," the boy retorted.

"Yes, but that was to cover us against people asking for money back who have not bought a ticket. I know all the tricks."

George was getting more confident. "I hope you do not demand your money back, because we need it too. Besides, if you do not like my show, Sherry Long-Barrow will sing for you, so it will be worth it even if you do not like my show. Now, I will start the show. I chose the first music-picture-story because Christmas is coming. The music is a song that has just come over from America. They say it is about Christmas, but it never mentions anything about Christmas. Here it is."

In a flash, the lights immediately went off, and the theatre plunged into darkness.

A three-piece choir sang *Jingle bells, jingle bells, jingle all the way* . . . Simultaneously, the projectors fired into action, and the 'Jingle Bells' music-picture burst into life.

On the screens, a very jolly Father Christmas, with foliage in his hair, was driving a sleigh. In the back, were a cartload of excited children. The cart bobbed its way over snow-covered fields and bounced over the gentle hills of England's countryside. The children rocked around in the back with delight. It passed through snow-covered villages with holly and robins adorning all the cottages.

It was a fun little show which lasted approximately three minutes, and the moving images worked their magic, thrilling the working-class audience as it had with everyone that had watched.

Someone stood up and shouted out, "No need for a refund, Tipton. We enjoyed it. Did we all enjoy it?" There was some clapping and whistling, and another shouted out, "Yeah, we enjoyed it, let us see some more of your moving pictures."

This sentiment was echoed by a few others, and George was relieved that the show was accepted. He was not sure about the next show, which employed the more expressly highbrow music of Gioachino Rossini.

It was something he had stored away in his memory after a visit he made to Venice in 1834. He recalled feeling guilty going to Venice while Charles was in prison, but nonetheless, it was an influential visit. He watched Rossini perform a piece called 'La gazza ladra', a fast and thrilling piece. A few years later, he put the piece to pictures, a sequence of a few hundred drawings that would make a moving picture show. Essentially, it was the wheel of a giant locomotive rolling into motion, steam everywhere, the rods pushing the wheel and gaining speed with unstoppable energy. The music getting faster and faster, the wheels accelerating. It was a mesmerising piece which threw the audience into some kind of stunned silence. George quickly popped up on stage.

"I have shown that moving-picture piece as a lead-up to the main moving picture show of the evening. The Tipton Show. The power of the machine is great, but who made it happen? It was the people of Tipton. The people of the Black Country, and all of you. Throughout the toil and the grind, you made it happen. Without you, it could not happen. This show is a tribute to you, and all who go through the toil and the grind. I built my show around Sherry's Black Country song."

Sherry appeared on stage and bowed, and everyone cheered. Most were familiar with her songs. She was renowned as having the voice of an angel that made your heart soar. Some were familiar with her Black Country song, but nobody had seen her song put to moving pictures.

Sherry thanked the audience and sat on a stool to play her guitar. She played for over two minutes as the lights dimmed down, and the theatre went into darkness. Then, Sherry's heavenly voice rang out along with George's visuals. There was an audible gasp at Sherry's beautiful voice, but it was much more than that. The pride and the pain on the smoke-filled faces that George had drawn. It echoed their own experiences. Some women began openly weeping. Some men tried not to weep too. Someone was expressing their lives for them, and it was heart-rending.

It affected Charles too. It actually mirrored his own sentiments and expressed them in a far better way than he could ever have done. Charles saw the reaction from the audience and was overcome. George was a master in his own way, and in that moment, he respected it would be George's side of the family that would be the rulers. He knew it would not be George. In that instant, he saw his prime role in life was to protect young George II who was sitting beside him.

George Tipton's 'Black Country Show' went on for another three emotionally-charged minutes. It followed the story, the feelings, and expressions, of Sherry's song which ended with the sentiment 'You are the salt of the Earth and will always be there'.

Some cried out: "Thank you, Sherry . . . Thank you, Mr Tipton." Some just cried.

There was a great adoration for George and Sherry for making them feel something deep. Feel they were worthy, and someone was speaking for them.

George was overcome with their praise. "Thank you, thank you," he said. "It is far more than I expected. Thank you." He waited for the applause to die down and said, "Up next, Sherry will sing a few songs for you. Then I have a surprise. A really big surprise!"

Charles, on the front row, began to get the jitters again as he wondered what this surprise would be. He assumed Figgis was behind it, and asked:

"What is this surprise about?"

Figgis said, "It would not be a surprise if I told you."

"Can you give a hint?"

Figgis lifted his beard and said, "No!"

Charles was not overly relaxed with this answer and sat tensely through the first of Sherry's songs. George joined him on the empty seat next to him.

"What is this surprise about?" Charles asked him.

"It would not be a surprise if I told you," George said.

Charles sat tensely through Sherry's second song, and he noticed a well-dressed man with blue eyes come in through the door. A Buckingham Palace man. A Buckingham Palace spy. The man surveyed the audience, surveyed it until he came to the front and looked directly at him. He went into overdrive and whispered to George:

"Can you wind up the show now?"

"Why?"

"Please, do not ask questions and just do it!"

George got up and approached Sherry on stage. He waited until she finished the song, then whispered in her ear:

"Charles has gone a bit batty," he said to her. "Let me do my surprise now, then carry on with the show."

Meanwhile, the man with blue eyes, having located Charles, left the theatre, and Charles went into full panic realising the man was getting reinforcements to arrest him.

On stage, George announced, "Due to a change in circumstances, I am going to reveal my historic surprise now. I said earlier that I was an orphan and grew up in an orphanage. That was because my father was in prison. Now my father is in charge of a prison up in heaven . . ."

The audience gave a nervous laugh.

"I always wanted to know who my father was and what he had done. My first music-picture-story was about that. We always thought the photographs were ruined. Now, my science teacher has managed to bring them back to life. They were taken in 1818 when I was eight. That makes them the world's first ever photographs! Yes, the world's first photographs! Historic! Here they are!"

George nipped back to his seat as the projector operators reloaded. The theatre dramatically went into blackness as George Tipton's first ever music-picture-story blazed onto the screen. One second, and one 'da' for each picture. It flashed by fast.

Da da da darr – WHO IS MY DAD? . . . Da WHO da **IS** da **MY** darr **DAD?**

It only lasted eight seconds, but it is surprising how those dramatic notes managed to inspire so much terror in Charles. They inspired terror now as they had inspired it in 1818.

Disobeying the terms of the trust. Now, he knew why the terms had been put there, and there was a degree of benevolence to them. Now the terms had been broken, it gave Zakamonsky a strange kind of legitimacy to quash his earlier instincts and liquidate them. That is how Charles saw it, and he grabbed George, and his son, and dragged them away. In the darkness and confusion, he hauled them through the theatre and out of the back door to the waiting cart.

"What is going on?" little George II demanded.

"Yes, what are you doing?" George shouted angrily. "I wanted to receive my applause."

Charles was shaking and sweating in extreme panic. "I will explain in a minute. We need to get out of here. Get onto the cart!"

Everyone climbed on, and Charles shouted to the drivers, "Get to the Iron Dock as fast as possible. Use the back roads!"

The cart shot off using tiny roads and alleys. George and son demanded answers. Charles gave a garbled explanation, and the cart reached the dock, stopping by the American steamer. It took three minutes. Before them, was the American steamer, and Charles demanded the drivers carry the trunk onto the boat. Grumbling, they did.

The guy with the sailor's hat called down and chuckled a little. "The man who embarrasses monarchs – is your brother coming with us?"

Charles looked at George. "Come on the boat, George. Let us escape England together."

"No. I want to take the pictures in Tipton."

The skipper asked, "Will you take the boat from Liverpool on Monday?"

"Yes."

"What about the boy?"

"I am going with my father," young George said.

Charles panicked, "Maybe young George is safer coming with me."

"How? Why?"

"Long journey to Tipton and Liverpool. He could get sick. It's safer he come now."

George thought about the child's safety. He had always successfully protected his son.

Charles was suddenly struck with his overwhelming responsibility to protect young George II, and it thundered through him like lightning. "It is best young George come with me," he insisted, and he grabbed the child, carrying him up the gangplank. The child wriggled strenuously. The vessel was building up steam. "Let us leave now!" Charles shouted at the skipper. The skipper was so surprised by the authoritative voice that he gave the order to leave. Young George was complaining and wrestling strongly out from Charles's clutches. "I want to go with Dad. I always go with Dad!"

Charles had an iron hold on the child, and it was too late. The boat had moved out of dock.

On the quayside, George ran after the boat in panic, but the boat was already in the river.

On the deck, little George was stunned. Wriggling helplessly and reaching out for his dad. His father was reaching out vainly for his son. The boat was mid-river, steaming towards London Bridge. George and son stared at each other helplessly until the vessel disappeared under London Bridge and they could see each other no longer.

CHAPTER FIFTEEN

50 – *The Journey to America*

The other side of London Bridge, young George was devastated.

"Why did you do that, Uncle Charles?"

"I thought it would be safer."

"I have always been safe with my father. He has always thought about my safety, he is driven by it. We have never spent a night apart."

"I am sorry. I am not sure what came over me. You will see him again in two weeks. In America!"

Charles was uncertain what had happened in that moment. Certainly, his sacred responsibility to keep the boy safe was part of it. Perhaps there was also a selfish desire to force his brother George to come to America. Keep the family together. If he had his son, it would force George to get on that boat in Liverpool in order to reunite. He would travel on the boat out of Liverpool with or without Sherry.

The boat steamed on down the river.

There had been Crown Wharf, Lion Wharf, Castle Baynard Dock, and twenty other minor docks before they reached London Bridge – the last bridge before the sea – and here, the major docks began. The largest set of docks in the world. Between here and the sea, nearly three hundred docks. Mile after mile of cranes loading and unloading. Ships sailing. About thirty miles of docks. Almost one quarter of all world trade passed through these docks. Ships of all shapes and sizes travelling to all parts of the world.

Charles stood on deck looking at this cacophony of maritime traffic, a little emotional at leaving England forever. It was a dark night, and he felt he had escaped unscathed, although he could not fully relax until they were out into the Atlantic.

It was over two hours by the time they reached the estuary and Tilbury, and another hour before entering the North Sea. Here, his first shift would begin. At first, Little George had been bright, but soon turned glum and silent on the journey. Charles settled him in their sleeping quarters, a small cabin in the bowels of the ship.

"Try to sleep," Charles said. "I have to work my shift. I will see you in the morning."

Little George nodded glumly. Charles returned to deck to start his shift.

His first task was to scrub the sails. They were laid out on the deck, and he began scrubbing along with another crew member. Soon they were turning the corner and steaming through the Strait of Dover into the English Channel. The night was dark, and everything at sea eerily quiet. He worked through the night scrubbing. They steamed for forty miles parallel to the southern English coastline. By Plymouth, the sails were deemed clean and were erected. It had been an extremely long and strange day. They sailed into the Atlantic. The shift ended. The dawn broke; it was a new day, although a dark one. He went down to check on little George. He was curled up on the floor in their small cabin.

"Did you manage to sleep?"

Little George shook his head. "Not much. I miss Dad," he said.

"We have to get through this. Need to be strong."

The little cabin, no more than a storeroom, was dark, lit only by a tiny porthole. Sacking had been laid on the floor to sleep on. He knew they would get through this. They would reach the safety of America, come together as a family. Start a new life and wait for the sign.

"I need to sleep," he said to little George. "It has been a very long day."

He lay down beside little George and fell asleep almost immediately.

Little George was comforted by Charles beside him but did not sleep. He lay awake, trying to make sense of his situation.

An hour later, little George shook Charles vigorously. "Wake up, wake up, wake up!" he screamed.

Charles woke with a start. Crates were hurtling towards him. He jumped up, but still managed to get hit in the leg. "Ahhhh!" he moaned. In addition to having only one tooth, he now had a painful injury to his thigh too. The crates came sliding back and forth. He grabbed little George and got them both out the cabin. The boat was rocking mercilessly in a heavy storm. Charles got them on deck. The storm lashed huge waves over the bow. There were railings to the side, and he guided little George towards them.

"Hold on to this bar, do not let go."

The wind was howling. It was a grey, grey day with an angry sky. A real winter storm in a heavy winter sea. An enormous sea. Nothing now between here and New York.

"Are we going to die?"

"We are not going to die. We are a special family."

"Special? In what way?"

Charles thought back to the meeting with his father. It seemed so long ago, so much had happened in the last few hours, yet the images from that encounter shone brightly. The golden age of human existence on the Earth that had happened many thousands of years ago. The war, the downfall, and the unique circumstances of his family's heritage that would one day bring human habitation back to that golden age. Navigating the dangers in between.

"Our family will do great things, deliver a new way of living to the Earth. There are great dangers, so do not ask too many questions."

Little George II was a bright, almost enlightened lad, and he simply nodded silently, acceptingly, as he desperately clung on to the bar, trying not to get swept overboard. Even in the midst of the unrelenting storm, there was light about him, and it inspired Charles.

The storm was over about an hour later, but the day was short. It was already getting darker. The shortest day, the winter solstice, was just over a week ahead. It was Friday 13 December 1850.

"Your father will be taking the photographs in Tipton today."

"Yes, those photographs were very important to him. He will go on to Liverpool and stay with Mr Figgis," little George revealed.

"Will he?"

"Yes. That is what he told me. That is where we were going to stay. He wants to persuade Mr Figgis to come to America."

"Does he?"

Charles felt a bit uneasy about this, hoping that Figgis would not spill the secret about his father. Charles could not get his brain around the mysterious relationship Figgis seemed to have with his father.

Charles quickly moved the conversation on. "Tell me about your mother. Where is she?"

Little George II lowered his head. "She is dead. Died when I was two."

"I am sorry. Did not know."

"I only have Dad. He is the only one I have."

Charles began to realise how dependent the two of them were on each other. "Maybe he will bring Sherry. We shall all be together again soon. I know it," he said, and he held his hand.

"Thank you."

The journey was gruelling. There was another storm the next day, but the ship sailed on. They were using both the sails and the engines. The so-called captain, the one with the peaked cap worn at the jaunty angle, wanted his boat to be the one with the fastest crossing between America and England. He pushed the boat to the limits and pulled out all the stops to do this. In fact, his boat was the second quickest, but he wanted to achieve the number-one slot. Charles admired his enthusiasm and experienced a slice of the optimism of America and began to consider his life on the new continent.

Several days later, they were in the middle of the ocean. It was a bright sunny day. Charles was on deck in a cheery mood.

"We are halfway through. Right in the middle of the ocean. Is that not amazing!"

Little George swivelled his head around. In every direction was sea. Thousands of miles of water each way he looked. Nothing else. "It is a very lonely position, very far from anywhere," he said nervously.

"Exactly, it is away from the authorities. Out of the jurisdiction of every country on Earth. Is that not great?"

"You are frightened of the authorities?"

"I have done ten years in prison. It makes you scared. Out here, I am free."

"What if the ship capsizes? There is nobody to rescue us."

"The boat will not capsize. We are a special family."

"If we are a special family, you should write down your thoughts. Put on paper how you think the world should be."

"What an excellent idea."

For the remainder of the journey, in what free time he had between shovelling coal and other maintenance, he committed ideas to paper. If he was to be part of this special family destined to bring peace to Earth, he could make a contribution. Even though his side of the family was the spare side, he could carve out a role for them. He wrote of the scenarios he wished to see from the alliance of the Quakers and the Communists. He added a long treatise that it did not have to be Quakers and Communists, but did need to include a plan, or plans, to ensure the spiritual and physical wellbeing of humans on Earth throughout the planet. Much of this was ideas they discussed in the theatre between the two halves of his show. This was the tenet of his plans. For the next few days, he wrote and shovelled coal.

The journey was hard. For Charles and little George II, who had never been to sea, it was incredibly arduous. Mainly wind and lashing seas, but they saw it through. After ten days they were once again on dry land.

On 23 December 1850, a few hours after landing and a train ride from New York, they sat on a platform at the main railroad station in Philadelphia, waiting for a train to Allentown, Pennsylvania. From there, they would negotiate a ride to Quakertown, a distance of twelve miles, and connect with Jeremiah, a Quaker comrade with whom Charles had formed a deep bond in prison. Beside them, the great trunk was parked, which Charles was bone-tired from dragging.

A cold wind whistled down the platform, and although exhausted, there was accomplishment on their faces.

"We made it," Charles said wearily.

"The first thing I want to do is have a bath. A nice hot bath. Does this friend of yours have a bathtub?"

"I hope so. After you have your bath, I want one too."

Charles's face was blackened through day after day of stoking coal, and his bandage, which he was still wearing, was near-black too. Little George was weather-beaten and exhausted but excited to be on dry land again with the prospect of being reunited with his dad.

"When will Dad arrive?" His expectant eyes accompanied his question.

"Very soon. He will be here in three days. The boat from Liverpool cuts a day off the journey, so he will arrive in three days. The day after Christmas. It is a shame we cannot all be together for Christmas, but they will probably have some party on the boat."

"He will arrive at the same dock as us in New York?"

"Yes."

"Let us all have a big breakfast in New York. I read New York is famous for big breakfasts. Let us have one to celebrate."

Charles brightened at the prospect. "That is a good idea. We can settle in with Jeremiah, and travel back to New York and meet your dad off the boat. I will ask Jeremiah about accommodation in New York. There must be a Quaker community there. The whole family reunited and starting a new life in America!"

This raised the mood as the day was bitterly cold.

The station was deserted except for a newsstand at the other end of the platform. Bundles of papers were unloading. The Allentown train was not due for another thirty minutes. Charles gazed down the platform at the newsstand. "I am going to buy a newspaper. Learn about the news in America."

Little George kept an eye on the trunk as Charles walked towards the vendor. He was surprised to discover he was from Bilston, just a few miles from his old home in the Black Country.

"Alright, mate, just got 'ere, have ye?" the vendor said.

"This morning."

"There be a lot of us 'ere. Better life."

He chatted with the vendor and found there was a big community from the Black Country, particularly in Bethlehem where their iron-making skills were much appreci-ated. He discovered too that the *Birmingham Journal*, the main newspaper serving the Black Country, was the one that had been delivered. He knew it was published once a week on a Saturday, and the one that had just been delivered was dated Saturday 14 December 1850. The vendor gave Charles a complimentary copy as a souvenir, and instead of buying an American newspaper, he returned with that.

It was a large newspaper, and he settled in beside little George II, flipping through the familiar pages printed with their usual blotchy black ink. The front page a regular hodgepodge of auctions, obituaries, and services, in six columns of tiny letters. Pages two and three consisted of bigger announcements, mainly of building societies and insurance companies, laid out in three larger columns. Pages four and five were titled 'Political and Domestic News of the Week'. Long opinionated articles he did not generally agree with, with odd snippets of hard news. On page six were letters, and page seven bankruptcy notices. He flipped back to pages four and five as something had caught his eye, though he did not know what. He found it buried away in a little box entitled: 'The Scourge of the Highwayman'. He buried his head in the two-page spread, not quite believing what he was reading.

> **THE SCOURGE OF THE HIGHWAYMAN**
> In the early hours of Friday 13th December, a stagecoach was attacked by a lone assailant ten miles outside Birmingham. One passenger only was killed, Mr George Tipton. A fellow passenger, Mr Marcus Smiley, reported the killer appeared to be a well dressed man with blue eyes and Nordic appearance. "It was truly horrific" Mr Smiley told us. "I had been to a show where Mr Tipton displayed his new invention. The audience loved it. I presume the killer was a rival show-man." The superintendant of Birmingham Borough Police has opened an inquiry.

Charles read this again, stunned, and clung to the newspaper like a quick-frozen statue. George Tipton dead!

After a minute of stunned silence, Charles lowered the paper and stared into space with a gaze reaching far into the abyss. A horrible truth dawned on him. Although Zakamonsky was psychotic, he still seemed able to give orders. This had ramifications far deeper than he could have imagined.

Little George looked up vacantly with tears forming. "Dad is not coming, is he?"

Little George II stared into the abyss too, tears dripping from his eyes. "Dad will never come to America. I will never see Dad again, will I?"

With eyes like tombstones, all Charles could say was, "We need to hide the trunk."

CHAPTER SIXTEEN

Hyde Park 2019

51 – Frederick Reveals Inside Information

"So that, in abbreviated form, was the life of the original George Tipton," Frederick said. "Field Commander Albrecht assassinated him on the outskirts of Birmingham."

I found myself asking, "Was Albrecht in England?"

"Yes, he was in England to formalise taking over the trust. It was Albrecht that was in the theatre, not someone from Buckingham Palace. He left the performance early so as to get ahead of the stagecoach that George Tipton was travelling on."

"Did this Zakamonsky character order Albrecht to do it?"

"Of course. Field Commander Albrecht would not have done it without an order from Mr Zakamonsky."

"I thought your son had told Charles Tipton that Mr Zakamonsky was too far gone in psychosis to issue orders."

Frederick shrugged. "We all make mistakes sometimes. Obviously, Zakamonsky was able to give orders even though he was bogged down in psychosis. I will be the first to admit George William is not perfect." He paused a little to give me a look at his beady eyes. "Zakamonsky had ordered Field

Commander Albrecht to dispose of the entire Tipton family, every one of them, but to get George Tipton done as a priority. He saw all of them as a threat to his eventual rule of Earth."

"Did it mean that Charles Tipton and George the Second slipped through the net and managed to escape?"

"Yes. Zakamonsky was furious about this and vowed very serious punishments if Albrecht failed next time around."

"I suppose he never got another opportunity."

"Not until now. Charles Tipton was extremely rattled by George's death and aware of his responsibility to keep the family safe until the time came. He knew they must become anonymous, so he changed the family name to Bethlehem. He created a powerful mythology about never discussing the Tiptons or the trunk. It became a taboo. Strange things, legends, very effective, and usually an element of truth in them. Charles got a job at the steel mills. The family lived in Bethlehem up until 1908. It was then that the third generation of Charles Tipton's, still called Bethlehem, got a sign that it was safe to change the name back to Tipton. Also, to move to Pittsburgh. Here, he bought a newly built house on the Brighton Heights estate. The one Charlotte Tipton lives in today. Interestingly, they lived in Bethlehem throughout the 1860s during the American Civil War, making steel."

"I would like to know about the lives of the Bethlehem's during this period."

"Not now, old chap. Things are coming to a head as we speak. Everything is about to explode."

"How?"

"The fear of the trunk was true, but not in ways anyone would think. Albrecht is after the trunk now. Charlotte Tipton's fears are correct. He is on his way to Pittsburgh as we speak."

"Albrecht? Is he still on the scene? That was hundreds of years ago."

"As I said, the Aurora genes last approximately one thousand years. Albrecht is nearly eight hundred years old. He is elderly and disgruntled. But still very fit and determined to fulfil his mission. Part of his mission is to dispose of the Tipton family. That he is attempting to fulfil right now."

"What has the trunk to do with this?"

"I shall tell you. In 1850, after the warning from Zakamonsky, Albrecht traced Charles Tipton's last movements in London and discovered the luggage shop on the Strand. He got the shopkeeper to identify the trunk that Charles Tipton had bought, then knocked him out, took that trunk, and had it shipped back to their Baltic headquarters for analysis."

"Why?"

"You must understand these Aurora are far more advanced than we are. He identified the chemical composition of every element of the trunk. This was so he could identify the location of Charles Tipton. Every time the trunk moved, he could track it. Once the location was determined, he could go there with a small party and bump them off."

"Somehow that failed?"

"Yes. By the time the similar trunk was shipped to the Baltic and analysed, Charles Tipton had the original trunk locked in a vault in Philadelphia. Dragging that thing all the way into the vault is another story. The fact is, the trunk has been stationary until now, and to trace its location, the trunk had to be moving. There were only two of these trunks ever made, and Albrecht had the second."

I started to understand. "We are now in 2019. The trunk has been stationary since 1850. Now, for the first time in a hundred and sixty-nine years, it has moved, and Albrecht can determine the location of the Tiptons."

"Precisely. This time he is one hundred and ten percent focused on getting the job done so he can reap the rewards."

"The rewards?"

"Yes, rewards, old boy. There is a new world order coming. This is inside information."

52 – The New World Order

"What are these rewards?" I asked.

"Let me explain it this way. For hundreds of years, Zakamonsky has failed, both in his rehabilitation of the Aurora race, *and* a method of getting them back to Earth. It is true he got Albrecht and his brigade back to Earth, but that was a special mission that took over a hundred years to accomplish. Zakamonsky was becoming desperate to fulfil his mission. His two-hundred-man expeditionary force was becoming restless too, one could say almost rebellious. Both Zakamonsky, and his expeditionary force, were approaching old age, some say the legacy age. An age where one has to aggregate their accomplishments in life. Both could only report failure. Zakamonsky tried a new approach. Artificial chemical growth of the Aurora genes on Earth. He is planning to have a new artificially produced generation of the Aurora People born here on Earth. He has three hundred million of them incubating in test tubes as we speak."

I looked at him grimly. "Zakamonsky has three hundred million beings of a different human race incubating here on Earth?"

"Yes, they are incubating in caves beneath a forest in Kaliningrad."

"Kaliningrad?"

"That is a Russian enclave wedged between Poland and Lithuania on the Baltic coast. The area has changed hands many times over the last few hundred years. Albrecht and his men have seen it all. Kaliningrad, that is where they are incubating. Nobody on Earth knows they are there apart from Albrecht and his team, me, and a few others."

I thoughtfully considered this notion of three hundred million superhumans secretly incubating near the Baltic coast. Soon they would be alive on Earth. This was big. "Would this be good for the Earth?"

Frederick scratched his chin. "Very hard to say. It could be very good, or it could be bad. Nobody knows. For Zakamonsky, it partly fulfils his mission in a convoluted sort of way."

"The rewards. You mentioned rewards for his expeditionary force."

"Ah, the rewards, yes. There are two hundred men in total of the advance repatriation team. They have been working diligently on Earth for nearly five hundred years under the orders of Supreme Commander Zakamonsky, who has so far failed in his anointed mission to repatriate the Aurora race. After dedicating over six hundred years of their lives without any noticeable benefits, they became restless and required rewards."

"Yes, what are these rewards?"

"They have been in this area for many years, seen many wars here, and the lands change many times. For the last thirty years, they have been living in the old Teutonic sewers underneath the city of Gdansk. The city itself has changed several times. It has seen German administration, Russian administration, and finally reverted to Polish administration, which the Poles are very happy about. New sewers came into operation in 1977, the Teutonic sewers were abandoned, and the advanced Aurora repatriation force moved in. It is like a small city down there, with all sorts of labs and experiments going on, and nobody is aware of it. There are various manholes to the city above, all of them locked from the inside. There is even a manhole near St Mary's Basilica, one of the greatest brick-built churches in the world. Sometimes they go to services in that church. They look exactly like humans and have become part of the living furniture of that city, although they rarely mix."

"Yes, what about the rewards?"

"The rewards, yes. There are three hundred million incubating beings with Aurora genes. Zakamonsky will keep two hundred million of them and give the remaining one hundred million to the expeditionary force. There are two hundred of this force, and they have each been promised equal shares. Each receiving half a million chemically produced Aurora beings. These are the rewards."

"The reward is each member of the team receives half a million Aurora beings?"

"Yes. Every Friday, Albrecht takes his brigade over the border to Kaliningrad. In the morning, they do exercises in the forest to keep fit. In the afternoon, they go down to the caves where the incubations are taking place. There is an area, deep down, that is divided into two hundred separate chambers. Each chamber contains half a million incubating Aurora beings. The group divide up and go to their own private chamber where they can spend a few hours with their personal half a million incubating beings. Their own future citizens that they will rule over. Here, they walk up and down the lines with a parental-like care, and they fantasise about how they will organise their personal kingdoms."

"Their personal kingdoms?"

"Yes. Zakamonsky has promised to hive off one third of the Earth for the expeditionary force while keeping two thirds of the Earth for himself. Each member of the expeditionary force will be able to rule their kingdom as they wish."

"How are they wishing to rule their kingdoms?"

"In different ways. Each have their own way. Some good, some bad. Some of the bad ones want to utilise Homo sapiens in their kingdom as slaves."

"Slaves? I thought the Aurora race was meant to be advanced enlightened people."

"Basically, they are, but the expeditionary force has been corrupted by hundreds of years of Homo sapien wars under the psychotic orders from their Supreme Commander Zakamonsky. That is where Georgina Tipton comes in. If she can liberate the Aurora People and bring out their true nature, we will be in for a good future."

"I thought Zakamonsky wanted to assassinate Georgina Tipton."

"He does, and Albrecht is on the way to do it. That is what makes it so exciting. We shall soon see if Georgina Tipton has the metal to overcome. The new world order does not just involve Zakamonsky and the repatriation of the Aurora. There is also George William and me on the other side. This is inside information, old boy. I need to ensure you do not divulge it to anyone else."

"How are you going to do that?"

53 – Becoming an Insider

In one lightning movement, Frederick reached in his pocket, withdrew some kind of bracelet, and snapped it around my wrist before I knew it. He looked at it, smiling.

"This will inform me if you tell inside information to anyone. It is vital to keep all knowledge of our plans, and knowledge of the Aurora, under wraps for the time being."

It was wafer-thin and did not have any joints, unlike anything I had ever seen. It appeared to be part of my wrist, and there seemed no way of getting it off.

He grinned. "We royals have access to some of the most advanced technologies. What is about to happen is crucial and must never get out. That wristlet will monitor every aspect of your movements. All interactions you make. It will act as a deterrent."

"What will you do to me if I do tell anyone?"

Frederick scratched his chin.

"Well, there is the dematerialisation aspect I mentioned. I am not keen to do that because I would like a person from outside our circle to talk to. We could go on a fantastic journey together. You could become an insider."

"What about my foot?"

"How is the ankle? Any pain?"

I thought about this and realised I did not feel any pain. He smiled.

"I thought as much. I took away the pain, and healed the foot completely when you were not looking. We royals are a little bit magical. That is what makes us special. A little bit of stardust. Perhaps we have a little bit of the Aurora in us. Not as much as Georgina Tipton. She is champion Aurora once she realises it. Come, walk. Leave the chairs for someone else. This is a beautiful park. We love beauty."

He led the way, and I followed. "I have an apartment near here," he added.

We walked up to the Serpentine, a sumptuous artificial lake, which divides Hyde Park from Kensington Gardens. Here, he stopped, breathed in, and happily sighed. "My mother had this lake done. Beautiful, isn't it?"

I had to admit that it was. The lake stretched out gracefully in a magnificent curvature.

"It was part of our garden. All of the park you see was our garden. My mother modelled it, and that is why I love it so much. I love beauty. We royals create beauty. We Hanoverians created the classical beauty of this country. I want to see a beautiful world. This was our garden. Let me show you our house."

We crossed back into the Kensington Gardens area of the estate, past the big round pond, and Frederick informed me this was also the result of his mother's refurbishment programme. Kids and their mothers were currently sailing toy yachts on its waters. Then his house came into view – Kensington Palace.

I said, "It does not look all that palatial."

"That is what is endearing about it. More of a large country cottage. That is how it started. Not royal at all. Originally owned by a commoner. Then, Dutchman William of Orange and his wife Mary Hyde bought it. It passed to my grandfather when he became king. Then, my father lived in it when he ascended the throne. Each generation extended it a bit. I lived in here as a child and played in this wonderful garden." We passed an ornate sunken garden and arrived at the humble entrance. He showed the ticket collector a pass. I supposed he had bought a yearly pass like any other member of the public as the house was now a tourist attraction.

We were in.

The entrance was like a country farmhouse, but upstairs was a series of sumptuous state rooms. A group of tourists ogled at the elaborately painted ceilings as a tour guide explained that King George I spent lavishly to create these magnificent rooms in order to have salacious parties in them.

Frederick shook his head disparagingly. "My grandfather was a disgrace. He nearly sunk us."

"I suppose you must hate the public trampling through your former home?"

"Not at all. The opposite. It gives me the opportunity to see how the public currently regard royalty. That is why I bought the yearly ticket. I can make multiple observations. Despite everything, they seem to be absolutely enchanted with us, and that bodes well!"

We moved through corridors to another room, and the guide rattled through a list of modern royals who had lived in the palace. They included Princess Diana and her two sons, William, and Harry. Apparently, William and Harry and their wives were living there now. We came past a door that had a notice which read *Private - No Public Admittance.*

I said, "I suppose they live through there."

Frederick nodded. "Yes. I would like to see what they are up to, but I can't." He stopped, looking at me a little seriously. "I will come clean with you, old boy. I am in the process of fully coming back to Earth, but for the moment, I can only materialise for an hour or two at a time. I am also allowed a few hours on Earth without materialising. In some ways, that is a better state in which to observe things. I can hover seamlessly in that state without being seen. I can travel thousands of miles in that state, even glide through walls."

I said, "Why not glide through the walls and into their apartments when you are in your dematerialised state?"

"Good question, yes. The answer is that young William has put up some strong forcefield preventing people like me from spying on them. It matters not. Our plans are more sophisticated than theirs ever could be. It is fine because he cannot see our plans either."

"What are your plans?"

"Don't jump the gun, old chap. Remember you are still under observation. If you behave, I shall let you into the new world order, or at least let you see what is really going on behind the scenes. I promised to show you my apartment. We must hurry. I only have a few minutes before I dematerialise."

He rushed me out of the palace and back into the park. He linked my arm, guiding me onto the main Boardwalk where people with skateboards and women with prams walked. We trotted briskly, heading north. He paused briefly a little beyond Kensington Palace. "It is a disgrace," he said. "Why cannot people leave things as they are?"

He was looking at the old Orangery building which had now been turned into a super-posh restaurant.

"Cannot people understand the pure genius of an Orangery? The unique delight derived from the scent of living orange trees in the middle of winter. I had my greatest thoughts in that building."

This time, I yanked him out of his thoughts. "I want to see your apartment before you disappear. Where is it?"

He smiled. "Quite on the ball, aren't you?" He took off again, heading north, and a couple of hundred yards later, veered off to the right, onto grass, and into a countrified area of the park. Here, sat up against the trunks of oak trees, were artists and poets doing their work. He took pleasure at seeing this. "My garden is giving inspiration to the world. It is on a significant energy point of the Earth," he said.

"That is a bit mystical, isn't it?"

Frederick shrugged. "A simple fact. That is what makes my garden an adorable place, and why I have an apartment nearby. Come on."

He took off again, heading east, and we reached the tip of the Serpentine and an Italianate garden. A few yards later, there was a gate. Lancaster Gate. We went through it.

The busy Bayswater Road was before us, and the fairy tale atmosphere of Kensington Gardens was no more. He ushered me across the road and indicated a big Victorian house which was painted bright white. "I bought an apartment in there a year ago in order to be near my garden," he said.

Although this was a very expensive part of London, I was a little surprised. I am not sure what I was expecting, but somehow, it was not a flat in a converted Victorian house. We approached the building. In a side road off the main thoroughfare, was a pillared entrance to the building, and he withdrew a key from his pocket and opened the front door. Inside, was a classically decorated hallway and a well-carpeted staircase. We climbed the stairs to a landing where there was another front door. He opened it with a different key.

Inside was a surprise too. It was entirely white: the walls, the curtains, the furniture, everything. There was even a white dentist's chair.

"You must like white," I said.

"Good, isn't it?"

I did not agree. It felt somehow funereal.

"I am going to keep you here for a little while."

"What do you mean?" I asked with a bit of anxiety.

All of a sudden, there was a click as though a collection of locks was being activated. Some shutters went down over the windows, and some men dressed in white appeared too.

"These men will look after you. It is about to come to a head. My son is fully back on Earth and about to start his mission. Figgis is with him."

"Is Figgis back on the scene?"

"Absolutely. We are now onto the fifth generation of the Figgis family. He is the cleverest of them all. The greatest robot and computer expert the world has ever seen. Quite frankly, he has got the Earth in his pocket, simply waiting for George William to give the go ahead."

"Is this what you mean by the new world order?"

"The cast is assembled." He rubbed his hands together excitedly. "I need to get off to Pennsylvania Heights while I still can. Georgina Tipton is crucial. I need to see if my son gets to her before that maniac Zakamonsky abducts her."

I remembered that Zakamonsky had gone psychotic because of the cruel treatment his father meted out to him due to the fact he had been bypassed for the emperorship. I became aware that Frederick had been bypassed for kingship by George William and had this sudden crazy notion that Frederick was going to bump off George William, and the rest of them.

"Are *you* the one that is planning to rule the world?" I asked.

He started disappearing. "No, not exactly," he said, giving me a curt look. "I shall be back for you soon to see how you are getting along. I promise I will be back." As he said this, he dematerialised.

CHAPTER SEVENTEEN

USA - 2019

54 - The Mission Begins

HRH Freidrich Ludwig, former Prince of Wales of the United Kingdom, father of King George III, floated over Pennsylvania Heights, or Brighton Heights if you wish to be more accurate, and landed himself inside Georgina Tipton's oak cabin to observe proceedings. Here, he found Georgina Tipton scrambling through the trunk.

Charlotte Tipton, despite her fear of the trunk, had become overcome with curiosity to discover what Charles Tipton's plans for the world had been and asked Georgina to search for it. So far, Georgina had been unsuccessful in locating the document.

"It must be in there somewhere," Charlotte urged.

"I am looking," Georgina insisted. "There is so much in here. It is a real treasure trove."

"I cannot approach anyone for a film until we discover what Charles Tipton's proposals were. It would be incomplete. Besides, my ancestor, my side of the family, could have some important solutions to the problems of the world." She plumped up her hair proudly. "I have been feeling in my genes an ability to improve the state of the Earth with some great ideas."

"I have found something."

"Is it Charles Tipton's ideas?"

"No, it is a notice that says *BEWARE OF ZAKAMONSKY.*" She handed it to Charlotte.

"Who is Zakamonsky?"

"I don't know." Georgina continued digging. A couple of layers down, she found another notice which read *BEWARE OF FIELD COMMANDER ALBRECHT. HE IS THE ONE WHO WILL GET YOU!* She gave this notice to Charlotte, whose enthusiasm now turned to terror. "No, please no!" Charlotte screamed. "It is happening! I knew we should not have tampered with the trunk. The legend is true. They'll be coming to kill us." As if to heighten her terror, the sound of a helicopter could be heard a mile or two away.

In the garden next to Charlotte's, an elderly lady, Mrs Malwhinney, was on her sun lounger, enjoying a gin cocktail, her poodle beside her. She loved this time of day and the quietness of the neighbourhood. She became mildly irritated by the sound of a distant helicopter.

In the cabin, Georgina found another item of interest, a small canister. Inside it was a note, a warning, from Charles Tipton. It read: *Once you read this, I, Charles Tipton, could be long deceased as I have arranged for this trunk to be locked in a vault for a very long time, nine years longer than the two hundred years life of the troublesome trust, which began in 1810 at the time of my birth. The truth of the matter is that my father, and George Tipton's father, is King George III, and because of this, a ruthless man called Albrecht is determined to extinguish the entire Tipton family. If you find this, please go into hiding and await a miracle. Good luck.*

Charlotte became faint with terror, too faint even to escape. The sound of the helicopter became louder, much louder.

In the next garden, the poodle began barking, and Mrs Malwhinney choked on her cocktail. "Holy Mother of Jesus," she exclaimed as the chopper appeared fifty feet above her garden. The chopper rapidly descended but landed in Charlotte's garden. As it landed, it sliced off a few prized shrubs, and an elderly figure jumped out dressed in a long black cape, sporting a lengthy white beard. He tapped on the window of the cabin. "Open up!" he demanded.

Charlotte, cowering in a corner, said, "Ask him if he is Field Commander Albrecht."

"Are you Field Commander Albrecht?"

George William said, "No, I am the king. Your great-great-great-great-grandfather, but Field Commander Albrecht is on his way. He signed off on a helicopter in Jersey City an hour ago. He should be here any minute. We need to get out of here as soon as possible."

Georgina, alert now and all fired up, took the situation in her stride, opened the cabin door, and held out her hand. "Hi, Gramps," she said. "I am Georgina."

"Yes, good." George William briefly took the hand. "Quickly now, there is no time to lose. Get the trunk out in the garden. We are taking it with us."

Georgina marshalled a totally confused Charlotte into action. They closed the lid and dragged the trunk onto the lawn.

"Figgis will now spray the trunk with his special solution."

"Who is Figgis?"

Aloysius Figgis, the fifth generation of Figgises, appeared out of the chopper door.

"This is Figgis," George William said.

"Why does he want to spray the trunk?"

"Because Albrecht can track where we are because of the molecules in the wood. To prevent Albrecht doing this, Figgis will neutralise the molecules."

Aloysius Figgis was a small, middle-aged, gnome-like man with a strange growth coming out of his head. He had an aerosol in his hand.

"It is not going to neutralise the molecules," Figgis muttered pedantically. "My concoction will change the structure of the molecules."

George William had a trace of irritation in his voice. "OK, it is not going to neutralise, but do something else." He grilled Figgis. "Is the trunk going to hold together with this new molecular structure?"

Figgis put his hands together in prayer. "I hope so."

"Have you not tested it?"

"How could I?"

Tetchily, George William looked at his watch. "Figgis – just get on with it. We have not much time."

Figgis sprayed the trunk.

George William asked, "What about the bottom?"

"Yes, the bottom needs to be done," Figgis said. "Would not be much point in this without doing the bottom."

At first sight, the general level of competence between

George William and Figgis seemed extraordinarily inept, but that is the way it was.

"You need to lift the trunk up so I can spray it," Figgis said.

George William got the girls to lift. It was extremely heavy, and they could not lift high enough. "Figgis, you need to lift the trunk up with the helicopter. There is some rope in the back. Get it."

Figgis got back in the chopper, flung out the rope, and got the rotors going. The girls tied one end of the rope to the trunk, and the other end to the chopper. Figgis revved up the blades and lifted off. Mrs Malwhinney, in the next garden, quietly went hysterical. The trunk lifted, and George William sprayed the bottom of the trunk.

George William shouted up, "Right, Figgis. We are done. Back down again."

Figgis lowered the chopper, and the trunk hit the ground with a thump. The girls quickly dragged the trunk away before Figgis crushed it with the chopper.

"Right, everyone get in, and we'll be on our way," George William said.

While Charlotte Tipton looked scared and confused, Georgina took it with surprising ease and shunted Charlotte in. George William climbed in and sat next to Figgis.

Figgis engaged the controls, and the chopper rose about seventy feet and stopped. The trunk dangled, swaying. Just a few feet above Mrs Malwhinney's head.

In the helicopter, George William pondered. "Hope the molecules hold together."

"Yes, hope so," Figgis agreed. "If it breaks, the contents will fall over that woman."

Georgina asked, "Why is he hovering and not moving forward?"

"He is learning the controls. First time he has flown one of these things."

Charlotte shrieked. Even Georgina looked unsettled.

"He is a quick learner though. Brilliant fellow, Figgis. Absolutely top notch. Have full confidence in him." He said this as a hope rather than with any certainty, but a minute or so later, the machine rapidly soared up and shot over the Ohio River. The velocity left the trunk trailing, swaying behind dangerously. They were heading for Pittsburgh International Airport, about ten miles away. Very soon, they were over Moon Park and, moments later, over the airport. Figgis landed on turf in a private area of the airport. A few feet away was the Learjet.

"Our Learjet!" George William exclaimed proudly. "This is no ordinary plane. Figgis has modified it!"

One of the things Figgis had modified, was welding some strips of metal to the side of the plane in order to carry the trunk.

"We need to get the trunk onto those strips," George William said to the girls. "Can you lift it onto them?"

Georgina surveyed the situation. "The rope is stuck under the helicopter's landing skids. Mr Figgis needs to lift the helicopter up again so we can release it."

"No time. Cut the rope," George William said, tapping his watch. "Albrecht is now just fifteen minutes away from your house. No time to lose!"

The rope was cut and, with enormous effort, Georgina and Charlotte lifted the trunk onto the metal strips. George

William ordered the remainder of the rope be tied around the strips for extra security and ushered the girls into the plane.

There were only four seats, two sets of seats facing each other on either side of a small aisle. A small plane, a small cabin. Everything plush. Very plush, and very fast. "Relax in the seats while we take off," George William said. "I need to have a chat with Figgis in the cockpit."

He left for the cockpit.

"Figgis," George William said. "Figgis - will the trunk perched on the side of the plane unbalance it?"

"I hope not."

"Figgis - you saying 'hope' all the time makes me feel nervous."

"What should I say?"

"I don't know. I shall think about it."

Figgis started up the engines. "I need to prepare for take-off."

"Fine. Think about balance, and make sure we do not crash."

"Alright."

Figgis filed a flight plan for Knoxville, revved up the engines, got clearance, and headed down the runway. George William, like Figgis, put his hands together in prayer. Figgis gathered speed down the runway, concentrated on the controls, compensated for the trunk, and got into the air without incident. A few minutes later, now in Jefferson County, Ohio, he rapidly dropped altitude, switched on jamming devices, and changed direction, heading for Arizona. He proceeded along a pre-planned route, flying low over isolated areas towards the secret underground fortress in the Arizona desert.

"We are out of range now, Your Majesty. It will take a very long time for Field Commander Albrecht to figure out where we have diverted to."

"Well done, Figgis. Now we can relax. We shall get the girls installed in the fortress, and tomorrow, we will begin the mission."

They travelled in silence for a few minutes. Then Figgis massaged the growth coming out of his head.

"My second brain, Your Majesty. It is really hurting."

"Figgis," George William whispered firmly into the Figgis ear. "Figgis, Figgis, Figgis. We are about to rule the world. We need all the extra brainpower your extra brain can muster."

"Isn't anyone else going to help us with ruling the world?"

"No! It is just you and me!"

"It is a tremendously big job, ruling the whole world."

"That is why we designed your brain to expand. As new challenges come along, your new brain will grow to deal with them. What length could your second brain grow to?"

"There are no limits. I will look like an idiot. Miles of brain trailing behind me."

"You will not look like an idiot. I shall make that illegal. We shall appoint an official brain carrier to walk behind you, maybe several brain carriers, and they will treat you like royalty. Now, tell me about our robot army."

Figgis brightened as he spoke of his great achievement.

"Well, Your Majesty, there are two hundred underground bases across the Earth, and each one has approximately one million robot soldiers. More are being manufactured every day. Approximately two hundred million so far. Then there are the policemen."

"Ah, the policemen, yes. Excellent." George William rubbed his hands together like an excitable child.

"We can control all of them from the robot command room at the Arizona base. You must see this room. It is amazing."

"I have been waiting for the day to see this room, Figgis. I cannot tell you how excited I am to see this room!"

"It is a big room, a huge cave. In the middle of the cave is the control desk. It has two chairs. One for you, and one for me. Here, we are surrounded by two hundred screens arranged in a big arc. One screen for each base. With the touch of a button, we can instantly summon the commander of any base on their screen and give him our orders for the day."

George William was becoming beside himself with excitement. "It sounds too wonderful for words. If only I had something like that in my day."

"You told my ancestor it was not the right time."

"True."

For the next hour or two they discussed plans, and in between times, George William popped through to the cabin to check on the girls.

Georgina was anxious to know more about her heritage, but George William was evasive, asking her to be patient. "All will be revealed in the fullness of time," he kept telling her.

In truth, George William was worried she would usurp him before he had his go at running the world. Before he had time to institute his plans. They were good plans, plans the Earth needed. He had pitched these plans for the best part of two hundred years, been accepted, was back on Earth, and he was not going to let go of all that yet.

Then there was Zakamonsky. He had heard that Zakamonsky was in the initial stages of getting back to Earth too. He had to fend off Zakamonsky and outwit him. He did not want Georgina meddling in that either.

On returning to the cockpit, he said to Figgis, "We must not tell Georgina about Zakamonsky."

"Why?"

"We do not want to overwhelm her. What we need to do, is ease her into our organisation and teach her, so that one day she will have all the tools needed to successfully take over."

"I will not mention Zakamonsky."

"Good. And don't mention our robot army either. Particularly do not mention the robot control room."

"Why?"

"She'll want to have a go. You know women. They'll want to have a go and make a complete dog's breakfast of the place. These are men's things; we need to keep it that way. The robot command centre will be our private den."

Figgis agreed wholeheartedly. "We shall keep the robot control room for ourselves. Just you and me. We will have hours of fun in there!"

George William felt satisfied that he could keep Georgina at bay until his plans were complete. However, his anxiety was raised a little as they travelled through Arizona. It was as they were nearing the fortress. As they approached, just a few minutes away from base, Georgina came into the cockpit. She hovered beside George William. They were flying low through the red rock area. The curious red rocks sticking up out of the desert like luminous needles. The sun bearing down produced a curious red-yellow light. Unique, and a little spooky, as if they were on Mars. The powerful red-yellow glow streamed through the split-screen windows of the cockpit, bathing Georgina in it, transforming her with a powerful, almost superhuman glow. In that moment, George William realised she was definitely the one. The true being that would deliver the Aurora People back to Earth. The legend was being fulfilled. He was awestruck.

Georgina uttered, "Do you know about the stone?"

"Stone, my dear? What stone?"

"I think it is in the coronation crown. The red-yellow stone. You must know about the stones and crowns of the United Kingdom."

"Oh, that stone, yes."

"If you want me to help, I need that stone."

George William laughed. "You will be lucky. It is in the Tower of London, one of the most heavily guarded buildings in the world!"

"I want that stone!" Georgina said with determination, and she left the cockpit.

"Another thing, Figgis. Do not mention the stone. Dial down all mention of the stone."

"Alright, Your Majesty. You had better buckle up. We shall be landing very soon. It may be a bit rocky. I have to land on the desert sand."

A few minutes later, he did land, and it was reasonably smooth. He taxied towards the entrance of the hidden fortress. Two of Figgis's humanoid robots were on the ground to welcome them. One to usher the party into the fortress, and one to park the plane in the hangar.

"Figgis, get one of your robots to keep an eye on the girls. We do not want them poking around."

"Will do. I shall also put a lock on our robot control room door."

"Good man."

George William left the plane with a mixture of excitement and nervousness. The mission he had been planning for two hundred years was about to begin.

Meanwhile, in London . . .

CHAPTER EIGHTEEN

55 – Into the Redemption Realm

As promised, Frederick did return.

"Ah, you are back," I said.

"Yes, old chap, I promised I would return, and here I am."

"Great, can I go now? I am getting hungry."

"Hungry, old chap? All you need to do is ask one of the servants."

"Those men dressed in white?"

"Yes, those ones. They are there to cook for you, and generally do everything to make your life comfortable."

Everything in here was white. Here, in his luxury flat overlooking Kensington Gardens. The walls, the curtains, the carpets, all white, even the dentist's chair. My spirits sank, realising he was determined to keep me here. "I suppose I will have to stay here until you have completed your new world order?"

"No," he said. He sparkled as if he had a great new idea. "No, you can be my eyes and ears. I want to send you to a very special place where you can report back to me on what is going on. A role as a spy! I told you I could find you a role, and now you have one!"

I was edgy. "A spy? What do I have to do?"

"Just report back to me. I assure you it is not a dangerous role; I have made sure of that. Report to me what is going on in there. I want to be ahead of the game. You and me ahead of the game! It is a very special place."

"Where is this special place?"

Frederick was bound up in his excitement. "I am so happy I found you a role. We can work together! It is a super-special place. You and me ahead of the game! It will be wonderful."

"Where is this special place?"

"You have to realise what a great privilege this is. It is unbelievable. You will be the only one that goes there out of the billions of people on Earth. Wewph, it is such a great honour!"

"Where is this place?"

Before I got an answer, I was already there. He had dematerialised me into a different realm.

The Redemption Realm.

My first instinct was that of horror.

I was not here in a physical form, and Frederick was right, I could not be harmed in a physical way. It was if I was in a physical body though. I could see, hear, even sense. Something like a spirit wandering around yet remaining aware of everything going on.

It was an environment shrouded in mist. Thick fog in places. Bluish and quite chilly. I noticed a forlornness, an all-pervading sadness about it. Every now and then, I saw glowing red spots - I was not sure what they were. Through the mist, I seemed to be travelling on a bluish path. I came upon a temple, and went in.

It was an odd temple. People were weeping. Everyone openly weeping. The whole congregation was sobbing. They were ritually praying for inspiration, and a way out of the desperate situation they were in. I got out of there and moved on.

Outside, on the foggy bluish path, mutilated people were stumbling around. Not exactly mutilated but covered in sludge. A sludge caked into their bodies like leprosy. Some more sludge-covered than others. A few were muttering their hope that Zakamonsky would cure them of the sludge and make them whole again. Make them beautiful like their race had once been. Somehow, I sensed Zakamonsky would not do this. As I travelled on, I came upon another temple.

In this temple, the same experience, but more explicit. They were weeping and praying for the redemption of their ancestors for not stopping the war. They appeared to retain hope in their hearts they would not be exiled for ever – they had already been exiled for 30,000 years – and they were praying for Emperor Zakamonsky too, in order that he be cured from his psychosis, and rule them properly.

You may think this was a thoroughly depressing place, and it was, but I found another side too. It cannot be denied, being exiled for 30,000 years sounds a horrendously long time, yet there was a beautifully inspiring aspect to this place too. I came upon a cultural centre.

In this tabernacle of heritage, there was brightness. Incredible light on many levels. For here, they performed plays about their prehistoric civilisation on Earth. These were uplifting in ways it is difficult to describe. It was a beautiful, exquisite existence that one could only dream about. They kept their prehistoric culture alive through hundreds of stories and plays. I will report back on some of these soon. It was not only plays, but they also had forums too. Discussion groups debating the way forward for their people and civilisation. They had to be careful though, as I heard that Zakamonsky randomly made inspections of these places, and if they crossed a prescribed line, they disappeared off the map. There was an underlying fear of doing this.

I had a brief glimpse, a kind of lightning flash, and it was of Georgina Tipton, and she appeared as the true saviour of this place, very strange. Unusual what you experience here.

As I write this account, I have been in the Redemption Realm for some while. I am not sure how long. It could be a few days, or it could even be a few years, time is very hard to judge here. I told you at the beginning, I was writing from a situation of captivity, and now you know where it is. I am a little dependent upon Frederick.

Frederick is turning out to be a wily old goat. He has got me reporting back from the Redemption Realm, and he seems to have his fingers in many different pies. All surreptitious. He is obviously part of this cabal set on taking over the Earth, but I am not sure what his own personal aims are. I have to keep in with him, so he can return me to Earth.

This is not my home, and I want to get back. I cannot stay here for much longer, or I may go mad. Frederick is not my only option, and I am planning an independent escape. There are plenty of scientists here who could help, but I need to be careful as there are many dangerous people around. Not least, Supreme Commander Zakamonsky. I have now acquired an independent contact on Earth, which is good news.

I will report back when I can.

WHAT NEXT?

Part 2 – Title 'COURTSHIP'
On the Earth realm: Georgina Tipton begins to discover her power. After an audacious robbery at the Tower of London, she launches into an astounding new stratosphere.

George William & Figgis get to grips with their two hundred million robot soldier army with their ineptitude knowing no bounds. They remain standing though.

Field Commander Albrecht plans a coup.

Emperor Zakamonsky finds his way back to Earth.

Part 3 – Title '2020'
Under the cover of the 2020 worldwide lockdown, all the parties seed plans for their new world order, and many other developments too.

Part 4 – Title 'AURORAHOOD'
What really happened 30,000 years ago?

Part 5 – Wait and see.

APPENDIX 1

George Tipton's Rule Britannia show

George Tipton's animated music-picture-story of the Rule Britannia song had over eighteen hundred drawings that illustrate forty-three battles fought between 1702 and 1846 that demonstrate the expansion and sometimes contraction of the British Empire. The song is sung with the missionary further that all is being done for the liberation of mankind. George Tipton was obsessed that everything should start in 1702.

BATTLES

1 War of the Spanish Succession 1702
2 Queen Anne's War
3 War of the Quadruple Alliance
4 Anglo-Spanish War
5 War of Jenkins' Ear
6 War of the Austrian Succession
7 First Carnatic War
8 Second Carnatic War
9 French and Indian War
10 Seven Years' War
11 Third Carnatic War
12 Anglo-Cherokee War
13 Pontiac's War
14 First Anglo-Mysore War
15 First Carib War
16 First Anglo-Maratha War
17 American Revolutionary War
18 Anglo-Spanish War
19 Fourth Anglo-Dutch War
20 Second Anglo-Mysore War
21 Northwest Indian War
22 Pemulwuy Resistance
23 War of the First Coalition
24 War in the Vendée
25 Hawkesbury and Nepean Wars
26 Second Carib War
27 Anglo-Spanish War
28 War of the Second Coalition
29 Irish Rebellion of 1798
30 Fourth Anglo-Mysore War

WORDS OF SONG

When Britain first, at Heaven's command
Arose from out the azure main;
This was the charter of the land,
The nations, not so blest as thee,
Must, in their turns, to tyrants fall;
While thou shalt flourish great and free,
The dread and envy of them all.
And guardian angels sang this strain:
Rule, Britannia! rule the waves:
"Britons never will be slaves.

Still more majestic shalt thou rise,
More dreadful, from each foreign stroke;
As the loud blast that tears the skies,
Serves but to root thy native oak.
"Rule, Britannia! rule the waves:
"Britons never will be slaves."

Thee haughty tyrants ne'er shall tame:
All their attempts to bend thee down,
Will but arouse thy generous flame;
But work their woe, and thy renown.
"Rule, Britannia! rule the waves:
"Britons never will be slaves."

To thee belongs the rural reign;
Thy cities shall with commerce shine:
All thine shall be the subject main,
And every shore it circles thine.
"Rule, Britannia! rule the waves:
"Britons never will be slaves."

The Muses, still with freedom found,
Shall to thy happy coast repair;
Blest Isle! With matchless beauty crown'd,
And manly hearts to guard the fair.
"Rule, Britannia! rule the waves:
"Britons never will be slaves."

APPENDIX 2

Georgina's Filmscript

This is the script that Georgina transcribed out of George Tipton's November 1850 film-strips and notes that accompanied them. Understandably it is devoid of the unique atmosphere in which it was performed in that grungy theatre in south London before it was knocked down.

INT = Interior
EXT = Exterior

```
INT BAPTIST MILLS, SALTFORD 1702 - NIGHT

An explosion. A furnace bursts into flames. A human body is
flung into the air and lands on the ground. A number of
people rush in, many with buckets. They are followed by
Abraham Darby I and his young apprentice. A doctor rushes
in. Two people lift the injured employee onto a bench. The
doctor administers first aid. Darby's apprentice assists
him, and the doctor instructs.
```

DOCTOR

First we loosen clothing and look for burns. We cool
the affected areas with water that is cool, but not
too cold, and we must realise the body is in shock
and treat for that too. The latest thinking of *The
Society* is to treat the body as a whole.

The apprentice nods attentively. Darby moves off to
inspect the furnace and the dowsing operation. He shakes
his head, distressed, and moves further down the hall to
where a pile of chopped wood is stacked, and a smaller
pile of coal. He looks at these piles, deep in thought.

The doctor finishes the first aid and the patient is carried
out on a stretcher. The apprentice looks for Darby and
finds him staring at the coal pile.

APPRENTICE

Thomas is being moved to the home of Lesley Sommers,
where he will be cared for. The doctor says he should
rest for the next two weeks.

DARBY

(distressed) These accidents are so regrettable. We
compromise on safety through commercial pressures.

APPRENTICE

Our pots are extremely popular and we must keep up with
orders . . . You were looking at coal deep in thought.

Birth of the Tiptons

DARBY

I am considering making our pots from iron instead
of copper.

APPRENTICE

Would that make the furnaces safer?

DARBY

It may. I am thinking about the fuel for the
furnaces. Of making a charcoal-like substance from
coal instead of wood. Something to burn much hotter
than anything at present. A heat to create a
stronger, tougher iron. We would have to redesign
the furnaces, making them larger and safer. With a
more powerful iron, we would use less of it and
produce more pots.

APPRENTICE

That is what we need. People love our cooking pots,
but we cannot make enough of them.

DARBY

Many experiments will be needed and it will take
time. There is something else I need to show you. I
will let you into my den.

The apprentice is led into the den which is lined with
shelves and a workbench. On the shelves are the company's
range of brass cooking pots. On the bench is a series of
large moulds in sturdy containers.

APPRENTICE

What are these, Mr Darby?

DARBY

Moulds. We have been making our pots one by one.
Spending hours hammering them into shape. With these
moulds we could make a minimum of ten pots an hour.
Men with hammering skills can be freed to make individual pots of artistic merit.

APPRENTICE

Ten pots an hour! Can that really be done?

DARBY

Ten pots an hour is only the start! Many experiments
still need to be done to perfect the moulds and mix
the sands and all ingredients into the exact
proportions.

APPRENTICE

(Full of wonder) You are a man of industry, Mr Darby.
One day you could be known as the man that started an
industrial revolution!

DARBY

I see this business expanding. I am sending you off to
business school.

Birth of the Tiptons

INT BAPTIST MILLS WAREHOUSE, 1707 – NIGHT

The warehouse is stacked with the company's signature
round-bellied cooking pots. The apprentice, fresh from
business school, looks around in wonder.

> APPRENTICE
>
> Who would have thought five years ago all of this
> could happen? Wonderful accomplishment, Abraham. I
> have obtained a patent for your moulds.

> DARBY
>
> What is that?

> APPRENTICE
>
> It means nobody can copy the formulation of your
> mould.

> DARBY
>
> Why do we need that?

> APPRENTICE
>
> A patent is the successful way to run a business.
> That is what I have been taught. It was you that sent
> me to business school.

> DARBY
>
> Maybe it will not matter as the new process is now
> ready.

APPRENTICE

That will need a patent too.

Darby, not enthused, becomes more passionate when
explaining the process.

DARBY

No more wood. We will be using a specially refined
coal in order to heat the furnaces hotter and more
efficiently than ever before. We will be able to make
iron in quantity. This formula will revolutionise
everything. Iron will be the material of the future.

APPRENTICE

This could increase production numbers and bring the
cost down.

DARBY

Yes! Many more people from around the world will be
able to afford our wares. People will be able to cook
hot nourishing meals in our big sturdy pots with
nutrients all sealed in. Be part of creating a
healthier world. We could be entering an age where
the Lord shines on a disease-free earth!

APPRENTICE

A wonderful vision, Abraham. I will help in any way I
can.

Birth of the Tiptons

DARBY

We need more space. And coal. A lot of coal and much
more space. What we need are new premises.

APPRENTICE

It is providence, Abraham. Last week I was told of
such a place. An abandoned furnace with much space.
It is near a newly discovered coalfield. A huge
coalfield.

DARBY

Where is this abandoned furnace?

APPRENTICE

On the River Severn in an area known as
Coalbrookdale. About one hundred miles upriver from
us here in Bristol.

DARBY

On the Severn? That would mean we could transport the pots straight into the Bristol docks
for loading onto international ships!

APPRENTICE

We have a community of Friends near there. On the
other side of the river in the village of Brosley. I
will arrange accommodation.

EXT RIVER SEVERN COALBROOKDALE - DAY

A few days later. Darby is with a 'Friend' from the
Brosley community. They view the abandoned furnace on the
banks of the River Severn.

                    FRIEND
    Shadrick Fox be a scoundrel. He abandoned this
    furnace and went to India. Left big debts, he did.

                    DARBY
    Would I be liable for the debts?

                    FRIEND
    No, Mr Darby. The landlord only wants to sell the
    lease now. There is not much call for iron in these
    parts.

Darby looks down the river. Its pristine waters running at
the foot of a high gorge, stunningly beautiful view.

                    DARBY
    It is a good maybe perfect spot. The furnace can be
    repaired but I need to be sure of certain things. We
    need to acquire more land. Build more furnaces. Who
    owns this land?"

                    FRIEND
    Most of the land here be held in trust under the
    Madeley Manor Trust. They be good people. Easy to

talk to. Let me show you a place where you could build a dock. The place you could load your ships bound for Bristol.

They walk along the river to a natural widening.

FRIEND

It is here. I have a solution for transporting the pots from the furnace to here. Friends in Nottingham have been experimenting with wagonways. They are wooden tracks laid parallel on the ground. The wheel of the wagon is designed to cling to the track and, with the horse, pulls the wagon along the tracks. It makes for a smoother ride with much less spillage.

Darby raises eyebrow at this clever pre-rail idea.

DARBY

About the coal field. I will need much coal. I do not want this coal field to run dry.

FRIEND

(laughs scoffing) The coalfield is huge. Twenty-five square miles or more. Be hundreds of years before it runs dry. Everyone is talking of coal now. Peat is becoming a thing of the past.

Darby nods to himself, assessing the situation.

FRIEND

Do it, Mr Darby. Move your business to
Coalbrookdale. It would be a great business for the
Friends to participate in. We could grow a fine
community with this business.

DARBY

I will do it.

INT COALBRROKDALE FURNACE – DAY

It is a few months later. The furnace has been repaired
and is in full blast. The noise is overpowering and everyone shouts to be heard. Darby is stressed and frantic.

DARBY

I need more coal!

APPRENTICE

The mine is running at full capacity. They cannot do
more.

DARBY

They must. Everyone is wanting iron. It is not just
pots anymore. We are going to need double the amount
of coal. Probably more.

Birth of the Tiptons

INT UNDERGROUND IN COAL MINE – NIGHT

A mine in Derbyshire. The drive to produce more coal has
led to accidents. Ten miners are trapped underground in
the aftermath of an accident. A shaft has collapsed, and
the mine is flooding. Escape impossible. They link arms and
boldly await their fate. As the water rises, they sway and
repeatedly sing the icy lament.

COMMUNIALLY

Farewell, farewell my wife so dear
I will be at rest, you need not fear
No anxious sorrow need you take
But leave our children, for my sake

Farewell, farewell my wife so dear
I will be at rest, you need not fear
No anxious sorrow need you take
But leave our children, for my sake

INT THOMAS NEWCOMEN'S WORKSHOP, DARTMOUTH – DAY

Newcomen has assembled a group of mine owners to demonstrate his new 'Atmospheric Steam Machine'

NEWCOMEN

This machine will drain your mines of water. It is
driven by the power of steam! It is the first ever
steam-powered instrument being offered for sale. It
is the first ever steam-powered apparatus to do

useful work. I am offering it to you, the very first
group of mine owners, at a special price.

The mine owners look sceptical

                    NEWCOMEN
I believe you should buy one. It is essential you buy
it. With the knowledge this machine exists you will
have riots on your hands if you do not have one.
Accidents will lead to death and deaths to riots.
Can you afford riots? Can you afford not to install
one?

                    CHARLES TIPTON (commenting)
This is the very beginning of our machine-driven
world. The very start of the industrial transformation that changed our world forever. This massive
change came on the backs of the miners!

INT. BOARTDROOM, COALBROOKDALE, 1712 - DAY

Abraham Darby and Thomas Newcomen sit at the boardroom
table.

                    NEWCOMEN
Since we last met, orders for my Atmospheric Steam
Engine have increased many times over.

Birth of the Tiptons

DARBY

I am glad your business is a success. I have lived in
Coalbrookdale four years now and those mining disasters haunt me badly. I feel responsible because of
my insistence on demanding so much coal.

NEWCOMEN

Worry not, Mr Darby. My atmospheric engines are efficiently pumping out water from the mines. Soon every
mine owner in the world will be installing one.
Flooding of mines will soon be a thing of the past.

DARBY

I hope you are right.

NEWCOMEN

It would not have been possible without your cheap
and excellent quality iron. You can take solace in
the fact that you have helped cure the problem of
flooding in the mines.

DARBY

Thank you, Mr Newcomen.

NEWCOMEN

You will have to get that old busy brain of yours
working hard again now.

DARBY

Why?

NEWCOMEN

We are going to need more iron and much stronger
iron. There are hundreds of inventors designing
machines made now from iron. We are coming into a new
iron age. You produce the best and cheapest iron.
You will have to step up to the mark. We'll need a
tenfold increase in iron at least.

DARBY

Impossible.

NEWCOMEN

You will have to. You are the only one who can do it.
You with your patents.

DARBY

I was advised patents are the way to do business.

NEWCOMEN

Business advice or not, the development of our
nation rests on your shoulders, Mr Darby. You and
your patents. On your shoulders.

Darby's shoulders twitch uncomfortably.

NEWCOMEN

I imagine you will have to build many more furnaces and
have to operate those furnaces all day and all night.

Darby looks horrified.

Birth of the Tiptons

Very soon thousands of products and infrastructure
will be made from iron. Bridges, boats, buildings.
My steam-powered machine will look primitive
compared to what will come. Far more powerful steam
engines will be produced and will need far stronger
metals to withstand the enormous pressures. This is
your challenge, Mr Darby, this is your responsibility. This is your destiny.

Darby becomes weighed down and heavy.

NEWCOMEN

There is a new world coming. Steam-powered engines
made from iron will replace horses and pull far
greater loads at far greater speeds. Steam-powered
vessels will navigate the oceans, no longer depend-
ant on the vagaries of the wind. Steam-powered
machines will plough the fields and release man from
toil. Steam-powered machines will make clothing.
Humans could be freed from toiling to explore higher
qualities. This could be your legacy, Mr Darby.
Mankind freed from toil. You are a religious man, Mr
Darby. Maybe humans will become giants in the image
of God. The future is with you. The future of human
development is in your hands, Mr Abraham Darby. You
and your patents. Good luck!

Montage of Darby working long hours experimenting

CHARLES TIPTON (narrating)

The idea of man being relieved of toil to pursue
worship of God had a profound effect on Darby. Over
the next four years he toiled so that others, in
future generations, would not have to toil. He
experimented for long hours all day and sometimes
long into the night to increase production and
produce stronger alloys of metal. His long working
hours meant being apart from his family, but occasionally the family were all together. On one occasion the whole family were together on a trip down to
London for the yearly Quaker national meeting.

INT. STAGECOACH, 1716 - DAY

Abraham Darby, his wife Mary Darby, and their children fill
the stagecoach. It jostles along the uneven roads on the
long journey to London. Abraham Darby appears exhausted
and grumpy. He chides sixteen-year-old daughter Mary for
asking about suitors in London. Wife Mary attempts to keep
everyone calm.

MARY DARBY

Your father has been working extremely hard for a
long time. After the yearly meeting he will have a
good rest. We will visit the London sights while he
rests.

DARBY

I need an important meeting with Mancroft.

Birth of the Tiptons

MARY DARBY

After his important meeting with Mr Mancroft he will
rest.

INT MANCROFT LIVING ROOM - NIGHT

Mary Darby along with the children and Mrs Mancroft sit on
one side of the room while Darby and Anthony Mancroft sit
on the other side in armchairs by the fire. The two men
converse.

MANCROFT

Abraham, you are the most innovative iron-maker in
the history of iron. It is an honour to have you
staying in my house. I am in awe. We all are. You are
a huge credit to The Friends!

DARBY

Thank you, Anthony, but you must not put me on a
pedestal. I am but a small cog in a big drama. I
can reveal though that a revolution is coming.
Steam machines will change everything everywhere.
They will do the work of dozens of men. Mankind
will be freed to pursue a life close to God. The
Lord is shaking up the world. There are challenges. I need to increase production and discover
a new alloy.

MANCROFT

(knowingly) You need finance and I will arrange it.
You know me, I shall arrange a share issue. Would you
consider opening a furnace here in Southwark?

DARBY

(hushed whispers) I do need finance. There is much to
do, but there is something else. Anthony, I am dying.
It is terminal and there is not much time. You must
not mention this to anyone.

MANCROFT

(whispering) Abraham, this is terrible. I will not
mention a word.

INT DARBY'S BEDROOM, MARCH 1717 - DAY

Darby is lying in bed with fever. Teenage daughters Anne
and Mary mop his brow. Young Abraham looks on, observing.
Wife Mary is hysterical.

MARY DARBY

Abraham, you are a monster. You never told us of your
condition and never left a will. No will. What am I
to do? How are we to live?

DARBY

(rasping) I have been so busy with my work I have
neglected you all and forgotten about the will. Now
it is too late.

Birth of the Tiptons

                    MARY DARBY

Your work, your work! How are we to live?

                      DARBY

I am sorry, so very sorry. (turns to daughter) Mary,
dear Mary, look after your mother. Look after the
family, it has to be you. Call on Richard Ford for
help. Richard Ford. (He turns to young Abraham) It
will be you, Abraham, many years from now, it will be
you that will carry on the family work. Learn the
ways of iron. Be diligent. Keep the faith, attend
the meetings. It will be you.

                CHARLES TIPTON (narrating)

It was five o'clock 8th March 1717 when Abraham Darby
of the first generation died. Two days later, a Board
meeting was convened.

INT BOARDROOM, COALBROOKEDALE, MARCH 1717 - DAY

Everyone is in mourning for the great founder. An executor
rises solemnly to address the meeting.

                     EXECUTOR

Considering the late Mr Abraham Darby left no will
it is my grim task to apportion ownership of the
company in the appropriate manner. Mr Thomas Goldney
of the second generation is awarded ten shares. Mr
Richard Ford is awarded two shares. Mr Joshua
Sergeant is awarded three shares and Mr Thomas

Goldney of the third generation is awarded one
share.

INT. DARBY HOME - DAY

Mary Darby dressed in black is in mourning.

                    EXECUTOR
My deepest condolences to you, Mrs Darby. It is
my grim task, under the terms, to inform you that
you have to leave your home. I offer my house for
you and your family to reside in on a temporary
basis.

EXT. RIVER SEVERN - DAY

A coffin is carried along the banks of the River Severn
followed by the Darby family plus the entire Brosley and
Coalbrookdale Quaker community.

                CHARLES TIPTON (narrating)
The stress was too much for Mrs Darby and she died
within a year. The children became orphans and the
situation remained desperate until Mary heeded her
father's advice and sought help from Richard Ford.
Soon they were married and the family went to live in
Ford's house. A semblance of normality came upon the
Darby children. In time Ford became chief of the
company and young Abraham the Second became his
apprentice. The company remained the predominant

purveyors of iron in the world and had many landmark
moments.

EXT COALBROOKDALE WORKS, 1728 - DAY

Richard Ford and twenty-year-old apprentice Abraham Darby
II stand on a platform where Abraham unveils an iron
wheel. Fanfare music plays.

> CHARLES TIPTON
> Young Abraham presented the world's first iron wheel,
> which enabled the inauguration of heavy industry.
> Steam locomotives and other heavy industrial items
> followed this invention. The company went on to
> prosper and Abraham of the second generation went on
> to marry. His wife bore him three children.
> Unfortunately this satisfactory state of affairs was
> destined to end abruptly.

INT THOMAS GOLDNEY'S BED CHAMBER, BRISTOL - NIGHT

Thomas Goldney lies in bed with his son by his side.

> CHARLES TIPTON
> You may remember Thomas Goldney of the second
> generation was awarded ten shares in the
> Coalbrookdale Company, making him the main share-
> holder. Regrettably he died and left his shares to
> his son Thomas Goldney of the third generation.
> Thomas Goldney of the third generation, who was

not a Quaker, had contacts in the armaments industry. Thomas Goldney of the third generation
turned 'his' Coalbrookdale works over to the
manufacture of swivel guns. The Coalbrookdale
Company had been a Quaker company and Quaker prin-
ciples were firmly against war and instruments of
war.

EXT RIVER SEVERN, COALBROOKDALE DOCK AREA – DAY

A line of dejected employees loads dozens of crates
containing swivel guns onto a ship bound for Bristol.
Abraham II is incandescent.

                        ABRAHAM II
    This is wrong, deeply wrong. Against our deepest
    principals as Quakers. We must stop this.

                         FORD
    We cannot. Thomas Goldney has every right to do
    what he is doing. Let us stand firm in our Quaker
    faith and practise and let the outcome be one for
    the good.

NOTE: At this point the show was suspended to have a wide-
ranging discussion about the situation, which apparently
lasted nearly two hours. The purpose was to come up with a
new world order where machines worked for mankind in an
equitable new and peacefully order without regard for
profit. The outcome of this discussion should come at the

end rather than here. This note is purely for the historical accuracy of Charles Tipton's presentation.

The show reconvened with this curious ending.

CHARLES TIPTON (narrating)
Abraham was not happy. He kept up his Quaker practice, but his life turned into an avalanche of bad
luck. First one of his children died.

INT. CHILDRENS BEDROOM – DAY

There are three beds in this room. Two are made. One has no
bedclothes. Undertakers lift a small coffin off a table and
carry it out. The coffin is followed by Abraham Darby and his
wife who is weeping.

CHARLES TIPTON (narrating)
His bad luck continued; a second child died.

In the bedroom a second bed is stripped of covers, and
only one bed remains made. A black down and up to reveal a
third bed stripped of covers, and undertakers carry out
another small coffin. Abraham and wife follow,
grief-stricken.

CHARLES TIPTON
Unbelievably, the third child dies. Abraham and his
wife cried for days.

INT. DARBY'S BEDROOM - DAY

A full-sized coffin is carried out; it is Abraham's wife.
Abraham's wife has died too. Abraham runs out of the house
screaming. The whole family is dead.

EXT. RIVER SEVERN - DAY

Abraham Darby II runs for miles along the banks of the
River Severn. He keeps running until he comes upon a small
stone church. He enters.

INT. STONE CHURCH - DAY

With tears streaming he makes his way up the aisle. Beyond the
alter is a stained-glass window of a shining Jesus. Weeping,
he addresses this stained-glass window.

                    ABRAHAM DARBY II
    Lord, I am overcome. Tell me what I should do. I know
    I have sinned. Done wrong, sinned badly. I have
    participated in supplying arms for war which I know
    is wrong. Please accept and forgive me. Please teach
    me in the ways of righteousness and put me on that
    path. I am broken, but ready to learn. Please give me
    the courage to learn.

A pastor sees Abraham and walks slowly up the aisle. He
has a look of empathy. He approaches Abraham with a
compassion and they look at each other for a little while.

Birth of the Tiptons

It is not the war you are being judged on, Abraham.
It is your Quaker faith. Give it up. Give it up now.
Come. Join us. Repent.

Abraham backs away and runs out the church screaming.

That is the way Charles Tipton's play ended, and there was an interval of two years before Georgina Tipton found the document Charles Tipton had written on the boat concerning his vision of a solution to the problems of human life and its organisation of world affairs.

BVPRI - #0006 - 120424 - CO - 198/129/17 - PB - 9781915972446 - Matt Lamination